THE SECOND CHANCE

A MARINA COVE NOVEL, BOOK FIVE

SOPHIE KENNA

The Second Chance

A Marina Cove Novel, Book Five

By Sophie Kenna

© Copyright 2024

Cover design by Craig Thomas (coversbycraigthomas@ gmail.com)

GET A FREE BOOK!

Sign up for my newsletter, and you'll also receive a free exclusive copy of *Summer Starlight*. This book isn't available anywhere else!

You can join at sophiekenna.com/seaside.

1

As the golden shoreline of Marina Cove swam into view from the ferry, Natalie Keller had only one thought hammering through her mind.

She was making a terrible, terrible mistake.

A puff of warm, saline air brushed across her skin as she took a breath to still the pounding of her heart. Natalie had been all over the world, but there was something different about Marina Cove, something that tugged at her somewhere in her solar plexus. Something soothing and thrilling all at once.

But there was another feeling, deeper, heavier, that gnawed away at her. That old, reliable companion of hers, the guilt-drenched shadow that followed alongside her for more than twenty-five years.

The memory of what she'd done.

Early morning sunlight reflected against the deep cerulean water, sending shimmering sparkles across its surface. Natalie arched her back against the painful tension that had developed between her shoulder blades and watched Hightide Port slowly march toward her, as though closing in on her. A prison cell, patiently awaiting her inevitable return.

Natalie shook her head, and idly ran her fingers over the smooth metal of the ferry railing, the gentle rocking against the waves almost a lullaby as they approached the shore. Stunning emerald-green forests and meadows of turquoise and violet wild-flowers sat on large, rolling hills that dropped into the sapphire sea.

She could just make out a small flurry of activity at the ferry port rapidly drawing near. People riding bicycles swept past shoppers milling around store-fronts on Ocean Avenue, and sailboats floated languidly to and from the shore.

Every person a story unto themselves, going through their lives on Marina Cove, carrying on all this time like she'd never been gone at all.

She sighed. How many years had it been?

A man and his young son appeared through the cabin door and walked past her, settling into seats on the observation deck. Natalie unconsciously ducked her head, turning from them to face the open sea.

Yes, it had been years since she'd been home, if that's what you could call it anymore. It had been too long. And after everything that had happened in Ireland...well. Natalie rubbed her wrists, phantom aches still running through them as she remembered the cold weight of the handcuffs clacking into place.

Her heart skipped a beat as she thought of the night leading up to her arrest. The smell of smoke, heavy and acrid in her lungs...the incredible heat of the flames. She clenched her hands. The pads of her fingers were still red and raw, inflamed.

After so many years running all over the world, after all the wild things she'd gotten tangled up in, Natalie was rarely unprepared.

But that night...that night, she hadn't seen coming. That was for sure.

She closed her eyes and took another steadying breath. After everything that had happened in Ireland, she needed to regroup. There was nowhere else to go, at any rate. Jess had gone away, who knew where, licking her wounds. They'd agreed to meet up with each other in another few weeks, once the dust had settled, a new house in Prague that Jess had arranged to stay at through one of her old network of friends.

And Harper...well. Natalie was done with Ireland, in any case. It was time to move on to the next city, the next adventure.

But right now, more than anything, Natalie wanted to hide out, to sleep away her fears, her guilt, someplace where she could just *stop* for a minute. She'd been calling the Seaside House for weeks as her life began to unravel, always hanging up as soon as someone answered, suddenly unable to speak. She certainly didn't want to see Ella...but she desperately missed Ramona. Not to mention Charlotte, Diane, Gabriel...who knew where they were, what they were up to?

A shock of regret punched into her stomach. Why on earth was it so hard to reach out to them? To give them a call, or, *the horror*, to visit them? It wasn't like she hadn't wanted to. Every time the desperate longing stirred within her, an invisible hand held her back.

She loved them, but her family had been broken

long, long ago. Irrevocably, most likely. What did she expect?

And so meanwhile, Natalie kept moving toward some unclear end. It was best not to think too far ahead, and in the meantime, in her own way, she loved her life, filled with constant adventures, thrilling days and wild nights.

And it wasn't like she was alone, at least not recently. Jess and Harper had become friends, great friends. She had nearly always traveled alone, leaving behind more than a few interested men who were probably bewildered by her sudden disappearance, but she'd unintentionally struck up a close friendship with the two women during the few months she'd lived in Reykjavik.

They'd followed her to Ireland, and she loved them for that. They had their own reasons for running, just like Natalie, and had bonded over their shared inability to stay in one place for too long.

Natalie shuddered as she thought of Harper. What had happened to her. She shook her head, and pushed down the bile rising in her throat.

She'd entrusted her meager belongings to Jess before she left for Marina Cove, including the only two possessions in the world she truly cared about, safely tucked away in her lockbox.

The two items were, by now, extensions of her own beating heart. She normally didn't trust anyone, but Jess and Harper had been different from the start. She hadn't wanted to travel with the items and risk something happening to them, risk damaging them or losing them somehow. Already she felt their conspicuous absence. She didn't know what would happen to her if she lost them. It wasn't an option.

However close she'd become to the women, they weren't family. After her arrest, she could no longer contain the ache to see someplace familiar...to see her family. Even if the last time she'd been home, Ramona had barely contained her hostility. Not that Natalie hadn't deserved it, of course, running away from everyone after their father had abandoned them all, leaving Ramona to run the Seaside House with their mother. It all seemed like a lifetime ago.

Dad abandoning them hadn't been the whole reason she'd left, not by a long shot. That wasn't what had sent her running.

It was just easier to keep moving. That way, she didn't have to think about the Year of Darkness, as she'd taken to calling it. She didn't have to think about *him*. About the decision that would change everything.

Even if that had all been more than twenty-five

years ago, Natalie would never forgive herself for that one. Not if she lived for a thousand lifetimes.

The ferry slowed to a stop, resting against the large wooden dock with a small lurch. The warmth of the sunlight against her skin did nothing to ease the tension rippling through her body like cords tightening, her heart thundering in her ears.

Just a few days. Just a few days.

It would be fine. She could hang out with Ramona and needle her relentlessly until she got past her harsh exterior to the warm, loving woman underneath. And it had been ages and ages since she'd reached out to April, her oldest friend, who still lived in Marina Cove with her husband. At least she thought she did. Natalie would definitely pay her a visit. It would be just like old times.

People began filing off the ferry onto the wooden dock. Natalie swept her blonde hair back and put on her sunglasses, hoisting her canvas messenger bag over her shoulders.

It would be fine. It was going to be fine.

Even though Prague was still weeks away, she knew she would be unable to stick around long. Ramona would understand.

She'd have no choice, really.

Her palms were sweating as she followed the

small line of people toward the ferry exit. As she brushed against a wooden railing, she felt a sharp pinch against her thigh as a splinter sheared into her skin.

"*Ow!*" she yelped, and then slammed a hand over her mouth. Several passengers turned their heads inquiringly. Heat rushed to Natalie's cheeks as she forced an embarrassed smile to her face. She swatted at her thigh and ducked her head. The last thing she wanted was to draw attention to herself.

As Natalie stepped onto the wooden dock, something shifted within her. Something about being on the solid ground of Marina Cove after so long...it sent knives of anxiety slicing through her. Her chest heaved up and down.

This had been a mistake. Obviously. It wasn't too late to turn back.

She glanced back at the ferry just as a handsome older man with windswept hair stepped out of the cabin.

Leo Sutherland, the old ferry captain. He froze in his tracks as their eyes locked, and shook his head as if to clear it.

Natalie? he mouthed. His head tilted to one side in confusion. She lifted one hand in an awkward wave and quickly turned to walk away, the boards of the dock rushing beneath her feet.

Well, now it was too late. Word would inevitably get around to her family that she was back now that she'd been recognized. She wiped away the tiny beads of sweat that had formed at her brow, ignoring the pulsing heat spreading from the splinter in her thigh.

What had she been thinking? It had been too long. She was going to turn up after all these years and expect everyone to just *accept* that?

After everything her father had done leaving the family, she'd gone and done the same thing to them.

Natalie didn't belong here. At any rate, she had no desire to see her mother. She was sick of pretending everything was all right every time they'd spoken over the years, and she was supposed to keep it up now, with everything else going on in her life? An unpleasant task, indeed.

And Ramona? It wasn't like Natalie could fall any lower in her estimation, anyway.

No. Now was not the time to re-open old wounds. It wasn't fair to them.

A flash of her father's face slashed through her mind. Hot tears brimmed in her eyes.

She checked the time on her phone. All she had

to do was get back on the next ferry and turn around. She could be on another flight within hours. A flight to...anywhere. Anywhere else. It didn't matter. Natalie could look after herself anywhere she had to.

As she moved toward the ferry terminal, pawing through her bag for her purse, invisible bands pulled across Natalie's chest. Her skin flushed, and she realized that she was having a difficult time catching her breath.

What was happening? She expected to have a hard time coming back to Marina Cove, but it was like she was having a panic attack, or...

Oh, no.

Her mind flashed to a day in the forest with her father, long, long ago. A fairytale clearing in the trees, a waterfall shimmering like a sheet of magical glass. It was an entire lifetime ago. She'd felt it then.

But how...?

Natalie's blood ran cold as she tugged at her shirt, the fabric wrapping around her throat. Her vision seemed to recede slightly at the edges, and before she knew what was happening, the world was tilting over, sending her stumbling and clutching onto a bench that sat on the boardwalk. A distant part of her registered someone gripping her elbow and helping her stand back up.

"Are you all right?" a voice asked her. Natalie shook her head, and looked up to find a man staring back at her with concern etched in his eyes. It was the man who had passed her on the ferry observation deck. His little boy stood next to him, his eyebrows furrowed.

"Please," she managed, and she swayed again, gripping the man's shirt for support. The sidewalk lurched back and forth as her heart slammed against her chest, her skin ice and fire all at once. Her thigh was now pulsing with acidic heat. "I need..."

But it was all going away now. And that was okay with her, just fine. She could take her hands off the steering wheel, *finally*. My goodness, what a nasty time it had been lately, hadn't it?

No need to worry anymore, though, nopey-nope-nope.... The man held her up with one arm and was dialing a number on his phone with his free hand. The boy was looking a little pale.

"Oh, don't you worry yourself, little man," she wheezed, and then for some reason, laughed. Her mind was wet cotton, but her stomach somersaulted as an image pierced the haze. Her lockbox, the two precious items inside.

What she would give to hold them now, pull them close to her chest and let everything else *go*.

And as it all went black, as she fell toward the wooden planks of the dock beckoning her like a plush feather pillow, something rushed through her that she hadn't felt in as long as she could remember.

It was relief.

2

Sylvie groaned as she turned over in bed and drew the blankets over her head, her lower back screaming with pain, her shoulders tight. A dull, tight ache spread from her fingertips through her wrists; she'd been clenching her hands when she was sleeping again. Her eyes burned with lack of sleep, as they always did nowadays. Certainly since...

No. Sylvie buried her face under the pillow and curled her knees to her chest. Time to push all that nastiness aside. What she needed was *sleep*, and she had nowhere to be. Not since...

Nope. Go to sleep, Sylvie. Sleepy time, *now*, please.

Another twenty minutes or so of sweaty

thrashing in her blankets, and Sylvie groaned again, loudly. "*Fiiiiiiiine*," she said to the empty bedroom, and poured herself out of bed, tangling herself in the sheets and tripping into her nightstand with her customary grace and poise in the process.

After a healthy breakfast that included two stale donuts she couldn't remember buying and a fistful of cheese-dusted popcorn, she poured herself a cold cup of coffee that she must have made last night, gulped it down, and got dressed. It was important to adhere to a routine, you know. Especially after spending the last weeks holed up in her bedroom.

On a normal day, if her life were the life of a normal person rather than whatever fun-house mirror version of life she was currently trapped in, she'd be on her way to work at The Windmill, the restaurant that until very recently had been her pride and joy, her baby. But since that was no longer an option, thanks to a certain special someone...

Well. Today she had plans, at least. It was something.

Sylvie brushed her teeth, half-heartedly yanked a brush through her knotted hair, and then stepped outside. It was still early enough...but she clicked the front door shut as quietly as she could anyway, and tiptoed across the stone path leading from her bright yellow beach house through her front yard, right past the garish orange tent.

Just as she reached the tall pine trees near the street, her stomach clenched as she heard a *ziii-iiiiip*.

Come on.

She broke into a jog, ignoring the burning from the unused muscles in her calves.

Just as she turned the corner, she glanced back once. Nick was standing there in front of the tent, days of growth on his face, a look of dismay in his eyes. Her heart squeezed. He said nothing, and after a moment, she gritted her teeth and rounded the corner, not looking back again.

~

DIANE CLOSED her eyes and shoved her feet against the pavement, pumping her arms and leaning forward as she tore down the street. Her lungs burned and her muscles begged her to stop, but she pushed on. Running, as much as she despised it with the intensity of a thousand burning suns, was the main way she'd learned to clear her mind recently. It was a small price to pay for the temporarily clean and pleasant clarity of her thoughts, which typically snaked through her mind like dense thickets of brambles.

The cool early morning breeze from the ocean swept across her skin, drawing goosebumps but making her feel cleansed, alive. The streets of Marina Cove were nearly empty, the sun barely above the horizon. Diane had snuck out of the Seaside House before anyone woke, or at least she thought she had—she noticed Mariah had left before her.

Who knew where she was going...Charlotte's daughter was clearly going through something. Diane made a mental note to try to spend a little more time with her niece, see if she could offer help in some way. Not that she was in any position to offer advice, not with the way things had been going lately.

A rush of prickling adrenaline shot through her, and she pumped her legs even harder in an attempt to burn it off. There was a lot to think about lately. Like what she was going to do with the rest of her life. When she would be going back to her home in Los Angeles...if she was going back at all.

How to reach out to her son, Jamie, who hadn't spoken to her in forever. How to forge a relationship with her daughter, Kayla, with whom she'd just taken the first few tentative steps in repairing the damage between them.

What to do about Austin.

Heat rushed to Diane's face. She had no idea what she was doing. And she wasn't getting any younger.

There was something blossoming between her and Austin, something powerful. That much was true. Their shared grief over the specter of the past, of Trevor, of Victoria's death all those long years ago...they'd been using music, writing together, as a means of working through it all. They had shared moments of intimacy so intense that it took Diane's breath away.

She had loved Grant dearly. And, after three years since his passing, she was ready to open herself up again.

Diane could see what was happening...it was something she couldn't help. She was falling for Austin.

Which made everything a whole lot more complicated.

Because what was she going to do? Leave everything in Los Angeles behind, her home, her old life? Austin was a wonderful man, a rare, good soul, but they'd only just begun their...whatever it was that was unfolding between them. More than anything else, though, she wanted to move on from her grief, the blame she'd placed on herself for so long over what had happened to Victoria. And that was going to take time.

All Diane could do was take things as they came, one day at a time. Anything else was folly.

Diane rounded the corner of Sea Star Lane, panting, and finally slowed to a walk. The air against the sweat on her skin felt wonderful, its cool touch caressing her and pulling the stress from her body. She checked her watch. The others hadn't gotten up yet, so she could head back and make breakfast for everyone.

Her stomach rumbled. Waffles sounded about right. And coffee. Diane smiled. Right now, life was good.

Her smile broadened as she thought about last night with Austin. They'd been writing a new song on the beach, something potentially to perform at the Marina Cove Music Festival that was approaching. A chance to win the audience favorite vote, along with ten grand. In the unlikely event they won, Diane privately planned to use her portion toward restorations for the Seaside House. Christian knew how to stretch money a long, long way considering his labor was already free, and any amount would help.

Every time she and Austin made music together, Diane's confidence in her singing voice strengthened. And with every word she penned, she felt the tension within her loosen, felt something give, a little piece at a time. They held each other as the sun set, and then danced under the starlight. Yes, she could see herself with Austin.

But the smile left just as quickly as it came when she thought of the unsigned note she'd been sent, the single line against the white page, etched in neat blue cursive.

Austin is lying to you.

She shivered. Something had definitely been going on with Austin...something was just *off*. The phone calls interrupting their time together, the flash of something unwelcome on his face. The night of their first open mic, how he'd suddenly left her standing there on stage, the look of fear in his eyes.

What could Austin possibly be afraid of? Or whom?

He'd apologized and told her later he was just dealing with some personal issues, not elaborating further. He didn't owe her an explanation, not really. They'd carried on like nothing was wrong, and

Diane hadn't been able to help being swept off her feet.

But still...

Diane shook her head. Who had written the note? What did it mean?

Was he lying to her?

She wasn't going to confront him about it...not yet, anyway. The situation was already delicate without adding further instability. She didn't want him to think she didn't trust him, and she wanted to give him enough space to open up to her on his own, without pressuring him into it.

But the question was a splinter in her mind. And despite her attempts to push it away, Diane had an unshakeable desire to find the answer.

∿

MARIAH DUG her toes into the cool sand, gritty against her bare skin, and breathed in the early morning air sweeping off the sea. Waves splashed against the shore, stopping just a few feet in front of her. The lavender sky was still a little dark in the west; the only sound at this hour was the calming, repetitive rolling of the waves and a few sea birds singing their beautiful songs.

The beach that extended down from the Seaside House curved inland in a small cove where Mariah sometimes came to think. Last night she hadn't slept again, and had snuck out here well before sunrise to get some air. Her eyes were burning, her muscles moving slowly, as if she were encased in wet cement. It was a feeling she was well acquainted with.

To still the pounding of her heart, she leaned back on her elbows, inhaled deeply, and watched the water. It really was beautiful here...the tangerine rays of sunlight against the water, the wisps of wind across the soft, golden sand.

Mariah again cursed herself for forgetting to bring her camera. It was a scene of pure tranquility.

She'd really gotten back into photography since she'd stumbled to Marina Cove what felt like a thousand years ago, but was really only at the start of summer. Photography had been like a salve, a wonderful distraction from what she'd left behind in Boston.

What she had run from.

Her family still didn't know why she'd taken a leave of absence from medical school, and she'd made it clear she didn't want to talk about it. She needed to reset, to be anywhere else for a moment, to catch her breath and figure out what was going on, what had been happening to her. What to do about it.

A crystal blue wave crested and splashed against the shore, ruby sunlight scattering through it like a kaleidoscope. It would've made an incredible picture. Not for the first time, Mariah felt an urge to drop medical school entirely and just become a photographer. She could travel the world, live a life of adventure, a new country every week.

But that was only the fear talking again. Mariah was *meant* to be a doctor. It had been the plan for years and years, all the way back to when she used to listen to her brother Liam's heartbeat with her toy stethoscope. It was her destiny.

She sighed, her fingers idly drawing shapes in the sand. It had all started out well enough. She'd been a star student, acing her exams, tearing through medical literature just for fun. So much had gone into where she was now: the years of studying, the incredible time investment, the interviews. She'd never forget her acceptance letter to the Boston University School of Medicine, showing her mother and dancing hand-in-hand in the living room, squealing like children.

But then she'd started her rotations, and every-thing changed.

Suddenly, she couldn't sleep. Her mind would grind on every little detail, terrified she'd made a mistake. It was a *dreadful* development, considering she was working twelve or more hours a day on top of her studies.

It was one thing to read about patients. But it was something else entirely to actually work with them. Her fellow students seemed to look at them differently than she did, like they were *units*, stripped of their humanity. When Mariah talked to the patients, she couldn't help but bond with them, to ask them about their lives, to listen to their stories. They were people, not *units*. People, with whole lives, histories, hopes and dreams and losses and loves. People.

And their lives were on the line.

In medical school, they used to teach how to separate from patients entirely, to disengage from them emotionally in order to remain objective. But the research didn't bear it out; in fact, it actually led to *more* burnout. And so students were now taught to strike a careful balance between empathy and objectivity, between bonding with patients and maintaining enough professional distance to make effective decisions.

Mariah hadn't yet been able to strike that

balance. And if she didn't...well. It was going to eat her alive.

She'd approached the problem like she always had—with determination, with a resolve to do better. She tried her best to take care of herself. To speak with her superiors, to listen to their advice. To research ways to strike that balance. She was just new, she reasoned. Med school was hard, it was supposed to be hard. She would get used to it.

But instead of getting better, everything just got worse. What had started as a few hours staring at the ceiling morphed into full-blown insomnia. She eventually stopped tasting food altogether. Weight had begun to slip off her frame. She started having panic attacks again, something she'd thought she had successfully learned how to manage in the past.

Mariah went through the motions of her days in a thick haze of terror, of uncertainty and doubt, desperate for the day to be over, dreading repeating it all over again.

Toward the end, she'd barely recognized herself in the mirror.

And then, at the worst possible time, came the night that had been the straw that broke the camel's back. The night that haunted her, that consumed her thoughts. The night that had driven her to take a leave of absence and flee to Marina Cove, to the safety of her mother's arms, where she thought she'd be able to collect herself, get herself back on track.

As she sat there in the sand, her heart hammering, the sounds of that night rang in her ears. Mariah feared she would never stop hearing them.

"*Mariah!*" a voice called in the distance. Mariah whipped her head around, still in a daze. She shot to her feet, her stomach clenching as her mother jogged toward her across the sand. Concern was scrawled across her face.

"Mom?" she called back. "Is everything all right?"

Charlotte slowed to a stop, out of breath. "Come with me," she panted.

3

Sylvie didn't slow the mad dash from her house until she turned onto Seaside Lane, a stitch in her side, drenched in sweat and gasping for air. Geez, couldn't a girl let her muscles atrophy in bed for weeks on end without getting out of shape? Ridiculous. She wiped her forehead with her sleeve and then plunked down in the middle of the street, resting on the heels of her hands, trying not to think about Nick standing there in her front yard, that hollow look in his eyes.

Today wasn't a day to think about Nick. He'd caused her to suffer enough. Right now, she just had to get through the next twenty-four hours. And tomorrow...well, that was future Sylvie's problem, wasn't it?

Today, she had plans. A walk on the beach with Charlotte, and then a shopping excursion to the mall with Mariah. Although Mariah was a lot younger than her, they'd struck up a great friendship since she'd mysteriously taken a leave of absence from medical school. Mariah had become like the daughter Sylvie always wanted.

All that walking, though...it sounded exhausting. Not to mention all those people...

She looked down at her orange T-shirt with several holes in it, her neon green pants. Nice outfit for the mall, *Sylvie*. Whatever. It didn't matter. It was good to have something to look forward to, rather than face the prospect of the man sleeping in a bright orange tent on her front lawn. Sure, the love of her life had suddenly disappeared with all the money they'd ever had in the world and then shown up at their front door out of the blue, weeks later... but a new pair of shoes and a Cinnabon would surely fix all that.

The sunlight dappled the ground around her, and she could just make out the gentle crashing of the waves against the shore. She furrowed her brows, shaking her head.

What did he think he was going to accomplish,

camping out in her yard? Like that was supposed to convince her of something? After what he had done?

Not a chance. He'd left her without a trace, abandoned her, and was gone for far too long. Too many nights of crying herself to sleep. She'd filed a freaking *missing persons report*.

What an awful mess.

When she'd first rung Lucia and Stefano, Nick's adult children from his previous marriage, she could practically hear the shrugs on the other end of the line. No, they hadn't heard from him. Yes, they would call her if they did, but maybe stop worrying so much. They'd never warmed to Sylvie, never even attempted, no matter how hard she'd tried over the long years she'd been with their father, and had been almost *aggressively* unconcerned at his disappearance. "You know how men are," Lucia had said to her without a hint of irony. She smacked her chewing gum idly. "I mean, maybe you, like, said something to upset him?"

After suppressing a wild scream of rage, Sylvie instead thanked Lucia for her *very helpful input*, hanging the phone up before anything else came out of her mouth. And then came the wild scream of rage.

Sylvie pressed the palms of her hands into her eyes. She had other problems to solve, at any rate. Like what she was going to do about the restaurant. There was something tangible, a task she could really sink her teeth into. How to reopen, and *fast*. How to get her life back on track.

Oh, wait. No money. *Right*.

Back to square one, then.

An image of that night passed through her mind against her will. Sneaking into her living room, dropping the baseball bat to ward off the intruder only to find Nick standing there with that horrible hollow look in his eyes.

It was at once one of the most relieving and one of the worst moments of her life.

She'd known at that moment that it was over between them. He was alive and clearly unhurt. And so whatever he'd been doing all that time she'd been unable to get out of bed, waiting for the police to ping a credit card he'd used or for someone to spot him, waiting for him to *call her*, to email her, send her a telegram, *whatever*, it didn't really matter, did it? All the times in the past he'd gone without letting her know where he was, always *meeting with vendors, babe*, all the fighting his casual relationship with time and basic communication had caused between them, he'd hammered the final nail in the coffin this time. This time, she hadn't even known where he'd gone. Who did that to their wife?

Whatever it was that had made him leave like that, it wasn't good, and it didn't change what he'd done. Because he'd betrayed her, betrayed her trust.

And he wasn't going to fix that. It was over. It was the very last thing she'd seen coming, the very last thing she wanted. The thought of being alone...it was a dark abyss whose depth she could barely fathom. But he hadn't left her with much of a choice.

And so as she'd stared at Nick, standing there in their living room with his mouth moving like a giant stupid fish, his grand re-entrance into the tragic comedy of her life, she cut him off with a wave of her hand. She was barely aware of the hot tears streaking down her cheeks.

"Is it really gone?" she managed, gritting her teeth to steady her voice.

His thick eyebrows drew together. "I, uh, I can explain, honey—"

"Don't 'honey' me," she seethed. "All I want you to answer is one simple question. Is. It. Really. Gone."

He tilted his head, apparently confused. "What are you—"

"*The restaurant, Nick!*" she screamed, stepping toward him. "All of our money! Our retirement! Our livelihood, everything we had, *everything I've worked for*. I don't want to hear anything else. I don't care where you were or what happened. *Is it really gone?*"

Nick stared at her evenly, letting out a long breath. His big, dark eyes bored into hers, making her shiver. He nodded once.

Fresh tears spilled from Sylvie's eyes. "Get out."

"Sylvie," he said, raising his hands in supplication. "I think we should talk—"

"Get out, Nick," she spat at him.

"Sylvie, *please*—"

"*Get out!* I don't care if it was another woman, or if you gambled it all away, or if you were abducted by aliens or whatever reason you've got lined up for me, I don't care, it doesn't *matter*—"

"You have every right to be angry with me—"

"Leave now, or I'm calling the police," she said with finality. His shoulders sank as he exhaled and nodded.

"All right," he said quietly. "I'm leaving. But at some point, you need to listen to me."

"Actually, *Nick*, I don't," she said, biting back more tears. "You're a smooth talker, you always have been. I'm sure you've got it all worked out, and what, you thought you would just waltz back into my life like you didn't rip a hole in my freaking heart? Like I haven't been crying my eyes out since you left?" She pushed against his chest, his strong, sturdy frame unyielding. "I was waiting to find out *if you were dead, Nick!*" She choked out a sob. "And so it doesn't matter. It doesn't matter."

Their eyes met. "Are you leaving me?" he asked.

She shook her head. "You're unbelievable. I don't want to talk to you right now. And you need to respect that."

He watched her for a long moment before nodding. "Okay. I understand." He turned to leave through the front door. "When you're ready to talk, I'll be here."

"Don't hold your breath," she shot back at him, with a lot more vitriol than she'd intended. And with that, he left. But the next morning, she'd seen a tent set up on the lawn. And every day since he'd been back, he sat there on the lawn outside his new sleeping arrangements, waiting for her. He'd honored what she'd said—he hadn't said a word to her.

She wasn't ready to talk. And probably never would be.

$$\sim$$

AFTER A FEW MORE MINUTES OF suffocation at the hands of her own thoughts, Sylvie stood, dusted off her neon green pants, and trudged toward the Seaside House. More than anything else, the real question she now needed to answer had become clear—where on earth had she even found these pants? Who in good conscience would sell something in this color?

She sighed heavily. Maybe instead of a walk at the beach, she and Charlotte could just lie on the sand and go to sleep for a month or two.

As she approached the inn, her chest tightened. A bunch of people were congregated around something she couldn't see at the side of the house. She picked up her pace.

"What's the story, morning glories?" she called. Charlotte and Mariah looked up. Ramona, Danny, Christian, Keiran, and Diane were huddled around them as well. Ella stood outside the group a bit, watching the sea. No Austin, though. Too bad.

She laughed inwardly. Diane had gone and

gotten herself a stone-cold fox. Sylvie would just have to settle for her usual harmless gawking with Mariah over Keiran the Hot Young Contractor.

But then Sylvie's stomach twisted like a rag at the expression on Charlotte's face. Sylvie ran up to Charlotte and began to ask her what happened, but looked beyond them, her mouth falling open.

The unexpected congregation had distracted her from seeing it at first, but the whole side of the Seaside House had changed entirely. The last time she'd seen it, the withered skeleton of an ancient garden had been completely overtaken by weeds and thickets, brush and rusted building materials and rotted lumber. But now, the entire area had been gutted, replaced with a stunning, overflowing flower garden, a secret cove from a fairy tale.

There were roses of every color, sunflowers, hydrangeas, tulips, zinnias; beautiful wooden trellises were strung with ivy and honeysuckle, and in the center was a dazzling stone fountain that splashed sparkling water into a basin that flowed into a little pond. Two wooden benches sat beside the fountain, beckoning her to sit down and while away the day in a hidden paradise.

"Whoa," she managed lamely. She turned to

Christian and Danny. "Uh, you guys really outdid yourselves here. When did you—"

"It wasn't us," said Christian. He looked down at an open note in his hand.

"What happened, Charlotte?" asked Sylvie.

Charlotte turned to her, and for some reason, she had tears in her eyes. Sylvie grabbed her hand.

"This was my dad's garden," she said, her voice hardly above a whisper. She glanced over toward it. "He dug it out himself, and every year..." Her voice caught. Mariah rubbed her shoulder comfortingly. "Those trellises...he built those with his own hands, carved in all that beautiful detail. I remember watching him build them. I thought they were destroyed, but he restored them. I never imagined..."

Sylvie shook her head, glancing at Ella, who was still staring at the water. "Who restored them? Who did all this?"

Christian handed her the note in his hand. Sylvie frowned, and read.

While I wish you hadn't kicked me off your property yet again, I get it. My father's done a number on you all. But I'm not him. I told you, you don't know the whole story.

Maybe this will show that I'm not out to get you. Let's talk.

—*Samuel*

"I walked right past it when I left this morning," said Mariah. "I don't know how he did it all so quietly, planting all this stuff, repairing the trellises..."

"He must have worked all night," said Danny quietly.

"What do you think he wants?" Sylvie asked Christian as she clutched Charlotte's hands. Charlotte was staring at the trellises, clearly lost in memories of her father. Her heart broke a little bit for her friend.

Before Christian could answer, Ramona huffed. "He's trying to scam us, just like Uncle Patrick. He wants to collect for the restoration work their little contracting company did before we found out what he was really up to. That's why he's been calling us incessantly for so long. That's why he turned up and tried to talk to us again during our barbecue. He's conning us."

"What if he just wants to help us?" asked Diane.

Ramona shook her head. "To what end? The goodness of his heart?" She scoffed. "I guess I should tell you all now, Uncle Patrick's lawyers sent us a letter demanding payment and threatening legal action if we didn't comply. It's an intimidation tactic, since all we signed was that contract for the charity, but still. He and Samuel are trying to squeeze us dry. And Patrick...he's got a lot of tricks up his sleeve, I think."

Charlotte shook her head, sadness in her eyes. Sylvie knew that Samuel had long ago taken over his father's contracting company, the company that had begun restoration on the Seaside House. They'd offered their help as a way to earn their trust, in exchange for the family signing over a percentage of their future revenue to a charity they'd later learned was fraudulent. The contracting company Samuel ran was one of a long list of businesses Patrick used to scam clients. They'd learned of his lengthy history of fraud, embezzlement, and deception, how he'd always gotten away the few times he'd been caught by throwing money at the problem, his team of lawyers and his extensive influence getting him out of everything.

There was no fighting someone with that much power.

Ella cleared her throat, and everyone turned to look at her. She let out a long sigh, and then approached them. Her eyes wandered over the garden, her expression distant and drawn. "Well, whatever his motivation, Samuel did a wonderful thing for us here." Her voice was wavering. "This is just like Jack used to have it. He...he would have loved this."

They all stood for a long moment, admiring Samuel's handiwork. The gentle falling of the fountain water was like peaceful rain, and a few songbirds already fluttered around the flowers exploding with bright colors. The trellises had been cleaned and revarnished, exposing intricately hand-carved flowers, birds, and long tendrils of climbing vines that must've taken Jack ages. It really was extraordinary.

"*Ella!*" cried a voice. Sylvie's head swiveled around, the sound snapping her from her reverie. Leo slowed his run as he came upon them, his hair windswept, always looking like he'd just stepped off a Viking ship. But his face was twisted in concern.

Ella swept toward him. "What's wrong, Leo?"

Leo's face was bright red, like he'd run a long way to get here. He doubled over for a moment to catch his breath, and then drew in a huge lungful of air.

"Listen, folks, ah..." he started, running a hand through his hair. "I got here as fast as I could. They, ah, they got her off to the hospital fast."

A chill ran across Sylvie's spine. "Leo, *what*

happened?" asked Ella, the pitch of her voice rising. "Who's in the hospital?"

He shook his head as if he didn't believe it himself. "I can't be a hundred percent sure," he said carefully, "because it's been so long—"

"Leo!" cried Ella.

He shook his head again. "I think it's Natalie."

4

"Daddy, are we almost there?" asked Natalie. She pushed a branch out of the way, carefully watching the gnarled roots that crossed the trail so she wouldn't trip again. Daddy squeezed her hand as he guided her underneath a low canopy of pine branches.

"Almost there, Nattie-bear," he said, turning and flashing her a smile, sending a big grin to her face. It was their day, Daddy-Nattie Day, and she'd been looking forward to it for weeks. Daddy sometimes took her and her siblings on solo adventures, a whole day just for them, and Gabriel had just had his turn last Saturday. For her seventh birthday a few months ago, he'd taken Natalie on a surprise rowboat ride down the coast for lunch, so that was gonna be hard to beat...

"Okay, close your eyes," he said. "And no peeking."
She could just make out the sound of rushing water. He
carefully led her by the hand through the forest they'd
been walking through for what felt like hours, lifting her
up over obstacles, a fine mist brushing her cheeks.

The sound of water was much louder now. Finally,
he stopped.

"You can open your eyes," he said. Natalie squealed
with delight as she blinked open her eyes to find a small,
wide waterfall rushing down from a precipice above
them. Water splashed into a pool that reflected the
sparkling sunlight shining through the thick canopy of
trees overhead. It was a scene from a fairytale.

"Can I touch the waterfall?" she asked tentatively.

He grinned at her. "Even better. Watch." He walked
toward the waterfall, and after turning his head to give
her a wink, disappeared into it. A tremor ran through
Natalie's body. He reappeared a moment later, drenched
and grinning.

Natalie laughed in delight, and she ran toward him,
scrambling over a few large rocks. He held her hand.

"One, two, three!" they yelled as they plunged into
the sheet of water splashing over them, saturating them
to the core, before they emerged behind the waterfall in a
little cove. They stood and watched for a long time, the

water shimmering like a sheet of sparkling molten glass, her teeth chattering and her eyes wide.

It was pure magic.

After a while of dancing in and out of the waterfall, they sat on a large boulder in the clearing, drying off in the warm air and eating snacks. Daddy packed all her favorites, cream soda and pretzels and caramel popcorn. She munched happily as Daddy told her stories about places he'd seen, adventures he'd been on. It was a perfect day.

Natalie suddenly heard a low buzzing sound, and then felt a terrible pinch in her finger. "Ow!" she yelped, swatting her finger and dropping her cream soda. Tears sprang to her eyes as she dragged herself backward on her elbows toward Daddy. "Something bit me, Daddy!"

He took her in his arms, examining her finger. "It's okay, Natalie," he whispered into her hair as he wiped the tears from her eyes. "You've got a little bee sting, that's all." He held her finger up, and deftly raked a tiny stinger that was stuck in her skin with his fingernail, like it had never been there at all.

"It hurts a lot," she whimpered.

"I'm sorry, baby," he said, his voice soothing. "Your first bee sting. I remember mine. You'll be all right, I promise. We'll just wash it out when we get home."

She nodded and snuggled up against him, her

pattering heartbeat slowing down as he gently stroked her hair.

But a few moments later, she couldn't catch her breath. Her tummy felt sick.

"Daddy," she said. "I don't feel right..."

He stopped stroking her hair. "What do you feel, honey?"

She paused. "Like...really nervous. My head hurts." Beads of sweat trickled down her forehead as he turned to face her. His eyebrows furrowed slightly before his eyes widened almost imperceptibly.

"Okay, honey, just take it easy," he said, shoving everything into his backpack. "We're gonna get home right now, okay?" He swept her up into his arms and started toward the trail. "You just relax." He broke into a jog.

"Daddy, what's wrong?" she asked, her voice cracking.

His chest heaved up and down as he barreled down the forest path back the way they'd come in. He looked down at her briefly, considering. "I think you might have a little allergy to that bee sting, baby. But it's okay, because we can get you some medicine for that. Okay?" He pumped his legs, in a full run now. "You're gonna be okay."

Natalie's chest hitched. "Daddy, I can't breathe," she squeaked out. He leaped over a fallen tree branch, clutching Natalie close to his chest. His eyes met hers briefly. He was white as a sheet and had tears in his eyes. Her blood ran cold.

"Baby, you're gonna be okay," he breathed, huffing and puffing as they tore through the forest. "I'm going to fix this."

Natalie started crying. Her chest was tight, like someone was hugging her way too hard. Everything was fading away. "Daddy, I'm scared," she said, tears pouring from her eyes. "I don't want you to go, please don't leave me—"

His eyes drilled into hers for an instant. "I'm never going to let you go, Natalie," he said, his voice cracking. He clutched her harder against him. "I love you so much, sweetheart. I'll always be here. Always."

The warmth of his arms, the beating of his heart, the deep notes of his voice. She released the horrible tightness in her tummy, and a tidal wave of relief swept through her.

Daddy would help her. Daddy would always keep her safe.

Everything would be okay.

. . .

"DADDY?"

Natalie stirred, and felt a hand interlock with hers. "Daddy, am I okay?"

A voice spoke from the thick haze. "Natalie," it said. Natalie forced her eyes open, blinking away the memory. Her eyes were wet with tears for some reason. "Natalie, honey...it's me. It's Charlotte."

Charlotte? Natalie must still be dreaming. Her thoughts began to sharpen. The last thing she remembered, she'd just gotten off the ferry. But Charlotte lived in Manhattan.

Time to wake up. She had to get back on that ferry, she had to leave Marina Cove, get on a plane to...

"Natalie?" another voice asked.

Huh? If she didn't know any better...the voice sounded suspiciously like Diane's. Bizarre.

Natalie groaned, stretching her legs and arching her back. A spot on her thigh was burning like someone had poured liquid fire all over it. But she could breathe again. She inhaled a long, slow lungful of air, savoring the clean, bright feeling in her chest.

As her eyes blinked open, she looked down and first saw...a hospital bed. Her pulse quickened. But then she glanced up, and her heart folded over entirely. Standing before her were Ramona, Charlotte, and Diane. She shook her head. Mariah was just behind them, worry in her eyes. Huh?

"Oh, Natalie." Charlotte leaned in and wrapped her arms around her. Tears unexpectedly sprang to Natalie's eyes. "Where on earth have you been? I've missed you so much," Charlotte whispered into her hair.

Diane and Ramona were next, both enveloping her in tight hugs. How did Diane get here already, all the way from Los Angeles? She must be visiting... and what was Charlotte doing here? And Mariah? A stale thickness hung in her mind.

At any rate, they seemed too stunned to speak. Which made sense. What did you say, anyway, to someone who turns up without explanation after years of radio silence? It was a good thing, though, because Natalie found she was unable to speak, either. Her head was still swimming, but her heart was full.

She had missed her family more than she'd ever be able to explain to them.

"Hi, Aunt Natalie," breathed Mariah as they embraced.

"Oh, Mariah," she said softly. "It's been forever, honey. What are you doing in town?"

Mariah seemed to pale a little, her eyes skittering to the heartbeat monitor for just a split second. "It's, uh," she stammered, shaking her head. "It's a long story."

Natalie frowned for a moment. But then tension stole over her as Ella emerged from behind them. Fear and confusion were etched into her mother's expression.

"Natalie, honey, are you all right?" she asked, pulling Natalie against her and stroking her hair. "We were so worried about you—"

"I'm okay, Mom," she said, extricating herself after a moment and swallowing the sudden irritation toward her mother. "I'm all right."

Ramona pulled up a chair next to Natalie's bed. "Natalie...what happened—"

At that moment, the door swung open, and an older, balding man with a stethoscope around his neck entered the room. He smiled warmly to Natalie as she pushed herself up on the bed. "Hello, Ms. Keller, I'm Dr. Grenier," he said, shaking her hand. He wore wire spectacles and had a soothing, grandfatherly air about him. "How are you feeling?"

Natalie's mouth felt like it was caked in sand. "I feel a lot better," she said. "I can breathe again."

He nodded. Ramona looked between Natalie and the doctor, frowning. "Ah, maybe someone can explain what happened?" she asked.

Dr. Grenier set down his clipboard. "Ms. Keller here has experienced a systemic allergic reaction. Restricted breathing, a sharp drop in blood pressure causing confusion and dizziness, and, ultimately, loss of consciousness." He looked between them. "In other words, she went into anaphylactic shock."

Charlotte brought a hand to her mouth. Diane bit her lip and reached for Natalie's hand.

Dr. Grenier continued. "But she's going to be just fine. Thankfully, she was quickly administered an injection of epinephrine, so we're keeping her here for observation for a bit, just in case her symptoms return." He turned to Natalie. "It looks to me like a bee sting is the culprit...that angry-looking welt on your thigh. She got you pretty good."

Natalie squeezed her eyes shut. She'd first thought it was a splinter from brushing her leg against the ferry's wooden railing, but as soon as she began to have trouble breathing, she remembered. She'd felt the feeling before, the one of impending doom, her throat closing up, the world coming in and out of focus.

The doctor lifted his glasses back up to his face and picked up his clipboard. "Now, Ms. Keller, have you experienced any previous reactions like this?"

Natalie thought again of that day in the forest with her father. The waterfall. Sitting on the rock in the fairytale clearing, eating snacks. The painful prick on her finger. Her throat tightened at the memory of his face.

"Yes," she said, and didn't elaborate further. Hopefully her family hadn't caught the slight tremble in her voice.

The doctor scribbled a note. "And you carry an epinephrine autoinjector?"

Natalie's eyes skittered to her sisters before she looked down at her hands folded in her lap. "No."

Ramona huffed. "Natalie, seriously? You know you're allergic—" Charlotte flicked Ramona's elbow, and she scowled.

Natalie stifled a small laugh. Good old Ramona.

She used to carry her injector everywhere she went. She certainly didn't want a repeat of what she'd experienced in the past. But somehow over the years, she'd sort of just...*stopped*. She was at a loss to explain why. Probably some deep, dark nonsense she had no interest in shining a light on. Maybe it was always being on the move, the day-to-day craziness that was her life...she was used to a lot more risk than *bee stings*.

Maybe she just preferred to leave things to fate.

Dr. Grenier looked down at Natalie over his spectacles, meeting her eyes. "I'm afraid I'm going to have to agree with your sister here. You're going to need to carry an autoinjector with you in the future." His eyebrows furrowed slightly. "I need to impress upon you the seriousness...I mean, your reaction was life-threatening, Ms. Keller..." He scribbled on a pad and handed it to her. A prescription. "Fortunately for you, you had a guardian angel today."

Natalie frowned. "What do you mean?"

Dr. Grenier lifted a blood pressure cuff from the wall, sat down on a stool next to her, and attached it to her arm, beginning to inflate it. "A man and his son were with you, apparently, and when he saw what was happening to you, he called an ambulance. He was a quick thinker, though, because as he was on the phone with them, he lifted you right up into his arms and ran you two blocks down to the urgent care on Ocean Avenue. It was faster than the ambulance was going to be able to get there. They administered epinephrine right away, and then you were transferred here for monitoring."

"Thank God he was there," said Ramona, almost to herself. Ella took out a handkerchief and dabbed at her eyes.

Natalie's skin flushed. She remembered now, the man and his son from the ferry. "Do you know his name?" she asked.

Dr. Grenier shook his head and removed the blood pressure cuff, scribbling another note. "I'm afraid I don't. I only know what your intake notes indicate. But if you ever do see him, shake his hand for me." He looked over his glasses again right into Natalie's eyes. "Because he probably saved your life."

An icy chill ran down her spine. She nodded, fidgeting with her hands in her lap. "Thank you, Dr. Grenier."

He nodded softly. "We'll be in to check on you in a bit. For now, please just rest. And do yourself a favor," he added as he stood up to leave, "and start carrying your injector. Please." He nodded to her family, and left the room.

Natalie swung her feet over the hospital bed to get up, but Diane put a hand on her shoulder. "Natalie, you should rest—"

"Oh, I feel fine," she said, rolling her neck from

side to side. But the looks on her sister's faces made her stop. She smiled and sat on the edge of the bed, letting her feet dangle. "All right. You win. I'll stop."

Natalie met Ramona's eyes. Ramona tilted her head to the side and moved her mouth to speak, but nothing came out. Her bottom lip wobbled, and she wrapped Natalie in her arms. A spike shoved its way into Natalie's throat. "I missed you, Natalie," Ramona whispered.

Something had changed with Ramona. She was...softer, somehow. That permanent line etched between her brows was gone. Another pang of guilt hit her as she thought of how little she knew of Ramona's life...of any of theirs.

They were all practically strangers by now.

Ramona released Natalie, her eyes red. But then she flicked Natalie in the arm, hard. "Thanks for calling, Nat," she said. "Way to keep in touch."

"Ow!" Natalie yelped, rubbing her arm. Then she kicked Ramona in the shin with her bare foot. "That hurt!"

Ramona stuck her tongue out, and then a slow smile spread to her face. A laugh escaped from Natalie's mouth, and Diane joined in, shaking her head. God, she'd missed them all.

"I have a confession, actually," Natalie said after

a moment. "It was me calling the Seaside House for the last few weeks. The old landline...it was the only number I had left in my phone."

Well...not the only number. A horrible lurch of guilt punched her hard in the gut. There was another number in her phone, the number she'd been holding on to for a long time. The number to the person she desperately wanted to reach out to, but knew she never would. Not after everything that had happened.

Ramona and Ella glanced at each other, a look of understanding washing over them. "I knew something felt familiar," said Ella. "I thought maybe...but we hadn't heard from you in so long—"

"Years," said Ramona, taking a chair in front of Natalie. "It's been years, Natalie. Without letting us know anything, how to reach you. If you were even *okay*." She pinched the bridge of her nose and sighed. "Where have you been?"

Natalie's stomach tightened. Here came the questions. "It's...I, ah..." She trailed off. How did you answer such a complicated question?

"We have a lot to catch up on, Natalie," said Charlotte. "A lot has happened recently."

Diane nodded, and then her eyebrows rose to her hairline. "Oh! Geez, Natalie, we don't have whatever number you use now, or we would have called you—you know we don't know how to reach you, right? You don't know yet! We found out—"

Ramona cut her off with a hiss. *Not now*, she mouthed to Diane, shaking her head. As if Natalie couldn't see it. Diane blushed and nodded.

Natalie took a deep breath. "I know you're holding back telling me right now, so let me put you out of your misery." She looked between her sisters, her throat constricting. "I know about Dad."

A thick silence hung in the air as Natalie watched their confused faces while they worked out what she'd just said. Pale sunlight shone through the vertical blinds against the large windows, sending a scattering of light against the walls. Ella pulled up a chair, her lips parted and her eyebrows furrowed.

"You..." Diane started. "How...?"

Natalie ran a hand through her hair and leaned back against the bed. "*That* is a very long story. I, ah..."

She trailed off as her mind began to race, images flashing through it. She thought of Jess and Harper. About the house in Prague. Suddenly, Natalie felt shackled to the bed. A prisoner. The walls were marching toward her, her family wrapping around her like a noose. Her skin burned like a furnace.

It was a feeling she knew all too well. The room closing in, the claustrophobia, the cabin fever heat nearly choking her. That old hidden guilt digging at her, clawing its way out from the dark corners of her mind, desperate to take hold and make her suffer for what she'd done. As if her suffering hadn't yet been enough...as if she needed *penance*.

And every time she'd gotten that feeling, she picked up and left. Which quieted the feeling like the flick of a switch pulled light from a room.

For a while, anyway.

Natalie looked at her mother, her sisters, sadness in her heart. She wasn't going to be able to stay for long. They would have to understand.

They hadn't gone through the things she had.

"Natalie." Ramona took her hand, squeezing it gently. There was that spike in her throat again. Never in her life had Ramona done something like that...a simple thing, but powerful. Something hard and heavy ached deep within her. "What are you doing here?" Ramona finally asked.

Natalie opened her mouth to speak, but couldn't. Suddenly, she could almost feel the heat of the flames against her skin, the burning house she'd come to call home engulfed in fire. *She had to go in. There was no choice.* The countryside sweeping beneath her tires. The cold clacking of handcuffs cinched into place around her wrist, digging into her skin.

Tears fell freely down her cheeks, and her family held her tight. She buried her face in Ramona's shoulder.

"I'm so tired," Natalie choked out. "I'm so tired of running. I'm sorry. I'm sorry I was gone so long." Her body shuddered as she wept. "I'm so sorry."

Charlotte tucked loose strands of Natalie's hair behind her ear and took her hand. "Natalie, talk to us. We're here for you." The others nodded as Mariah handed Natalie a cup of water from the table, which she drank in one go.

Natalie took a long, deep breath, shaking her head. She looked up at them, her mother, her niece, her sisters. Her family who loved her, even after she'd abandoned them for so long without a single word. Just like her father had.

She was very lucky indeed to have them.

And so why did she feel like she was suffocating?

She closed her eyes, twin trails of tears cutting down her cheeks, and said nothing. After a while, Charlotte leaned over and kissed her on the forehead. "You rest, honey," she whispered. "We'll stop in later to check on you."

After they all hugged her goodbye and quietly left the room, Natalie closed her eyes, took ten slow breaths, and then swung her feet over the edge of the bed and stood up, momentarily dizzy. She found her clothes on a shelf against the wall, stripped out of her hospital gown, and got dressed.

A few moments later, she was gone.

lick. Click. Click.

C Mariah lowered the camera and checked the digital screen. Close, but no cigar. Her nimble fingers smoothly rotated the zoom ring slightly as she moved down the sand to get the focal length just right. Without directly thinking about it, she opened the aperture as wide as she could and simultaneously raised her shutter speed. She wanted the focus as shallow as possible.

Click.

She glanced at the screen. That's the ticket. She looked up just as the small flock of piping plovers she'd been photographing flew up from the sand and away into the sky at the same time a man with a dog came running past.

"Oh, sorry!" the man called back to her. It didn't matter, she'd gotten the shot. She sat back in the sand and shuttled through the images she'd taken.

Her skills had definitely improved. And in a pretty short amount of time. There was just something that made sense about photography. She'd think about what she wanted, and her hands took over. A thrilling sense of satisfaction swelled through her as she looked at the last photograph with a sort of pride she couldn't remember ever feeling.

A split second later, as if on cue, a familiar pressure bubbled up from her chest and into the backs of her eyes. An image of a hospital bed, the sound of a heartrate monitor. Nurses in blue scrubs pushing past her. Her heart skipped a beat, sending a spluttering cough from her throat as she placed her hands over her face and squeezed her eyes shut.

Not now. She grabbed hold of the tendrils of thoughts snaking through her mind and stuffed them back into the corner where they belonged. She rubbed her eyes hard with the heels of her palms, took a few deep breaths, and looked out over the water.

Her eyes settled on a group of surfers treading water a few dozen yards out into the deep blue sea.

White sunlight dappled the rolling waves, illuminating them with a sparkling glow. They called to each other and began swimming toward a large wave heading in their direction. Mariah raised a hand over her eyes to shield the sunlight and squinted.

One of the surfers hollered into the sky with glee just as the wave crested over him. Mariah held her breath. It looked like the wave was going to swallow him whole. She couldn't tear her eyes away.

At the very last second, the surfer pushed himself on top of his orange surfboard and stood up, deftly balancing just as the wave caught the tail of the board and swept him with incredible force parallel to the shoreline. She leaned forward slightly, furrowing her eyebrows. The guy was like a slab of pure lean muscle, and a dense sleeve of tattoos reached from each shoulder down to his wrists. Wet, dark hair whipped in the wind as an expression of pure delight crossed his face.

She smiled at the familiar curve of his jaw, the necklace of round sandalwood beads he always wore. Keiran, one of the young contractors Christian had hired to help him in the seemingly endless challenge of restoring the Seaside House. She laughed inwardly as she thought about ogling him with Sylvie on the inn's porch whenever he'd pass them, his tight sleeveless shirts clinging to his chest, a sledgehammer perched effortlessly over his shoulder. Calling out, *"Hi, Keiran,"* in unison before dissolving into giggles like two high-school girls. Harmless summertime fun.

Mariah found herself raising the camera to her face, felt her fingers unconsciously dialing the shutter speed way up, closing down the aperture. *Click.* Keiran turned his board slightly to shoot above the wave, one hand on the side of his board, before disappearing with a giant splash beneath the water.

Her mouth felt dry, and an embarrassed swell of guilt rushed into her cheeks. He was going to think she was a stalker. She quickly turned her lens on some of the other surfers. *Click. Click.*

Something needled at her as she lowered the camera and flipped through the pictures. It was probably just everything with Aunt Natalie.

A few moments later, she sighed heavily. That wasn't it.

But then she remembered, as she always did. Every time she'd let her guard down, every time she lost herself in enjoyment or quiet or calm, it was there, always there, always ready. That night, the night that was going to torture her forever.

She pushed it back as her fingers quickly shuttered through the pictures, her eyes not quite seeing them.

"Hi there," someone standing above her said in a slight Southern drawl.

She dropped the camera clumsily and yelped as it banged against her knee. Swearing, she frantically brushed the dust from the lens.

"Oh, sorry to startle you," he said, sitting down in the sand next to her.

Mariah looked up at him, heat rushing to her cheeks. "No, it's fine. Butterfingers." She reached out a hand. "We've, ah, never properly met."

He took it and shook once, his hands wet with saltwater and sand. "Yep. I'm sorry I haven't formally introduced myself before. I'm a little shy, I guess." He laughed. "Christian talks a lot about you."

She smiled, trying not to stare at the way his tattoos rippled over the sharp curves of his arm muscles. "Is that right? Well, glad to officially meet you. You guys have quite a job ahead of you with the inn, huh."

Keiran laughed again. "You could say that. We really need a proper crew of contractors, but..." He trailed off, scratching the back of his head awkwardly.

"But there's no money," Mariah completed the sentence. "It's okay. I know all about it."

She had been trying to help out while she was here by working at The Windmill. But of course, that was no longer open.

Mariah shuddered as she recalled the petrified look on her mother's face when she'd first explained what had happened with Nick, about her dream job being unceremoniously ripped away from her. She tried hard not to think about what it would all mean for them. For her mother.

He nodded. "That's cool. Are you moving here too? I know your mom lives here now."

A swell of anger rose in her throat as she thought of Sebastian. It was replaced quickly by a heavy pit of sadness. "I'm just here temporarily. My mom lives here because my dad, or rather the guy I've been calling 'Dad' my whole life, cheated on her and ruined everything." Her voice warbled. "I'm sure Christian has told you that he's my biological father."

Keiran watched her for a moment and then nodded, not elaborating. He dug his toes into the sand and looked out over the water. "I'm sorry to hear about your mom."

Mariah quickly swiped away a tear rolling down

her cheek. "No, I'm sorry. I don't know why I said that. I don't even know you."

They sat in silence for a while, watching the waves lap at the shore. He reached down and sifted sand through his fingers, letting it fall into the cool breeze. "If it helps at all, Christian is a great guy. I've been working with him for a long time. He's...helped me out a lot. I don't know where I'd be today if it weren't for him."

She looked up into his eyes. Sunlight glimmered against his golden-brown irises. She tried to speak, but couldn't find the words. Navigating her new relationship with Christian had been just one of the many recent shifts in her life. She'd been feeling like she was trapped on a merry-go-round spinning wildly out of control, trying desperately to hold onto something to keep her from flying off into the abyss. She quickly looked away into the sand. "Thank you for saying that. I know he's a good man. I'm happy for my mom. It's just...there's just a lot going on for me right now."

Another stretch of silence, this one a little less uncomfortable. He pointed at her camera. "That's a really good camera...hard to find. Where'd you get it? I love the detail it gives in low light."

She raised an eyebrow. "You're into photography?"

He shrugged. "Sort of. Just a side hobby. I'm not good. Like, at all. But it relaxes me. I love the feeling of getting the sunlight just right, dialing everything in perfectly...that satisfying *click*. I like the idea of freezing these fleeting moments in time. A way to remember." He looked at her. "Sorry to wax poetic."

"No, I know what you mean." She idly ran her fingers over the camera. It had been a gift to her from her mom...and Sebastian. All those years ago. Another rush of heat rose in her chest.

"Can I see some of your shots?" he asked.

Mariah debated for a moment, then handed over the camera. He deftly pulled up the playback menu and scanned through her shots. "Whoa. You got some great shots of us surfing. I almost look like I know what I'm doing." He laughed. The ghost of his Southern twang wrapped around her like a warm blanket.

She leaned over to see the screen. Now he was scanning through the shots from earlier, the sparks of sunlight against the sand, the piping plovers taking flight, the expanse of the Marina Cove shoreline.

"You're a heck of a lot better than I am, that's for

sure," he said. "You'll have to show me how you get shots like these someday. You're a photographer back home, then?"

She slowly shook her head, and a strange, faraway voice answered. "No, I was in med school..." Her heart beat hard against her temples. "I, ah, I'm on a break..." A frightened panic stole over her as her lungs reached out to take a breath but found nothing. Her chest tightened as she heard the steady, rhythmic beeps of the heartbeat monitor, the sharp, clawing smell of disinfectant. People racing past. A hospital bed. Someone yelling at her, her mind working too slowly. She needed to make a decision, but what? The beeping of the heartrate monitor rang in her ears, pounded against her eardrums. *Beep-beep. Beep-beep. BEEP-BEEP.*

A hand on her forearm made her jump. She looked wildly around. "Are you okay?" a faraway voice asked her. She felt weak and listless, like she'd just run a marathon without any water.

"Mariah?" the voice asked again.

She shook her head and shot up in the sand. "I'm really sorry, Keiran," she heard herself say. "I have to go..." Her appetite was gone, replaced with a roiling nausea. "I'll see you around."

She turned and trudged across the sand, her legs

heavy, like they were encased in blocks of cement. "See you later," Keiran called out from behind her in what she distantly registered as a bewildered tone. She broke into a jog, not caring how much she'd just embarrassed herself.

As her feet kicked up plumes of sand behind her, she wiped hot tears from her eyes. She didn't slow down until she got to the road leading to the Seaside House, where she could go to the bedroom floor she slept on and curl up under a blanket and get away from everything. Her feet sounded like drums against the pavement, the breeze like a tempest. She squeezed her eyes shut and clutched her camera against her chest like a child with a teddy bear, desperately wondering how she'd gotten here, lost and spinning out of control.

6

A s Natalie walked up Cedar Canyon Drive, she couldn't help her awe at the breath-taking view of Marina Cove's southern coast. From this height, the view was panoramic—she could see the boats coming in and out of the harbor, the rise and fall of the wildflower meadows and the forests, the long, untouched stretches of sand. She recalled climbing to the top of Monte Solaro on the Isle of Capri a few years ago, taken aback at the otherworldly beauty of the view, but it was nothing compared to this.

Her heart ached. There was no doubt that she missed it here.

She ripped her eyes away from the endless blue

horizon, and followed the road as it turned slightly into a forested area. A small pang of guilt hit her as she thought of Dr. Grenier stopping back into her empty room, but she felt totally fine. No sense in sticking around in that tiny prison cell of a room for no reason.

Natalie's feet moved of their own accord up the steep incline. She'd made the walk hundreds of times when she was younger on her way to see April.

A smile spread on her face. April had been her best friend their whole childhood. They'd grown up together, always in the same classes, chasing the same boys, bailing each other out of trouble. April had shared Natalie's wild spirit, and together they'd explored Marina Cove's vast wilderness and hidden secrets, feeling like pioneers.

But then April had gotten married and settled down, and then came the Year of Darkness. Marina Cove was suddenly too small for Natalie. Too painful.

They'd shared a teary goodbye, promising to keep in touch, but as Natalie stayed on the move, without any demonstrable plan, she found it harder and harder to reach out. Their lives were just too different. April had moved into a house at the top of Cedar Canyon Drive with Garrett and began working a dead-end 9 to 5, something with account-ing, or insurance. When Natalie changed her number for the first time, she had debated which numbers to copy over, ultimately deciding a clean slate was the best approach.

It was nothing personal...they were just too different. They'd had their time, and they'd grown apart. That was life.

Despite all that, the few times Natalie came back to Marina Cove, she always made a point to stop and see April and check in. She never regretted it. She would always be a dear friend, no matter how much their lives diverged.

As Cedar Canyon Drive leveled off, Natalie breathed in the fresh scent of pine and saltwater, a smile breaking across her face. It was good to have a plan. A visit with April, a trip to the urgent care center to try to get the name of the man who had saved her so she could thank him personally, back to the Seaside House for the night to touch base with the family, and then the first ferry out of Marina Cove in the morning.

It was a shorter visit than she'd planned, but there was no escaping the claustrophobia that had already been tickling the base of her spine...and there was only one way out of it. She had an old acquaintance in Nova Scotia she could drop in on and stay with for a few weeks, and earn a little cash helping out at her bookstore while she waited for Jess to square things away for their new digs in Prague.

And after that? Who knew. There were countless places she hadn't been yet. Countless adventures waiting for her. A lifetime of possibility.

As Natalie rounded a curve, she slowed her walk as a group of people milled around at the edge of the forest line. A young man in a ridiculous sombrero was chattering into a phone as several others circled him, looks of concern on their faces. Then a man cupped his hands and faced the forest, yelling, "*Caleb! Caaaaaleeeeeb! Graaaaaayson!*"

"What's going on?" Natalie asked a woman in a wide-brimmed hat, a deep frown on her face.

"We're on a tour of the island," she said, gesturing toward the young man on the phone. "And there were two boys with us. Our tour guide was supposed to keep track of everyone, but somewhere along the way, they got separated."

"Oh, geez," said Natalie, peering into the forest. She could just make out the distant cerulean water through the dense treeline. "Where was the last place anyone saw them?"

A balding man with an orange zippered pack around his waist turned to them. "It was a while ago. The trail split off in a couple directions, and *Zane* here got us lost," he muttered, casting a glare toward the young man still chattering away on the phone, one finger in his ear. "I think somewhere in those twists and turns...we should've all been keeping an eye out, but honestly, we were all feeling a little stressed getting lost..."

Natalie surveyed the group and then scanned the treeline. It was easy to get lost in there—even if you followed the sea way down below, there were sometimes steep cliffs of rock separating the forest from the shore.

She closed her eyes, mentally wandering through the forest up here. She remembered a place where the trails separated out, some heading out to rocky overlooks, some heading down to secluded beaches, and one heading right toward...

"I'm headed in there," she said to the woman in the hat.

"I don't think that's a good idea, lady," chimed the balding man, eyeing Natalie up and down like she was a child. "You'll just get lost too."

Natalie smiled politely. "I can take care of myself. But thanks for the concern, mister." And with that, she turned into the forest that she knew like the back of her hand.

Ten minutes later, she came upon the split in the trail, slowing her run to catch her breath. The path forked off in six different directions. Her father had always called it "Cedar Spokes" when he used to take them on hikes through here. Her stomach immediately twisted at the memory.

What was she doing here again? The surly balding man, with his little orange pack and his socks tucked into sandals, was probably right. This had been a bad idea. The kids could've gone anywhere in this forest. The sun was already beginning its march toward the horizon. For the first time in a long time, she felt the uncomfortable prickling of fear across her spine.

Who did she think she was? It was just like her to jump first, and think second. When was she going to learn?

Natalie took a long breath and wiped her forehead with her sleeve. A moment later, she turned northeast and began to run again. It was just a hunch, but if the kids had a decent sense of direction, this would've taken them back the way they had likely come. When she was a kid, there was an older man who used to run a little touring outfit from the eastern shore. He probably didn't run it anymore, but who knew? Natalie had learned to trust her instincts.

A few minutes later, the trail leveled off against a wide clearing of rocks that overlooked the shore below. She could just make out Shannon Pier in the distance, the old Ferris wheel still going strong. A rush of nostalgia flared deep in her heart.

And sitting there, on a large, flat rock that jutted out toward the edge, were two young boys.

A branch cracked underneath Natalie's foot, and they both jumped to their feet in surprise. And then the younger boy ran toward her, his eyes red with tears, and wrapped his arms around her, pulling her tight.

～

BLUE and red lights were flashing through the treeline up by Cedar Canyon Drive as they wound their way up through the forest. It sent a nasty rush of memories through her, and for a moment, she could swear she felt the cold pinch of handcuffs around her wrists.

She took a deep breath and squeezed the hand of the younger boy, Caleb. The older boy, Grayson, who looked to be about twelve, was apparently his neighbor. Neither of them had said much on the walk back. They were clearly spooked. Natalie had done her best to keep them calm, telling them stories of some of her adventures abroad to take their minds off things.

Natalie led them through the last line of trees. A small crowd of people had gathered at the edge of the forest, flanked by two police cars. At the sight of them, a woman yelped and ran toward her, lifting Grayson off the ground and pulling him into her arms. "Oh, Grayson, baby, I'm here, I'm here," she cooed. She had tears in her eyes, and mouthed *thank you, thank you* to Natalie while clutching her arm.

Caleb released his grip on her hand and began running toward a man, no doubt his father. The crowd had broken into applause, and people came up to her to shake her hand and pat her shoulder, thanking her for finding the boys. Heat rushed to her face as one of the police officers ambled up to her, grinning.

"Thank you, ma'am," he said. "That was really something."

"It was nothing," she said, a little breathlessly. It had been mostly luck, but it warmed her heart to see

Grayson's mother clutching her son, happy tears trailing down her cheeks.

She stepped through the small throng of people, wanting to make sure Caleb had found his father. She came upon a man kneeling in front of Caleb, stroking his hair and whispering into his ear. He looked up, and their eyes locked. An electric shock rushed through her body.

It was the man from the ferry. The man who had carried her in his arms to safety.

The man who had saved her life.

"Oh, my God," she heard herself say. She shook her head as if to clear it. But it was definitely him, standing before her.

His head tilted slightly before recognition dawned on him. He slowly stood to his full height, his lips parted slightly.

"It's you," he said softly.

Natalie was hypnotized and could only nod. He took a step toward her.

"Theo," he said. She could feel the heat coming off his body in waves.

"Natalie," she managed, unable to tear her eyes away from his.

He glanced down at Caleb, reaching for his hand, and then back up at Natalie. "You found my son. I..." His voice cracked. "Thank you," he whispered.

Tears rushed to Natalie's eyes, and she did nothing to stop them. There was something about him, the intensity of his gaze, that took the oxygen from her lungs.

"I should be thanking you," she said. "You saved my life."

He ran a hand through his dark, wavy hair, graying ever so slightly at the temples. "I only did what anyone would have done."

Natalie took a tentative step toward him and shook her head, her body feeling strangely numb. "No. Not anyone. But seriously...thank you. That doesn't even begin to...I don't know what to..."

A corner of his mouth turned ever so slightly upward. He squeezed Caleb's hand. "Well, I guess this makes us even, then."

Natalie laughed, tears trickling down her cheeks. Her face was on fire, her heartbeat thundering in her ears. They looked at each other for another long moment before each of them laughed nervously.

"I'm sorry your son got lost in there," she said. "It can happen to the best of us."

Theo's eyebrows drew together. "Well, it shouldn't have happened. Zane's a new tour guide of mine...he was under strict orders not to let Caleb and Grayson out of his sight." He rubbed the back of his head with his hands, strong and weathered. "I had to catch up on work today. I thought it would be more fun for him than hanging out in the office. I never..." He shook his head, and blew out a breath. "Zane and I are gonna have to have an uncomfortable talk later."

Natalie forced herself to draw breath into her lungs, realizing she'd been holding it for some reason. "You're the owner of—"

"Marina Cove Adventures. Yeah."

Natalie nodded. "I knew it when it was run by old Mr. McAllister."

He grinned. Her heart beat a little faster. "So you're from here, then. That was my father. I took it over when he passed."

They watched each other for another wordless moment, the world seeming to fade away around them, before Caleb tugged on Theo's shirt. He laughed, redness touching his stubbled cheeks. "Well, Natalie—"

"I should probably—"

They smiled nervously. Natalie cleared her throat. "I don't want to keep you."

He shook his head. "You aren't. I, ah..." His eyes

crossed back and forth over hers, making her stomach tighten. "You really know your way around out there, I guess." He ignored Caleb tugging on his shirt again.

She nodded. "I was something of an explorer when I was a kid. I'm pretty sure I know every square inch of this island."

A small line appeared between his brows as he seemed to consider something. Natalie wiped her palms on the back of her shirt, hoping he didn't notice. Against her will, her eyes traveled to the fingers of his left hand to check for a ring. Where was the boy's mother?

She pressed her eyes shut. Did that matter? What was her plan here? She was leaving. Whatever was happening here...it was very much unlike her.

At this particular moment, though, she found that she couldn't care less. Let future Natalie unravel it all.

Have fun with *that*.

"This is a strange thing to bring up," he said, rubbing the stubble on his chin. "Considering we just met and I have no idea what your situation is. But if you ever want to, I don't know, pick up some extra income, I could really use someone on my staff who knows what they're doing. I could work around your schedule..."

Natalie froze, her stomach twisting. "No," she said too quickly. "No, no, no no. No. Ah. I don't..." She couldn't be sure, but it looked like his face fell. He nodded slowly.

She dug her feet into the ground, her cheeks burning. "I don't live here anymore." She laughed nervously. "I'm sorry I just said 'no' so many times. That was a weird thing to do."

He laughed at that, hard, sending a strange warmth through her. "No, it's okay. It was weird for me to offer. I'm just a little desperate for good help, that's all." He glanced down at Caleb. "Long story."

Natalie's mind was in knots. Something horrible squeezed at her throat, a terrible desire to abandon her plan to leave in the morning. To stay here, right here with Theo, to keep him talking, no matter the cost. To delay the moment when they would part ways. Their eyes lingered on one another's for too long.

Theo finally broke the silence. "Well. Ah. At least let me buy you dinner." His cheeks reddened again. "To thank you."

She stared into his eyes, transfixed. Her mouth was dry. "Yes," she said softly, before she knew what she was saying. The word carried on the wind and swirled around them.

His lips parted slightly. "Okay." A slow smile spread on his face. Natalie shivered.

Caleb tugged on his shirt again. "Dad, I have soccer tonight."

Theo closed his eyes. "Right." He moved imperceptibly closer to Natalie. "Can we plan for tomorrow night?"

Natalie paused for the briefest of moments. She'd been planning to leave on the ferry first thing tomorrow.

Well. That was going to have to wait.

"Tomorrow is good," she said lamely, and grinned.

He pulled out his phone. His scent drifted over the soft breeze, like captured summertime, saltwater and cedarwood and fresh-cut grass. "Um. So, ah, how can I reach you?"

Natalie hesitated. She almost never gave out her number. Her own family didn't even have it.

His eyes lingered on hers for a moment before he began searching through his pockets, pulling out a small slip of paper and a pen. He scribbled on it and handed it to her. His ferry ticket stub, with a phone number on the back. "How about this. If you find yourself up for it, maybe you can call me tomorrow," he said. "We can figure out a time that works for you."

Natalie nodded, and squeezed the ticket stub in her hand. "I will," she said, her voice barely above a whisper.

He smiled. "I better get this one home."

Caleb looked up at her before giving her another bear hug. "Thank you for finding us," he said. Natalie forced back the tears forming in her eyes.

"It was nothing," she said.

Theo took Caleb's hand. "Thank you again, Natalie. Really," he said. His eyes blazed with intensity. "I hope to see you again."

Natalie nodded, unable to think of anything else to say. He smiled, and turned to leave.

She stood there for a long time as the crowd dispersed. Eventually, she sat with her back against one of the trees at the edge of the forest, trying to gather her thoughts. Trying to figure out what had just happened. What the feeling of unreality washing over her meant. She stared at the ticket stub in her hand, at the phone number etched against it, her thumb rubbing idly against the ink over and over again. After what felt like hours, she shook her head, and gritted her teeth against the wave of claustrophobia washing over her.

And then she looked at the ticket stub one last time, tears blurring her vision, before ripping it into a hundred little pieces.

But try as she might, she couldn't force away the phone number that had been burned, indelibly, into her mind's eye.

7

The sun was just dipping below the horizon as Diane stepped onto the field of swaying sea grass leading to the lighthouse. Crickets chirped and fireflies were just beginning to light up around her. A cool breeze swept off the coast below as she began the ascent, her heart fluttering.

As she navigated through the tall grass, she checked the time on her phone. Austin would be done with work at the restaurant by now. Tonight, they were going to hang out at the top of the lighthouse, write some music, spend some time together. Diane had been looking forward to it all day.

She approached the battered wooden door that was the entrance to the lighthouse. The latch was still there, but the lock had been long removed. She lifted the latch and pulled a few times to get it open, the weathered wood scraping against the frame. A wonderful old smell washed over her as she stepped inside, old dust and saltwater and driftwood.

After climbing up the old spiral staircase, distantly concerned about it collapsing on her and sending her to an untimely end, she finally pushed through to the observation deck, sat down against the wall, and breathed in the fresh sea air. The view was panoramic. Out across a large bay where the land curved back out sat the silhouette of Shannon Pier, the roller coaster, the Ferris wheel, the place of a thousand memories. For a brief moment, she remembered plummeting down on the old wooden rollercoaster with Trevor after they'd broken into the pier with Austin.

So much had changed so quickly. It seemed like a lifetime ago.

Just as she pulled her legs underneath herself and breathed a long, peaceful sigh, her phone rang. Diane frowned. She thought she'd put it on silent for tonight. She didn't want to be interrupted.

Her eyebrows rose as she saw the name on the screen and answered. "Hello? Teagan?"

"Diane!" said a chirpy voice on the other end.

"It's been a million billion years! How are you doing?"

Diane grinned. Teagan had worked at Nicholls+Kline with Diane years ago, and she'd been sorry when she left. "It's been forever, girl. I'm, ah... good. I'm good. How are you?"

"Oh, you know," she said, the sound of rush hour traffic in the background. "Living my best life. Sitting in twelve lanes of standstill traffic, breathing in the smog, trying not to tear my eyeballs out. The usual."

Diane laughed. She knew all too well the existential despair that LA traffic brought. "So what can I do for you?" she asked.

The sound of a horn blaring cut through the phone, followed by Teagan yelling a few choice words through her car window. "Geez, some people," she muttered. "Sorry about that. Survival of the fittest out here. Anyway," she said, her voice dropping. "I heard about what happened. At Nicholls and Kline. That you just sort of...stopped working there."

Diane's heart sank. She thought of the last email one of the managing partners had sent her, the one firing her. She'd left them no choice. Even before getting wrapped up in everything with Trevor, the writing had been on the wall for a long time. She'd long lost her passion as an advertising executive.

"Yeah," said Diane slowly. "That...that's sort of a long story—"

"Oh, I'm glad you're gone," Teagan interjected. "They were holding you back, Di. I never liked it there. And the clients...I mean, detergent? Popsicles? Vegan bratwursts? It's amateur hour."

Diane bristled slightly. "I think we did okay."

Teagan scoffed. "Yeah, because of you. You're a great writer. Everyone else there is a joke." Another blare of her horn. "*Hey, watch it!* Look. I'll cut to the chase. Me, Tara, Hot Adam, remember him? We started a new agency just a couple of months ago. And guess who we just bagged as our first major client."

Diane frowned. Mostly, she didn't care about this, but Austin was running late. Everything that had happened recently just made that whole life, getting wrapped up in all the glitz and glamor, seem...small. "Who?" she asked, trying to keep the impatience from her voice.

Teagan paused. "Spectra."

Diane leaned forward. "You're kidding."

"I swear."

Diane whistled. Spectra. They were a huge up-and-coming smartphone company, a major disruptor rising like a shooting star. Diane knew their past work well—their last agency had won numerous awards for their marketing efforts, but Spectra was never satisfied. They had what was effectively an infinite budget, and put huge amounts of money toward campaigns that they'd kill at the last second for reasons unknown. But the commercials that did air were incredible, the best the industry had to offer.

Working with them was a massive boon to whatever agency they shone their light on. Everyone dreamed of someday bagging Spectra.

"How—" Diane began.

"It still feels like I'm dreaming," she said. "But it's real. We already have our budget. They liked our initial pitches, but they want more. They've got a new phone releasing in the fall, and we're going to push it." Teagan blew out a breath. "And that's where you come in."

Diane's heart thudded in her chest. "What do you mean?"

"Diane," she said slowly, "we want you to be our creative director."

It felt like all the air had been sucked from her lungs.

It was the opportunity of a lifetime.

Thoughts spun through her mind unbidden. It

was the answer to all her problems. Money. Security. Prestige. A chance to use her talents in a huge arena.

But immediately, that all crashed away as she thought of her family. Of Austin.

And besides, she was leaving all that noise behind. Wasn't she?

This...this was different, though. A different story entirely.

"I...ah..." Diane stammered. "I'm staying with my family right now, in Marina Cove. I—"

"You don't have to answer now," she said. "I get it. You're taking a breather. You do you, Di. Have a reset. But I wanted first dibs on you before someone else snatches you up. I assume you're keeping your options open, but you and I both know it doesn't get any better than this." She hesitated for a moment. "I want you, Diane. I always thought your talents weren't being fully utilized. I'll need to know your answer in the next few weeks, okay? It'd be a five-year contract, minimum, we need someone for the long haul. I'll obviously have to look elsewhere if you've already got other plans, so let me know as soon as possible. We need someone, like, *yesterday*."

Diane heaved out a lungful of air in a huge *whoosh*. "I don't suppose this could be a remote working position?"

Teagan was silent for a moment, and then laughed, hard. "Right? Can you imagine? We should all be so lucky." She laughed again. "That's hilarious. Spectra would just love that. The head of creative calling in from across the country on an itty bitty screen. But seriously," she said, her voice now a little wary, "we need boots on the ground here as soon as possible. And Diane?"

"Yeah?" she managed weakly.

"This is your big shot," she said. "You'll win awards. You'll make lots of money. I've always had massive respect for your work. This is your time, Diane. Your time to shine."

Diane jumped as the door to the observation deck swung open. Austin appeared a moment later, his rosewood acoustic guitar slung around his shoulder and a grin on his face. Diane raised a finger to him, mouthing, "*I'm sorry.*"

"Okay, well, I've got to run," said Diane, her voice hoarse. Her skin felt numb. "I appreciate you calling. I'll have a think on all that. Mmhmmm. Okay. Bye."

She hung up the phone, her mind reeling. What had just happened?

"Hey, cutie," said Austin, leaning down to kiss her forehead. He rested the guitar against the railing and sat down next to her, frowning. "Everything all right?"

"Oh," she said, fire rushing to her cheeks. "Uh. Yeah. Yes. Fine."

His frown deepened, but he didn't ask anything further. He took her hand and squeezed. "You're a sight for sore eyes," he said, his gaze wandering over the sea below. "Today was a killer."

Diane swallowed hard and turned to him. She looked into his eyes, trying to steady her breath, watching the light of the setting sun glimmer against the golden threads that swirled in his hazel irises. A little smile spread across his cheeks. Diane leaned forward and pressed her mouth against his, her heartbeat hammering against her temples. Everything seemed to slow to a stop around them.

After a long moment, she slowly pulled away. Austin's face was flushed. "What was that for?" he asked.

Diane smiled. "I missed you," she said, pushing back the lump in her throat. "I really did."

The corners of his mouth pulled up into a grin as he ran his hand over the back of his head. "I missed you too," he said softly. He kissed her again. It did wonders to still the tangled web of thoughts in her mind.

They leaned back against the wall of the lighthouse, watching the colors of the sky deepen. The lights of Shannon Pier were just beginning to pop on. Her mind jumped to Natalie, and her shoulders slumped. They'd stopped by the hospital to check on her earlier, but she was already gone. For all Diane knew, her sister was already on her way to wherever her next stop would be.

"We don't have to play tonight, if you want to just hang out here a little," said Austin.

"No," said Diane quickly. "No, I want to. I could use a distraction."

His brows drew slightly together, but then he reached for his guitar. Diane watched him pull it lovingly into his lap like it was a baby, watched his fingers gently make the shape of a chord against the steel strings, his eyes wandering over the fretboard in admiration. After so many years without playing, Austin still handled his guitar with incredible respect, with wonder.

She turned to face him, already feeling better as she drew a lungful of bright summertime air, that unique seaside scent that seemed to make the lungs sparkle, that seemed to rinse troubles away. He looked into her eyes, strummed the first few notes, and began to sing.

Oh, another day's gone
And I'm waitin' for dawn,
I can't close my eyes, can't face what I know again...

Diane watched him with admiration, lost in that deep, gravelly voice laden with incredible emotion, sad yet hopeful, a voice that brought goosebumps to her skin. It was a song they'd been writing together, unfinished as of yet, but Diane knew it was powerful. As Austin wrapped up the first verse and began to sing the chorus, Diane joined in, letting her voice harmonize with his automatically, just letting go and matching his rises, his falls.

Been waiting for you
Been waiting for so long
Never knowin' where to go, never knowin' where to run...

In just a few days, they were going to meet up for a concert in the park with the rest of Silver Hollows, the indie band that Austin used to lead with his ex-wife, Kate, before their marriage fell apart. She hadn't met the other band members yet, and was nervous, knowing that Kate's shadow loomed large. And how many people would be there in the park? What was she even doing, anyway? She didn't belong.

Austin had reassured her that everything was

fine, that the rest of the band wanted badly to perform again, and that there was no pressure. But Silver Hollows had been famous in the indie rock scene, and despite Austin's encouragement, she still felt like she was a child playing with the big kids.

Suddenly, Diane felt everything around her slow to a crawl. The sounds vanished, the wind froze, the breath in her lungs locked in her throat.

Kate.

Diane shook her head slowly. How did she not think of that sooner?

Kate, Austin's ex-wife. Kate, the missing member of Silver Hollows, the woman with whom he still owned and operated a slowly failing restaurant. Kate, the woman Austin had unwittingly involved himself with because of the striking resemblance she had to Victoria.

He'd never gotten over his guilt, over blaming himself for the car accident that took the life of his first love. And once he'd realized what he'd done, the marriage was doomed. Austin had seen that he'd been with her for the wrong reasons, and she hadn't taken it well, obviously.

Kate was probably still in love with him. And she was probably the one who had sent her the note. *Austin is lying to you.*

Kate was trying to scare her off.

Diane gritted her teeth. She really didn't need any more complications in her life right now. And she hadn't done anything wrong. She didn't deserve getting that note. Maybe she could do something about that.

Maybe it was time to pay Kate a visit.

Diane pulled in a breath. It actually felt good, having a plan. Not knowing...that was the real killer. Now she knew what to do. What a relief.

She pushed back the doubt lingering in her mind, the doubt that asked what she'd do if Kate hadn't been the one to send it. The doubt that wondered if Austin really was keeping something from her.

Austin bent down over his guitar to pick a complicated pattern for the bridge. Diane's chest tightened as she watched him. The way his mouth moved. His tousled hair, a lock falling over his eyes. The look of concentration, the way he bit his lip when he focused on a complicated chord. His fingers nimbly crossing over the fretboard.

He looked up at her suddenly, and her heart lodged itself in her throat. Teagan's words echoed through her mind, reverberating like a gong. He set the guitar down carefully, tilted her chin up, and kissed her softly on the mouth. A gust of wind blew across them from the ocean below, whipping her hair wildly and bringing goosebumps to her skin.

"I'm really happy to be here with you," he said. The wind ran through his tousled hair, his sparkling eyes settling on hers. "I'm happier than I've been in a long time." He took her hand and squeezed it gently. "A very long time. And that's because of you."

Butterflies danced in her stomach as a grin spread helplessly across her face. "Oh, Austin," she said, "you have no idea..." She shook her head. "These last few years have been hard on me," she said, swallowing hard. "Well and truly hard. Grant, Trevor, coming to grips with Victoria. I've lost my job, I'm making up for *years* of lost time with my family, my son hasn't spoken to me in years..." She blew out a long breath. "It's too much, really, for one person to handle. And you've helped me so much. You've listened to me, you've held me when I needed to cry. You've been there for me. You're a good man, Austin," she said, her voice warbling. "I'm lucky you're in my life."

Austin wrapped an arm around her, and they watched the stars come out over the endless sea before them. The spokes of the Ferris wheel on Shannon Pier lit up, painting the water in a dazzling array of colors. In between gusts of wind, Diane could just make out the delighted screams of people riding The Rocket, the old wooden roller coaster. She rested her head on his shoulder and smiled.

"Diane," Austin said, his voice barely above a whisper. She turned her head up to look at him, and then sat back. There was a line between his eyebrows.

"What is it?" she asked.

His lips parted slightly, his eyes seeming to bore into hers. A shiver ran down her spine. He took a long breath and then let it out, his shoulders slumping.

And Diane knew.

She knew what he wanted to ask. It was the question that loomed in the air between them, always, working its way into every open space and pulling hard at the seams.

Thoughts began spiraling through her mind. The offer from Teagan. It would be enough money to help her family reopen the inn, even if it meant she would no longer be living in Marina Cove. Wasn't that the right thing to do? They needed her help. And it would set her up for a long time, probably for the rest of her working career. After Grant had gambled away all their money and their retirement, she needed to think about her future. She may have developed a deep-seated disdain for the world of advertising, but a girl's gotta eat, right? There was no work in Marina Cove for someone with her specialized background.

What on earth was the long-term plan here?

Diane's heart was thundering in her ears. She planted her feet into the wooden beams of the observation deck, feeling the weight of the solid ground. They both turned to look out over the crashing waves below, leaving the words unspoken. He held her tightly against him, and she rested her head on his chest, listening to his heart beat, her eyes welling with tears. It was going to be a problem for another day.

Right now, they were here together, and no one could take that away from them.

8

Darkness had settled over Marina Cove when Natalie finally turned onto Seaside Lane. Fireflies dotted the quiet street, and the sound of ocean waves lapping against the shore carried over the warm breeze. Despite the tranquil scene, nausea rolled through her stomach in small waves.

One night. One night.

As she approached the old house, her heart skipped a beat. She slowed to a stop, the feeling draining from her fingertips.

The Seaside House was practically in tatters.

Natalie bit back tears as her mind raced. Ramona and Ella had been having trouble making ends meet for years...but something else had happened. Black scorch marks ran up the side of the house, ending in sections of the roof that looked to be temporarily patched over. There had been a fire?

Weathered siding hung haphazardly all around the second story, broken windows and missing shutters and splintered wood. It was like an upside-down version of her memory of the beautiful inn she had called home for so many years.

What on earth had happened here? How had things gotten so bad? Her heart broke for Ramona. Natalie knew how hard she had worked to keep things going.

Again, she fought back tears. Of course she didn't have any idea what had gone wrong. She'd made herself unreachable. She had been gone far, far too long.

Natalie began to run toward the house, her heart in her throat. Why had she waited so long to come back? Why had she been so *selfish*?

As she neared the front porch, several figures stood up, illuminated only by dim candlelight. Natalie took a long, deep breath. But before she could say anything, Ramona stepped down onto the sand to meet her.

"Natalie, what were you thinking—" she spluttered.

"Look, I'm sorry—"

"Ramona," interjected Diane. "Hang on a sec—"

"*No!*" Ramona yelled. Natalie's chest tightened. Ella and Charlotte stood back on the porch. "I'm not going to tiptoe around it. Natalie. *Come on*. We were worried about you, obviously. You were supposed to be at the hospital—"

"I know, I was fine—"

"—we came back, and *of course* you were gone. I mean...I don't even..." Ramona threw her hands up in the air, shaking her head.

Natalie bristled, but only for a moment. She and Ramona...they always had a special connection. She understood her baby sister, always had. What others took for brashness, Natalie knew was Ramona just being direct, no-nonsense. Underneath was a strong, loving woman, one of the most caring people Natalie had ever known. Despite Ramona's current anger, her edges had definitely softened a lot since she'd last seen her.

"I'm really sorry," said Natalie sincerely. "I mean it. It was selfish and inconsiderate. Old habits and all..." She sighed as Ramona's face softened. "I wasn't skipping town or anything, I promise. I, ah, went to go visit April."

Natalie left out the part about searching for the boys in the forest. About meeting Theo.

After she'd picked herself up out of her strange stupor there at the edge of the forest, she'd gone to April's old house, only to find she no longer lived there. It was a shame. It had been a beautiful place. April had loved it up there.

Something bothered her about April not living there anymore, though. She hadn't been able to put her finger on it.

Ramona approached her slowly before wrapping her arms around her. "I thought you left already."

Natalie shook her head. "No. I don't know how long I'm staying." She gestured up toward the house. "I was hoping to stay here for the night, but..."

Ramona nodded. "Yeah. It's a long, long story."

"Is it even, like, habitable anymore?" Natalie asked.

"Sort of," Ramona said, smiling ruefully. "If you like your showers ice-cold, your electricity unreliable, and parts of your house burned out."

Natalie blew out a breath. She needed to get away from the house. Something heavy sat on the center of her chest. "Maybe we could all go for a walk on the water and you guys can catch me up a little?"

Ramona glanced toward their mother and sisters, and took Natalie's arm in hers. "Natalie, honey," she said, shaking her head. "Buckle up. Because a lot has happened while you've been gone."

~

HOURS LATER, Natalie stood with her feet buried in the wet sand, letting the cool water rush over them before it swept back out into the darkness. The moon was gone tonight; a billion tiny points of starlight blazed in the sky, a brilliant, shimmering pool of diamonds. It took her breath away.

She leaned down and lifted the tennis ball washing up to the shoreline, and, grinning, threw it back into the water. A very excited Ollie divebombed into the waves after it, tongue lolling out, taking several breaks to bite the cresting waves. Natalie laughed in delight. Charlotte's furry best friend was a *very good boy*, no doubt about it.

She turned to Charlotte standing next to her. They made eye contact for a moment, unspoken words passing between them, before they both stared back out over the dark expanse of the sea.

Her mind was reeling as she heard everything that had been happening in her family's lives. They'd told her about Charlotte's plan to restore the Seaside House, the fire, the lone one-star review from Felix. Her dream job, and how it had been torn away. Sebastian, and Christian. Ramona losing her home, getting sober, reuniting with Danny. The whole business with Patrick, and his son Samuel, how he'd restored their father's garden so beautifully. Diane losing her husband, the whole mess with Trevor, the first steps with Austin. Ella told her all about Leo, about their new life together, their new adventures.

They'd eventually talked about all the intervening years since Natalie had first left home, everything that had brought them all together here in Marina Cove. It was so much more than her mind could process in one night.

The only one missing was Gabriel. Natalie missed him terribly, so badly it physically hurt. Despite their attempts to reach out to him, he apparently hadn't been interested in a family reunion after they'd told him about Dad.

Natalie couldn't blame him. When Dad left, it had broken the family apart.

Gabriel had always been enraged with their father, not caring *why* he left. Which was ridiculous. He had his reasons for leaving. And Natalie had long ago given him the benefit of the doubt. She always would.

And she'd been right all along, now that she knew the truth. He was a broken man. It didn't excuse him abandoning them, sure, but Natalie didn't care. In her mind, he really could do no wrong.

But for those he left behind...they all had their reasons for coping with life the way they did. And so you didn't just snap your fingers and come back together like nothing had happened, sappy reunions and hugs and kisses and newfound trust and support. All that had to be *earned* again, didn't it? Real life was never so cut and dried. Real life was messy.

Beautiful, *and* messy.

Diane, Ramona, and Ella joined them, silently watching the waves roll in, enjoying the cool water rushing over their feet. A long time passed before anyone spoke.

How was she supposed to leave now? She shuddered involuntarily. She obviously couldn't leave so soon, not after they had all poured their hearts out to her. Not after she'd seen how hard they were struggling. There wasn't much she could do to help them; she had enough money to get by, but nothing more. And she could no more help with restoring the house than she could building a rocket ship. The least she could do was to stick around for a few days...

Or not. She could still leave tomorrow, after she found April. She could just visit home more often, then...

Natalie pressed her eyes shut. It was all too much. They probably wouldn't believe her, but she had missed them, badly. A desperate urge surged through her to hug her sisters, to pull herself against them and bawl her eyes out and just *hold* them, to wrap herself in their embrace. The force of it knocked the wind from her stomach, nearly brought her to her knees.

Natalie loved them, loved them more than she would ever be able to explain to them. Her family was the most important thing in the world.

And so why had she stayed away for so long? Why had it been impossible to reach out to them?

Why had she wasted so much time?

Natalie shook her head. She couldn't believe what she'd done. That invisible hand had always held her back each time she wanted to come home, to stop *running* and to be with familiar people again, to be with people she loved. The rush of claustrophobia, the walls closing in any time she *stopped*. It was too much to handle.

Natalie clenched her fists and bit back tears pricking the corners of her eyes.

"I'm sorry I missed everything," she said, her voice small and tired. "I'm sorry I've been gone so long. I don't know what to say."

Charlotte rubbed her shoulder. "At least you're here now," she said softly. A heavy silence ensued. The breeze grew slightly colder, sending a shiver down Natalie's spine.

"So what have you been up to all this time?" asked Diane. Her voice was tentative.

Natalie dug her toes deeper into the coarse sand to keep them warm. "Oh, you know..." She didn't know how to begin, how to end that sentence.

"Uh, *actually*, we don't," snapped Ramona.

Natalie slowly rose her eyes to meet Ramona's. That old hard line was between her brows. Natalie couldn't stop the corners of her mouth from turning up. Ramona's face softened. They both began laughing. "Sorry," said Ramona, her face red. Natalie let out a long breath, her shoulders relaxing a little.

"What made you come home?" asked Ella.

Natalie ignored the bite of resentment toward her mother, pushing *those* thoughts down. No point in dwelling on that now.

Instead, she reached down for the tennis ball, held it out for Ollie, and gave his ears a good scratching. He howled with contentment before jumping up on her, giving her cheek a wet, sandpapery lick, and dashing back down the coastline. Natalie couldn't help but laugh. She and Ollie were going to be very good friends. For a little while, at least.

"I just needed to get my head on straight for a while," she said finally.

Charlotte splashed the cool water with her feet before turning to Natalie. "Did something happen in Ireland?"

Natalie thought of the horrible burning smell of smoke. She unconsciously clenched her fists, the skin of her hands still inflamed and aching.

That story...well, she wasn't quite ready to tell that one. It didn't matter, anyway.

She shook her head. "It's complicated, guys," she said. The first fingers of the space around her closing in brushed against her chest. Natalie looked up at her family helplessly.

She didn't like being like this. She knew it wasn't fair to them.

They had given up ages ago asking why she was always gone, why she was always moving around. They'd had some epic fights about it. Natalie had never been able to explain it to them in a way they'd understand. The horrible claustrophobia, the only solution to keep moving. How every time she sat still, she thought of *him*. Of Joel.

Joel. Her stomach tightened. What could have been. What *should* have been. She had loved him desperately.

And she had ruined everything.

The guilt had nearly driven her mad.

After one particularly uncomfortable phone call with Ella and Ramona while she was living in Amsterdam years later, Natalie had chucked her cell phone into the depths of the Herengracht. With all her contacts.

She was officially off the grid. At least as far as her family was concerned.

And then somehow, more years had passed, and she'd never managed to give them her new number. It hadn't been conscious, exactly.

It had just sort of...happened.

Natalie let out a long, shaky breath. "I'm sorry," she said, not knowing what else to say to them.

Diane came up next to her. "Maybe you can at least tell us how you found out about what happened to Dad?"

Natalie met her eyes, and a long moment passed. A cool gust of wind swept off the dark incoming waves and whipped at her hair. She blew out a breath and nodded slowly. They moved a little closer to her, but this time, Natalie didn't feel quite so trapped.

"I was in this random pub in Ballaghaderreen with a friend of mine, Jess," she began, digging her feet deeper into the sand. "We were on a little road trip up to Sligo one day. And I overhear this guy, this super old guy, three sheets to the wind. He's in from a few towns over, yapping up a storm to the locals. He starts telling a story about an older woman who had been visiting a good friend of his. A woman whose husband had disappeared decades earlier, and she'd managed to track him down. And then I heard him say the name 'Jack.'"

Diane put a hand to her mouth, glancing over to Ella, and back to Natalie. "You mean—"

"Yeah," said Natalie, nodding. "I got up so fast my

glass shattered against the ground. He didn't have much when I grilled him. But he told me his friend's name. Maura." She met her mother's eyes. "And he thought the woman who had been visiting her was named Ella."

Ramona blew out a breath. "So you went to go see Aunt Maura."

Natalie nodded. "I wasn't sure if I had ever even *met* her when we were kids. You know how Dad was about his family." They all nodded solemnly. "So Aunt Maura told me everything. I made her promise not to tell anyone I had been there, that I wanted to talk to you all myself."

Ella shook her head. "I was in Ireland to find his gravesite. We were so close. I wish I'd known."

Natalie ran a hand through her hair. "Well, a few days later, I started calling the landline at the Seaside House. I wanted to...I don't know. Get back in touch, I guess. Things, uh, weren't going so well in my life, you could say. After I found out he had died, what had really happened, I guess I just wanted to hear a friendly voice. I figured it was a good time to come home, to take stock for a minute." She looked between them, her throat tight. "I missed you guys, I really did."

Natalie could almost feel their desire to

approach her, to wrap around her in a beautiful, comforting embrace and let everything go. But they didn't. No one quite knew how to navigate it all. Natalie wondered if they ever would.

"We missed you too, Natalie," said Ramona. Their eyes met, and they both smiled.

"What brought you to Ireland in the first place?" asked Diane. She knelt down to grab the tennis ball and tossed it back into the waves for Ollie to splash after.

Natalie thought for a moment and then ran both hands through her hair, damp with saltwater. She was breathing a little easier now. "Well," she started. "When we were younger, Dad told me this story from when he was a kid, maybe a teenager? He was climbing Mount Carrauntoohil, this mountain off the Ring of Kerry. I think it held some special significance to him, but he didn't tell me what that was, only that it was complicated."

Natalie laughed inwardly. *That* sounded familiar. "Anyway, he'd gotten lost...I guess he wandered off the trail, or wasn't following the trail at all. It was getting dark, but he was stubborn. He was only getting more lost. It was when he finally gave up, when he decided to head back down, that he ran right into the trail." She let out a long breath. "There was a lesson in there. There always was. But he made it to the top that night. The moon lit up the land like new-fallen snow. He said it was one of the most beautiful things he'd ever seen."

Ella drew in a sharp breath. "I've never heard that story," she said quietly, almost to herself.

"There was a lot we didn't know about Dad," said Diane, rubbing her mother's back comfortingly.

Natalie's brows drew together. Her family had gotten closer in her absence. She pushed back the sting of envy.

"So," she continued, "I go to Ireland every year, and I climb up that same mountain. This year, I just happened to stay longer than I intended." She paused. "I can't explain it. But walking in his foot-steps, knowing he was *right there*..." Her voice cracked. Charlotte took her hand. It felt warm, and safe. She looked up at her younger sister, tears pooling in her eyes. "I miss him. I wish...I wish I would've known what he was going through." She shook her head and dug her feet further into the sand. "Maybe I could have helped."

"We all have our regrets," said Ella, staring out over the water. "But there was nothing any of us could have done."

"You don't know that," snapped Natalie, too quickly. A silence hung thick in the air around them.

It was a terrible thing. There was no sugar-coating it. Dad was gone. And he was never coming back.

They could've had a lifetime together...so many more years. People always think they have more time.

You just never knew.

Natalie willed back fresh tears forming in her eyes, clenching her fists at her sides. Her heart ached horribly, like someone had it in a vise, slowly crushing it. She could no longer speak.

A while later, bone-tired, she found herself falling back against the couch in the common room of the Seaside House. The inn no longer felt like it was theirs. It no longer drew Natalie in with its warm embrace, no longer held that indescribable feeling of *home*. It broke her heart.

She may as well have been sleeping in another hostel, another stranger's couch, another night in a foreign place, unanchored and drifting out to sea.

Natalie tucked herself in with the blanket they'd given her after she insisted on sleeping downstairs, and stared at the ceiling for a long time, thinking about her father. About how his leaving had been the first toppling domino that had set everything else in motion. She thought about her sisters, how much they'd all been through, how she barely knew them at all. The festering resentment toward her mother. About meeting Theo, how she'd melted into a pathetic puddle.

Jess, and Harper.

The lockbox.

As her eyelids grew heavy and her body finally gave into exhaustion, her last thoughts were of Joel, and what could have been.

9

Natalie slowly inhaled the bright, clean seaside air as she worked her way up toward the northwestern part of Marina Cove. It was a perfect summer day—the locals were out and about in their shorts and sandals, eating ice cream cones or sipping cold drinks, bicycle riders looping around town, kids playing in the parks, families under umbrellas on the shoreline. The pressure that had been sitting on her chest was gone, her lungs now able to draw a full breath.

Once she'd fallen asleep on the couch, she'd had a surprisingly great night of sleep. She couldn't remember the last time she'd woken up feeling so refreshed. Her body must have just finally given up under the stress of the last few weeks. Months.

Natalie shook her head. Years, really.

Her feet carried her unconsciously toward her destination. After about ten seconds on the internet this morning, she'd found April's new home address and her cell phone number. Guess some people just didn't care about privacy.

At any rate, April had been thrilled to hear from her, and invited her over for lunch. After Natalie helped her sisters make a huge breakfast of pancakes, scrambled eggs, bacon, and pastries, she'd excused herself, telling them she was going to see April for a few hours. She agreed to meet them later for a trip to the beach.

But before she'd begun the trek to April's house, Natalie stopped at the ferry terminal, and bought herself a ticket for the last ferry out for the day.

Guilt stole over her. It was time to go. She'd known as soon as she sat down to breakfast with her family. She just wasn't cut out for it, sticking around like this. She'd catch up with April, head to the beach with her family for one last outing, try her best to forget all about Theo and his piercing eyes, and then get on the late ferry to the mainland. Nova Scotia was calling her name. She already had it all lined up with her old acquaintance there, who immediately offered her some work at her bookstore.

It was horrible to leave now, she knew it was. But she told herself she could just visit more often. It didn't have to be so all-or-nothing...there was no reason to let this much time pass. Maybe she could come back for Christmas this year?

A memory cut through her with the force of a sledgehammer. Running up the old wooden stairs, seeing her mother on the bed, the letter. That fateful Christmas Eve, the last time any of them ever saw Dad again.

She shivered. Maybe not Christmas, no. Maybe she could come back for New Year's instead.

It was better than what she'd been doing. One step at a time. You couldn't change everything all at once.

Speaking of which. Natalie pulled out her phone, shielding the screen with one hand from the sun overhead, and pulled up the encrypted messaging app she used in lieu of regular texting. It was how she communicated with everyone. That way no one would ever have her number.

Natalie hammered out a text, an unconscious smile forming on her lips.

Hey, Jess! You all good out there, wherever you are?

Before she could put her phone back in her pocket, the three dots wiggled, showing Jess was typing.

Natalie! What's up, girl? We're all good. Staying with a friend in Malta at the moment. Far enough away from Ireland, hopefully.

Natalie's chest tightened at the memory of what Jess had gone through. She tapped messages back and forth, feeling better with each step.

Prague was only a few short weeks away. It was good to have something to look forward to. A smile broke on her face as she wondered what adventures awaited her there.

By the time they'd typed out their goodbyes, Natalie had turned onto April's block. She put her phone away, another punch of guilt hitting her as her fingers brushed against the ferry ticket for later that evening. She swallowed hard, and stopped in front of April's house.

It was a nice little cape-cod style house, red brick and white trim on a block full of similar houses. Neighbors mowing the lawn, sitting on their porches, happy people, all going through the same motions, *Hey Bill, hot enough for ya? Hahahahaha*, day after day after day after day…

Her shoulders tensed. Places like this, they always felt like a prison to Natalie. She looked over April's new house. It was nice, but they were crazy to leave that beautiful old house up on Cedar Canyon. Toys were strewn across the yard, the grass nearly at knee level. Paint was chipping on the house exterior, and the trash cans were overflowing. Things weren't run down, exactly...it was all just unkempt. April and Garrett had three young children, who could blame them? She pushed back the prickling of claustro- phobia, and took a long, deep breath.

After a moment, Natalie trotted up to the front door, nearly faceplanting after stumbling over a pink tricycle. A gigantic, gleaming silver SUV sat in the driveway, in front of a covered boat on a trailer. Before she could knock on the old front door, it opened, and April shot out, pulling Natalie into a crushing hug and practically lifting her off the ground.

"Natalie! Oh, God, it's so good to see you!" she yipped. Natalie squeezed her friend close, breathing in her scent, her heart dancing with delight.

"I missed you so much," said Natalie. "It's been forever. Way, way too long."

April released her and led her inside. "I'm so sorry about the mess," she said. "Things have been a little crazy lately..." Her phone chimed. April pulled it out, frowned, and shoved it back into her pocket.

Natalie waved her hands dismissively. "The place looks great. I can't imagine what it's like, three young kids." April led her through the dining room, which had been converted into a play area, stepping carefully over toy cars, plastic blocks, torn books, dozens of stuffed animals. "You're in full-blown Mom mode. It's what you always wanted." She glanced into the living room. The most enormous flat-screen TV she'd ever seen was perched above a decorative fireplace. In front of the TV sat a lone leather recliner next to a tiny end table. Garrett's throne, apparently.

April laughed as she led Natalie to the small kitchen, gesturing toward a wooden table in the corner. Her phone chimed again. "It's a lot, for sure. I don't think I've slept a full night since my oldest was born. But I'm managing." She pulled out two mugs. "Want some coffee? Some tea?" She looked at Natalie, her face flushed. "I can't believe you're here. It's...surreal." *Chime. Chime.*

Natalie grinned, ignoring the constant texts on April's phone. "Tea sounds lovely, thank you." She watched her oldest friend busy herself around the kitchen with a practiced hand. It was a far cry from the girl who used to break into abandoned buildings in the middle of the night with her, who she used to sneak into high school parties with. The girl who once held her hand as they jumped off Gambler's Leap on the north shore of Marina Cove together, screaming wildly into the night, sailing through starlight and plunging into the icy pool of water below.

"So where are the little rascals?" Natalie asked as April handed her a mug of tea and sat across from her. Natalie noticed for the first time the dark circles under April's eyes.

Chime. "Oh, Garrett took them to his parents' house so we could have some quiet time together," she said, gesturing around. "A rarity around here. His parents live just around the corner."

Whoa, too close for comfort. "How nice for you guys," she said. "I actually tried to visit you yesterday. I went to your old place up on Cedar Canyon."

Something clouded over on April's face, sending a prickling sensation over Natalie's arms. "Yeah, ah, we moved a while back," she said, not meeting Natalie's eyes. "Garrett's a powerlifting trainer at a gym over here, and he wanted to be closer to his clients." She lifted her tea bag in and out of her cup. *Chime.* "I miss the old house, of course, but I like it here."

Natalie nodded. Suddenly the room felt a little hotter. She tugged at the neck of her T-shirt. "So. Tell me everything. What've you been up to all these years?"

April laughed. "Oh, you know. Working. Kids. It's funny," she said, meeting Natalie's eyes, "there's simultaneously more than I could ever tell you, and also very little to tell you. The days seem to burst with insanity, but in a way they're all the same. I feel like I'm in one of those dreams, where I'm doomed to repeat the same day over and over again for all eternity." She ran a hand through her hair and sighed. "I'm making it sound worse than it is. The kids are great, they really are, they're a dream come true. Garrett's kids from his last marriage are all grown, and I did always want kids. They're not the problem." She shook her head quickly. "There is no problem. I'm great. We're great." *Chime.*

Natalie glanced down at the table. "Do you need to get that?"

April shook her head, tapping the phone to put it on silent. "No. Sorry." But she didn't elaborate. Something caught in the corner of her eye, through the front window. A blazing red pickup truck slowly passed the house. "Enough about me, though, I want to hear everything you've been up to. Natalie the

Wild Child, the world traveler, the great explorer. Let me escape my humdrum life for a while and hear about yours," she said on a laugh.

Natalie pushed back the odd tension in her stomach and told her a few stories of her travels. Sailing the Galápagos Islands. Her solo trek across the entire Icelandic wilderness. The year she spent on a motorcycle across Europe with a man named Esteban, who spoke no English. She had a deep well of experience from which to draw, and April was a good audience; she clearly missed her own wilder days.

But an odd thing happened as Natalie recounted some of her stories. They seemed to follow a similar format, a formula; picking up on a whim and randomly choosing a new location. Exploring, making friends of circumstance, bursts of whirlwind romance that dissipated as fast as they'd begun, and then that irrepressible need to move on.

Lather, rinse, repeat.

It wasn't all that different from how April was describing her own life. A sickening lurch rolled through Natalie's stomach.

She glanced out the window to see the gigantic pickup truck monstrosity slowly rolling by the house again, the brand-new paint gleaming in the sunlight, piercing her eyes.

Chime. Chime.

April leaned on her elbows, pinching the bridge of her nose. "So how long are you in town?" she asked her tea.

Natalie looked up at her friend, momentarily speechless, and then somehow saw April through different eyes, just for the briefest of moments. Hunched over the table, clutching her mug. Her eyes bloodshot, weary. Her expression distant. Another cold shiver ran down Natalie's spine.

Something was wrong.

Natalie set down her mug and reached across the table, taking April's hand. "April, I've known you for a long time. A long, long time," she said carefully. April's eyebrows drew together slightly. *Chime.* Natalie leaned forward. "You can talk to me. Is everything okay?"

April stared at Natalie for a long moment, and then her eyes welled with tears. There was a horrible hollow look in her gaze. Finally, she opened her mouth to speak, but then the screeching of tires in the driveway tore through the house. April frantically wiped her eyes and shook her head.

"What the..." Natalie said, standing up. "April, what's—"

And then Garrett barged through the front door, holding a young boy who looked no more than three, followed by two more older children. He was wearing a white tank top and gym shorts, the sharp edges of his muscles bulging like they were about to pop like a balloon. The two older kids ran right upstairs as Garrett lumbered into the kitchen, plopping the boy down on April's lap. She flinched.

"He needs a snack," he said as he pulled a glass from the cupboard and filled it with water. He pulled down a large plastic container, some sort of supplement, and began dumping the powder into his cup.

"Uh, hello, Garrett," said Natalie, something hot stirring in her chest as she sat back down. Garrett had been the one texting her the whole time, obviously rushing April. So much for giving them time to catch up.

Garrett glanced down at her. "What's going on, Natalie?" He eyed her up and down, too slowly. Natalie crossed her arms over her chest automatically. "Been a minute, yeah?"

She frowned. April set the boy in a chair at a little square table in the corner of the kitchen and began pulling food from the fridge. Natalie didn't know what to say. After loudly gulping whatever mixture he'd concocted, Garrett belched, snuck one more glance at Natalie's body, and then pointed at the boy. "Give him some pants, April," he said. She flinched again as he passed her. "My mom said his legs were cold."

April nodded as Garrett left the room, plonking down on the leather recliner in the living room and turning on a hockey game. She left the kitchen, leaving Natalie alone with the boy.

Alarm bells were ringing in Natalie's mind. She turned to the boy, who had a giant grin plastered on his face. "I'm Timmy," he said, standing and doing a little hopping dance on the floor while waving a slice of cheese in the air. At least he was oblivious.

"Hi, Timmy," she said. Her mouth felt like it was caked with dust. A moment later, April swept back in with a pair of pants, and set them on the counter. "I'm sorry to cut things short," she said over her shoulder. "I, ah, I've got to get dinner started, I've got laundry, cleaning..." She began pulling cans and boxes from the cupboard. "Garrett's had a long day..." she said, like it was an explanation.

Natalie felt like she might jump straight out of her skin. April was living Natalie's worst nightmare.

Trapped, with no escape. A prison of her own making.

What had happened? Back in the day, April had been so strong, so independent...

She watched April for a moment, stunned. A memory filled her mind, back to something April had told her when she and Garrett had first gotten married. She'd always wanted it in a church, had it all planned out, and then changed it at the very last minute to the fire hall. Garrett was a self-professed atheist, looking for any opportunity to sling it into a conversation. Until now, she'd never put it together. Even back then, he'd been pulling the strings.

Whatever was happening here, there was a long history of it.

As Natalie rose from the table, April met her eyes. She held a box of dinosaur-shaped macaroni in one hand and a pot in the other. April briefly glanced toward Garrett in the living room, and then back to Natalie. Their gaze lingered on one another's for what seemed like a long time. There was a look of something in her expression that was almost pleading. It chilled Natalie to the core.

"Listen," said April softly. A tear trickled down her cheek. "If you're still in town later this week, maybe we can grab lunch or something." She looked around helplessly. "Out of the house this time. I'll figure something out."

Natalie approached her and wrapped her friend in a hug, leaning up to whisper in her ear. "April, are you all right?"

April nodded. "Really. Things are fine." She forced a laugh. "I know what you're thinking. But Garrett...he's not like that. He's just rude sometimes. His job is stressful. I'm sorry about all that." April squeezed her hard. "It was really good to see you, Natalie. I missed you terribly."

"I missed you too, honey," she said, forcing back the lump in her throat.

A few moments later, she was standing back on the street, a feeling sweeping over her like she'd just surfaced after being underwater. She inhaled the fresh air for a long time, her mind racing. The whole visit had shaken her.

April needed her help. At the very least, she needed a friend.

She pressed her eyes shut. Well. That did it. With her family struggling the way they were, and now her best friend trapped in a suburban nightmare with a man who, at the bare minimum, had no respect for her, there was no way she was going to leave Marina Cove right now. Prague was still going to be there in a few weeks. Right now, there were people who needed her.

Natalie reached into her pocket, pulled out the ferry ticket, and tore it in half.

She was going to stick around for a while.

Her stomach was knotted, icy chills crossing over her skin. This hadn't been part of the plan. But that was life. She could manage. She *would* manage.

And before she could stop herself, she pulled out her phone, her heart fluttering. Her fingers dialed the number that had been swimming in her mind.

If she was going to stick around for a while, she could earn some extra money. She could stockpile a little cash to tide her over for the next stretch of... whatever it was she was going to do next. Future Natalie's problem, and all that.

And Theo...well, he had said he was desperate for help. It would certainly be more interesting work than her usual travel go-to of waitressing. And while she was here, there was no harm in having dinner with him, was there? Except she would take *him* to dinner. She owed him that much for what he'd done.

On the third ring, he answered. "Hello?"

"Theo?" Natalie said, her voice trembling slightly with adrenaline.

A beat passed. "Natalie," he said, sounding

genuinely surprised. "I was hoping you'd call." Natalie's stomach somersaulted.

Out of the frying pan, into the fire.

"Theo," she said, exhaling slowly. "Would you like to have that dinner with me?" She was suddenly overcome with a sensation of crossing over some invisible threshold.

And she had no idea what it was going to mean.

10

"Well. I could get used to this," said Sylvie, taking a long slurp from her chocolate malt shake. She turned to Mariah, wiggling her eyebrows. "You gonna finish that?"

Mariah guarded her shake and stuck her tongue out. "You stay away."

Charlotte laughed, leaning her face up toward the sunshine basking down on them. In the distance, thunder rumbled, but for now the sky was a crystal clear blue. "Nobody makes them like Jerry."

The three women were slowly making their way down the stretch of sand. They'd just had what turned into a lunchtime feast at Jerry's Diner. After weeks of barely tasting her food, Sylvie was beginning to get her appetite back. It was a tremendous relief. A delicious cheeseburger, hot, crispy french fries, and fresh-cut watermelon had been just what the doctor ordered.

And chocolate malt...well, that had always been her weakness. She grinned as she polished off the rest, and then glanced longingly at Mariah's, emitting an exaggerated, plaintive sigh. Mariah giggled and kicked sand at her shins.

Sylvie let out a long, slow breath, noticing the sun warming her skin for the first time in what felt like a long time. The ocean sparkled beside them, the water rushing over the shoreline to meet their feet. It was a beautiful day, it really was. She hadn't been noticing them lately, and that had been a real loss in a place like Marina Cove.

"So, what's on the docket today?" asked Sylvie. "You guys talk to Samuel yet?"

Charlotte and Mariah exchanged glances. "Not yet," said Charlotte. "Ramona doesn't want to meet with him. She's suspicious, and has every right to be."

Sylvie nodded. "Still. That garden paradise. That was a pretty cool move, you have to admit."

"It really was," said Mariah. "I still don't know how he managed all that in one night."

Charlotte's brows drew together. "I don't think Samuel has any idea what that meant to me, to our mom..." She sighed. "I think we ought to hear him out, whatever he has to say. I don't trust him either, but whatever he wanted to tell us about Uncle Patrick sounded ominous, and I don't like not knowing what lurks in the basement, know what I mean?"

Yeah, after all the things they'd learned about that scumbag Patrick, who knew what else he had up his sleeve. Poor Charlotte...she didn't need to be dealing with this on top of everything else. Like, just off the top of her head, Sebastian most likely *going to prison*. She shuddered.

"I could talk to Samuel for you," said Sylvie. "On the sly, yeah? Ramona will never know." She gave a wink.

Charlotte laughed and shook her head. "I think Ramona just needs a little more convincing. I'd like to see what he has to say. Find out what he wants."

They all stopped at the water, admiring the waves gently rolling against the shore. A small flock of seagulls circled overhead, calling out into the wind. The sky had darkened considerably, dark clouds slowly working their way toward them.

Mariah met Sylvie's eyes. "Have you decided what to do about Nick yet?"

Sylvie barked a loud laugh. Mariah had inherited Ramona's directness. It was something she appreciated. "Oh, man," she said, shaking her head. "No. I have no idea. Right now, I sort of like the idea of him suffering out in that tent on our lawn. There's a sort of poetic justice to it, after what he did to me."

Lightning flashed somewhere out over the water. The air had that dense, earthy smell just before rainfall. Sylvie debated for a moment, then furrowed her brows in resolve. "On that note, though," said Sylvie, "I did want to talk to you guys about something."

Charlotte and Mariah moved closer. "Anything," said Charlotte.

Tears nearly sprang to Sylvie's eyes. It was so wonderful having Charlotte back in her life. She was fortunate to have such a good friend. And Mariah had been a wonderful surprise, an old soul, someone she just naturally clicked with.

It was going to be brutal when Mariah left to go back to med school. Whenever that was.

"I have a plan," Sylvie said slowly. Thunder boomed, getting closer as the sky darkened. "A plan to reopen The Windmill. And I'm going to need your help. Both of you."

Mariah yipped. A smile spread across Charlotte's face, and she pulled Sylvie into a hug. "You know I'm down with that," she said.

She and Mariah exchanged a high-five. "What can we do?" asked Mariah.

"Nothing just yet," she said. The plan was still just a baby plan, something that she'd been circling in her mind for weeks. "But I've got an old friend who might be able to help."

Just then, lightning crashed in the sky, and buckets of rain began pouring over them in a deafening roar. In a matter of seconds, Sylvie's clothes were plastered tightly to her skin. She began cackling, and then turned to face the sky.

"*Woooooooo-HOOOOOOOOO!*" she yelled, laughing as the rain pattered against her face. Mariah spun around, her arms outstretched, and Charlotte splashed into a large puddle that had formed in the sand. The cool rain felt wonderful against her, cleansing.

It was exactly what she needed.

Charlotte held a hand over her eyes to shield them. "Want to come back to the Seaside House? We can make a fire, rent a movie, order some pizza later..."

Sylvie tapped a finger against her mouth, mock

debating. "Hmmm...I don't know, I was gonna wallow in my tub and cry into some ice cream..." Charlotte laughed, but then Sylvie groaned. "Shoot," she said, looking up at the sky. "I left all my windows open...I've gotta run home and batten down the hatches." She gave Mariah and Charlotte a quick hug. "I'll be over in a little bit. Later, gators!" She ran over to the water's edge, gave one large leap into the air, and came splashing down as hard as she could right into a cresting wave, before skittering past a giggling Charlotte toward her house, feeling more alive than she had in a long time.

$\sim$

SYLVIE TOOK her time walking home, her skin tingling pleasantly against the crashing rainfall, her mind wandering aimlessly. She thought about being a little girl, how she'd climb up on the couch and lean up against the windowpanes at the first sound of thunder, watching the dark sky swirling, the first drops of rain tinkling melodically, the sweeping tones of the windchimes carrying over the wind. That spark of excitement, nothing to do that day but watch the rain, to enjoy her mother's homemade tomato soup and play checkers and tell scary stories by candlelight.

Everything had been so much simpler then. And she'd had no way of knowing it. The great paradox of youth.

After her mother had passed when she was ten, Sylvie's father had done his best to raise her. But he had to work so much...Sylvie had always felt alone. And when he was around, he was always so tired, she never wanted to burden him. So she kept her problems to herself. And then when he passed unexpectedly when she was sixteen, she was really out to sea. She resolved to not let it define her life, to define her character.

There was a lot more to her, a lot more she would do. Her story was only beginning.

Sylvie had overcome a lot in her life. She'd learned to manage herself well, to put on a brave face and push on. To not rely on others, to keep herself from becoming dependent upon someone.

And then came Nick, and it all changed.

Between the disaster of his previous marriage and her desire for independence at any cost, they'd decided early on not to formalize their relationship. To simply commit to each other as partners. The idea of getting married...it had seemed to Sylvie like a cage, something that would crush her down into a subservient role. She considered him her husband, though, even if they didn't have a sheet of paper to prove it.

They were together, and that was enough.

And as they grew closer and closer, it didn't seem so wrong to let up a little. To open up her heart.

To let herself learn to rely on him a little. And then a lot.

Now that hadn't gone too well, had it, *Sylvie*? Look where it had gotten her.

Well, she wasn't going to make that mistake again. Just as she would shutter the windows against the incoming storm, it was time to batten down the hatches of her own life. Somewhere along the way she'd become complacent. That time was over.

In a twisted way, taking control again was thrilling. She didn't need anyone else.

By the time the outline of her sunny yellow house emerged through a curtain of rainfall, she was shivering, goosebumps prickling her arms and legs. Right now, more than anything, she wanted a hot shower. And a cup of coffee. And maybe a donut.

Her stomach twisted like a wet dishrag as she approached her front lawn. Nick was on his hands and knees outside his tent, using his arms to slough away layer after layer of water that had flooded his makeshift home. His white T-shirt clung to the broad, tight muscles of his back, the hard ropes shifting rhythmically as he fruitlessly tried to stem the small river now running through the front yard directly into the entrance of the tent. He ran a hand through his hair, water pouring down his face in rivulets, and then sat back on his arms, finally giving up. His eyes were pressed shut.

Sylvie's heart fluttered. He looked like such a sad sack, nothing like the man with the booming voice and the poker face. There was something humanizing about him this way. Almost...endearing.

At that moment, Nick looked up at her through the sheets of rain, and a rush of adrenaline shot through her. They looked at each other for a long moment, Sylvie's teeth now nearly chattering.

She took a few steps toward him, her feet sloshing in the puddles of the yard. "You look ridiculous," she yelled over the falling rain, keeping her gaze on him. "And you need a shave."

His eyes bored into hers, sending a chill across her skin. The corners of his mouth began turning up. And then he laughed, quickly stifling it.

Try as she could, Sylvie couldn't suppress the horrible laugh building in her throat. There was nothing funny here. But the laugh poured out of her anyway, the lightning crashing above them, both drenched to the core. The way he was looking at her...it was unraveling the tightly knotted ball her heart had been in. His eyes were tired, pleading. Innocent like a child's.

Sylvie blew out a long breath and held out a hand. He looked at it like he didn't know what a hand was. She shook her head. "Come on," she said. "I can't leave you out here like a sad puppy dog, obviously. You're lucky I'm feeling magnanimous today."

He took her hand and hoisted himself up, towering over her, the heat drifting off his body through the chilled air. It took everything she had to stop herself from yanking off his wet T-shirt and kissing him hard in the rain like the cover of a trashy romance novel. *No, Sylvie. Bad Sylvie. Remember what he did to you?*

She swallowed hard, turned, and marched inside without looking back, Nick following quietly behind her.

❧

SYLVIE SET two cups of freshly brewed coffee on the kitchen table and sat down across from Nick. He was running a towel through his hair and over his face, and set it on his lap as he accepted the cup. He held it up to his face, slowly inhaling the scent, letting the steam waft over his skin, his eyes squeezed shut.

After stripping off her wet socks, Sylvie held her feet out next to the vent underneath the table now blowing deliciously warm heat against them. She took a sip of coffee and looked up at him, the rain still smacking against the house in waves.

"What are you even eating out there?" she asked. Because that was just the sort of thing she really needed to know right now.

He raised his head, that old twinkle in his eyes. "Oh, you know," he said. "Living off the land. Berries, grass, leaves. The occasional pine cone." She laughed, but then stifled it with a mouthful of scalding coffee. He smiled. "I went to Darren's and bought out their stock of freeze-dried food. He looked at me like I was crazy." He looked back down at the table. "I've been okay."

A long silence hung between them. Sylvie let her eyes wander over him when he wasn't looking. It was a strange sensation...this man she'd known so well for so long, but also now a stranger. She fought back the tears threatening in her eyes.

"I wanted to thank you," Sylvie said softly. "For

respecting that I didn't want to talk about...
everything."

His shoulders rose and fell almost imperceptibly,
his eyes locked on hers, as he nodded simply. They
sat for a while sipping their coffee, listening to the
rain, the tension easing in Sylvie's muscles.

Despite everything, there was no denying that it
was good to have someone else in her home for a
change. Another warm body, another beating heart.

As they drank from their cups in silence and
Sylvie watched out the front window, the clouds
slowly broke apart in the sky, and the rain slowed to
a stop. Shafts of sunlight played against the ground,
a dancing, glimmering prism. Nick tilted the mug to
his lips, drained the rest, and then stood up.

"Thank you," he said quietly. "I really appreciate
it. I'll get out of your hair now." He moved toward
the front door.

But then Sylvie's hand shot up, grabbing his
wrist. He stopped in his tracks and turned
toward her.

Sylvie's breathing became labored, and she
squeezed his wrist. Tears sprang to her eyes. "Nick,"
she whispered. "Where did you go?"

He swallowed hard. Their eyes met. Her heart

was thundering in her ears. A significant part of her just didn't want to know.

But she couldn't take it anymore.

Nick let out a long breath in a whoosh, and sat back down. He set his hands on the table and looked down at them. His eyes clouded with tears.

"I ruined everything, Sylvie," he said, his voice hoarse. His fists clenched on the table. "I ruined everything, and I'm so, so sorry."

Sylvie wiped her eyes and ran a hand through her hair, trying to steady her breathing. He looked up at her, a pleading expression etched against his face.

"I thought I knew what I was doing," he said. "With our business. I thought I knew how to manage it. That I could learn, you know? I really thought..." He sighed, shaking his head. "My old man never amounted to anything. He was a deadbeat. A leech. And I wanted to change all that. I really did. I wasn't happy in my old work, I hated accounting. I thought I was going to be mediocre, to be barely better than he was. But when we decided to go all in on the restaurant, for me to leave my job and work together, everything changed." His eyes blazed into hers, sending a shiver down her spine. "I felt like I was finally making something of myself. For the first time in my life, I had a purpose."

He leaned back, running his hand over his face. "I thought my accounting background would just sort of...carry over. But it didn't. Working with vendors, keeping the books, payroll, supplies, health insurance, workers comp, safety, health inspectors, all of it...it's so much, it's so much harder than people think it'll be to run a restaurant. As you well know. I thought I was doing it, that I was learning. You brought me into the business, and I didn't want to fail you."

His brows drew together. "As it turned out, I didn't know what I was doing. We were *hemorrhaging* money, Sylvie. And I kept trying to fix it, to cut costs, to advertise, cut deals with vendors. I still don't know where I went wrong. Things just kept getting worse. And I tried to shield you from all that. So I lied," he said, his voice wavering. "I lied about how well we were doing. About the state of our finances. I lied to you. I thought I could turn it around, and no one would ever know. And eventually, there just wasn't any money left."

Sylvie ran over the last few months in her mind. She really hadn't known. Nick had somehow kept everyone on payroll, and the quality of their food hadn't suffered. In her role managing the front-of-house, nothing had seemed amiss. The fact that he'd kept it so well hidden was impressive, in its own grotesque way.

Nick fiddled with his hands on the table. "And so I panicked," he said finally, a tear rolling down his cheek. "I panicked *hard*. I've never been so afraid in my life. Everything was crashing down around me. I cracked. And I did what I thought I was never capable of, what my old man did to me and I swore I would never repeat. I ran." His body shook for a moment in a silent sob. "I ran because I had *no idea* what else to do."

Sylvie leaned forward, trying to wrap her head around everything he was telling her. "Where did you go?"

He let out a shaky breath. "I went to stay with my old college buddy, Judah. I don't know if you remember him. He's out in Nevada, in the desert. I don't know how to describe it...I wasn't myself. I had totally cracked. I drank too much, slept too little, tried to drown the reality of what my life had become. That I'd become everything I swore I wouldn't. I went on a bender, I'm not proud of it. I hid under a rock like a coward."

He looked up at her, his eyes wide and afraid and

sad. "I never should have left. I went to a dark place and I didn't know how to get myself out. I'll never forgive myself, and I certainly don't expect you to, either. But I never stopped loving you, Sylvie," he said, his voice thick with emotion. "I came to my senses, and I want to make things right. I want you back in my life. I don't know how yet, but we can get back on our feet. I will do whatever it takes to make things right again."

Sylvie let the tears fall down her face, and shook her head. "Nick, what do you want me to say to all that? You shouldn't have left me here!" She gritted her teeth, her throat shrinking down to a pinhole. "*I didn't deserve that, Nick!* I was all alone! And now you turn back up, and I'm supposed to just *trust* you again?" She scoffed. "That's assuming you're even telling me the truth here. I mean, I'm only human, Nick! It doesn't work like that!" She clenched her teeth and swiped the tears away from her face, and rose from the table. She stepped into the kitchen, poured herself a glass of water, and gulped it down, trying to catch her breath. Her chest felt like someone was crushing it.

Her mind was a mess of racing, tangling thoughts. It was far too much to process all at once. She turned to him, and wiped her eyes again. "I hear what you're saying. I do. And I'm sorry you went through all that. But you could've trusted me, Nick. We could've figured things out together." She shook her head. "You shouldn't have left. And now I can't trust you. I just can't. I don't know what else to say right now."

He rose as she approached him, but she moved past him into the hallway. She came back with a stack of towels and handed them to him. Nick accepted them wordlessly, and walked to the front door. He turned around to face her.

"I love you, Sylvie," he said, defeated. "I always have." And then he pushed through the front door, clicking it shut behind him softly.

Sylvie's mind was skipping around like a broken record as she watched him dry out his tent on the front lawn, her heart twisting.

What was she supposed to do now?

The ground beneath her seemed to crumble away, sending her into freefall just as she thought she'd been back on solid ground.

11

Mariah pressed her feet into the boardwalk and took another lick of her chocolate ice cream cone, not really tasting it. She was staring out across the water on her favorite bench on Shannon Pier, mesmerized by the way the sunlight sparkled off the water's surface like dancing pinpoints of light. Sounds of children laughing and squealing on the roller coaster down the pier carried over the gentle breeze.

She grimaced at the painful ache spreading through her temples after her long shift on the phones tonight, her mind frantically replaying the calls, unsure if she'd said the right things, if she'd taken the right steps. If she'd made some horrible mistake.

Mariah hadn't told anyone else in her family that she'd taken a temporary job working on a crisis hotline, after everything with The Windmill. She reasoned that the exposure to callers' traumas would be good for her while she was waiting to go back. Now she wasn't so sure. That same part of her that fixated obsessively on her work, that endless mental grinding, was already wearing her down even further, making things worse.

But Mariah was a worker. She always had been. She had to do *something*. And since helping out at The Windmill was no longer an option, she needed something to push her, something to get her ready for what was inevitably coming. Her stomach twisted hard as she found herself back at the hospital for a split second, that horrible inter-minable beeping, the shouting, the crying.

Closing her eyes, she willed back the choking feeling, the heaviness that began deep in her chest and tore into her throat like wildfire. She lifted the phone in her other hand and opened the email that she'd read at least three dozen times since she received it after her shift on the crisis hotline tonight.

Ms. Carter,

I hope this email finds you well. I am emailing to

check in with you regarding the upcoming semester. I know you are on leave for personal reasons, and of course I respect your privacy in this matter. I do hope you are considering your return, however, so that you do not fall behind or delay your graduation any further.

On a personal note, I just want to say that you were doing a great job. You have a talent and will make a wonderful doctor someday. I do not make any assumptions, but I would wonder if your leave may have anything to do with what transpired the week before you left.

If so, I do hope that it will not pose a roadblock for your continuation in the program.

I've always taken a special interest in you since you have started with us—I believe you are a great asset, and I look forward to your return. Please let us know your plans for the upcoming semester as soon as possible.

Best,

Dr. Meyers

Mariah felt the hot sting of tears in her eyes as she gulped a lungful of air, suddenly lightheaded. Some distant part of her had hoped to never hear back from her med school program, or especially her mentor Dr. Meyers...but she had to face reality sometime.

It didn't matter what the email said. It didn't matter that they wanted her back.

Mariah knew what had happened was her fault.

Her issues had started long before that night, to be sure. Every time she'd looked in the mirror in the last few months, she was a little thinner, a little weaker. Proper sleep was nothing but a distant memory...dark circles had seemed to permanently etch themselves underneath her eyes. She hadn't remembered the last time she'd tasted food, actually *tasted* it.

And then that night...

Mariah had never, *never* in her life quit anything. She pushed forward no matter what, always straight As, always another extracurricular activity, always receiving glowing praise for her work. It was just...in her blood. She loved to learn, to master, to achieve. It was thrilling to get lost in her work, to squeeze out every drop of potential she knew she had in her, no matter the personal cost.

And Mariah had given up an awful lot over the years.

She dug her fingers into her palms to stop them from trembling. After that night, what now seemed like a lifetime ago, she'd lasted another few days. It was hazy. She was maybe sleeping an hour a night.

One morning, she'd woken up, forcing her eyelids open like they were made of concrete, and had immediately fallen to her knees, dry heaving and coated in cold sweat.

She had nothing left...and had no other alternative but to stop.

At least for a while. It wasn't quitting, she'd told herself. It was a pause. A...personal break. To get back in the right headspace, shake everything off, and get back to business. It was what she did. Her body, her mind, they had failed her. That was all. A temporary setback where she would come back stronger, better, more resilient.

So in the meantime, she kept busy, ever busy. Decided to stay in Marina Cove, to get the job waitressing at The Windmill to help her mother and her family with the catastrophic debt and problems they'd found themselves in during the restoration process. Dove deep into her photography, the ultimate salve, something in which she could get lost forever. Spent time with Christian, trying to forge a relationship with him. Preoccupied her mind with her anger toward Sebastian, the lying, cheating, disgusting excuse for a father. Mariah knew the moment she'd left that she would be back. She'd never quit anything before, and wasn't about to now. It was shameful enough, taking this personal leave.

Yes, it was time to go, before she fell too far behind, before she racked up any more debt. Marina Cove had been a great vacation, a wonderful escape from the harsh reality of the real world.

But it was just that, a beautiful dream.

"Uh, I think you might need a napkin there," a voice said next to her. That subtle Southern twang.

She whipped her head up, frowning. "Huh?"

Keiran leaned an arm against the wooden railing of the pier's edge, squinting in the sunlight and smiling. He was in swim shorts and an old black cutoff T-shirt, exposing the long sleeves of tattoos that spread up his muscular arms. He gestured toward her hand, raising an eyebrow.

Mariah followed his eyes to her right hand, her mind fuzzy and thick. She distantly registered the sticky, wet feeling of her fingers wrapped like claws around her waffle cone. The ice cream had melted completely, flowing through the cracks in the cone and all over her hands, trailing down her arm like a river, and finally pooling on her jean shorts in a dark, gooey puddle. She watched it with fascination, and a bubble of laughter forced its way from her stomach out through her mouth. Her stomach clenched as more laughter escaped against her will, her body breaking out into hard guffaws. Her eyes watered as she looked back up at Keiran, breaking out into more laughter at his bemused expression.

"You okay?" he said, laughing with her as he sat down next to her.

Mariah nodded, wiping her eyes. "Oh, yeah. I'm peachy. Just enjoying this delicious ice cream cone on this glorious summer afternoon. Don't mind the crazy girl." Something spiked like thorns wrapped around her chest. She began crunching her way through what remained of her waffle cone.

They sat in comfortable silence for a few minutes. Mariah wiped off what she could of the chocolate on her shirt, not caring at the moment how insane she looked. Keiran didn't seem the judgmental type. She leaned back against the bench. "What brings you to the pier? Figured you'd be out in the water on a day like today. The waves look, uh, surfy today."

He laughed. "They were definitely extra surfy today. But today's a rest day. I like to come here to the pier sometimes to watch the water. To relax, I guess, and to think."

"Ponder the mysteries of the universe, and so on?"

He glanced at her. She noticed how the sunlight played in his golden-brown irises like shards of glowing glass. "Something like that. This place, it calms me down." He looked behind him, down to the pier's entrance. She followed his eyes and saw a security guard pacing back and forth.

"Did you hear what happened here earlier this summer?" he asked. "Apparently some people broke into the pier, and, like, opened up the whole park. The Ferris wheel, the bumper cars, all of it." He smiled. "I heard they fired up the roller coaster."

She looked up at him. "Really? Ha. That actually sounds super fun. Stupid, but fun. I never do anything impulsive."

A shadow seemed to pass over his expression, but it was gone in an instant. He blinked and shook his head almost imperceptibly before turning on the bench to face her. "Listen. I've been meaning to talk to you. I was wondering if you'd be interested in a little...opportunity."

Mariah watched him impassively as she idly tried to wipe the stickiness from her fingers. Her mind began to drift to med school against her will. "What sort of opportunity," she asked, her voice seeming distant.

"Well," he said, his eyes lighting up, "you know I

surf. Marina Cove has an annual surfing competition. It's not a big deal or anything, I just do it for fun. I came close to placing last year, but I wiped out spectacularly. So I've been training a lot this year. There's a cash prize. I could really use the money."

Mariah forced herself not to let her eyes wander to his arms, to the chiseled abs she knew were just beneath that T-shirt. He was in spectacular shape. "So where do I come in? You need a cheerleader?"

He grinned. "No. Since the waves are so good on the north shore, people come from all over to compete. It's really blown up over the last few years...attracts a lot of attention from sponsors and whatnot. *Surfside* magazine covers the local competitions around here, and last year they did a whole series documenting some of the surfers, the training and everything leading up to the actual competition, and then they do a big profile of the competition itself."

He ran a hand through his hair, and heat rose in Mariah's cheeks. "I know last year they were pretty unhappy with the photographer they hired. His stuff just didn't look very good. Blurry, and whatnot. Anyway, a few weeks ago, I was catching up with the guy who interviewed some of us last year, and he said they aren't too happy with the new guy they hired to do the photography this year either. I forgot all about it...but I was thinking about those shots you got of us. And so naturally, I thought of you."

Mariah frowned. "To what, be the photographer? I can't do that."

Keiran tilted his head slightly. "Why not? I wasn't just trying to flatter you when I told you how great your shots were. I mean...we looked..." He looked into her eyes. "Awesome. I know that sounds stupid. I swear, I'm not a narcissist or anything. But I love to surf, and I think you'd do a great job. I could put you in touch with them. If you wanted."

"I'm not a photographer," said Mariah, running her hand over the back of her neck. "It's just a stupid hobby."

Keiran shrugged. "You point your camera at things and then take pictures of those things. I think that means you're a photographer."

Mariah furrowed her eyebrows and looked out over the water. Out in the distance, she could just make out a small group of surfers trying to catch waves. "What would it entail? If, in theory, I was interested?"

"You'd follow us around and just document what we do. Practicing, training, whatever. The day of, you'd take all the competition shots. Everything would be printed in the magazine. They're big... you'd be surprised how many people buy the issues that cover this."

Well, not that surprised. A magazine full of action shots of hot, ripped surfer dudes with killer tans tearing through the ocean waves on an island paradise? She wouldn't say no to a copy.

"It pays, of course," he added. "I have no idea how much. But like I said, it's a pretty big event. I'd imagine it's good, whatever it is." He inhaled the clean saltwater air and let it out in a slow exhale, closing his eyes. After a moment, he put his hands on his knees and pushed himself up, groaning and stretching. "Aaaanyway. I'm sure you're super busy, I just thought I'd give you a heads-up. Let me know. You know where to find me."

He gave her shoulder a small squeeze before heading back toward the pier's entrance, sending a thrill of butterflies through Mariah's stomach. She pushed down the feeling. "See you, Keiran," she called to him. He glanced back at her and grinned before turning down the stairs toward the sand.

Mariah sat on the bench, wiping her sticky hands on her shirt and watching the waves roll in. She grimaced as the old swell of thoughts began to poke at her before pulling her phone out and automatically conjuring up Dr. Meyers' email once again. She read it several times, her heart beating faster and faster.

She thought of Keiran. That little bit of Southern drawl, the way she warmed up every time he smiled, the kindness in his eyes...

But no. He was just another beautiful distraction. She didn't live here. She was going to be back in school. There was no harm in a little flirting...the guy was gorgeous, and she wasn't dead, after all. He probably had a line of girls waiting for him a mile long, how could he not? It was fun to daydream, though.

Getting paid for something she loved to do for free would be fun, for sure. Sitting on the beach, taking photos of all those guys? Please. What was stopping her?

That little voice called from somewhere inside her, the voice that was impossible to ignore. The voice that told her to push harder, to work longer, to achieve at all costs...the voice was telling her something. That if she took the gig, there was something there, something else. Something that would be hard to extricate herself from. For some reason, she knew it went down a road that would change things somehow. It would change the plan.

It was a warning.

She shook her head and pulled up the email from Dr. Meyers once more, and touched the Reply button. A few minutes later, she'd drafted out her response. Enough was enough. Time to get back to the real world.

Her finger hovered over Send Message. Mariah frowned. She willed her finger to press down...but it wasn't responding.

Something held it back like it was being pulled by invisible bands.

Her eyes found Keiran's distant form down the coast as he reached down and skipped a rock across the water's surface. Mariah exhaled slowly and put her phone back in her pocket, her mind turning and turning its endless rotations, an infinite spinning windmill.

It could wait one more day. She wasn't quite ready to send it. Not yet.

12

D iane double-checked the map on her phone, frowning, before looking up and turning left. She wasn't all that familiar with this part of the island. Her feet seemed to cross over the pavement separately from herself, like someone else was puppeteering her body. Her mouth was dry.

Austin had the morning off from work, so Diane decided that today was the day. She reached into her pocket and ran her fingers over the sheet of paper, the unsigned note that had been left for her and was slowly but surely eating away at her.

It was time to have a little chat with Kate.

Diane wiped her forehead with her sleeve. The day was already warm, and it was a long walk from the inn. As she turned right and began a slow ascent to what looked like a street filled with restaurants and cafés, her mind turned once again to the phone call with Teagan. The offer to be creative director at her new agency.

It just wasn't so simple. It wasn't as simple as choosing love, or choosing family, or choosing work over everything else. Diane had to think about the future. She needed a plan, one that made sense even if it wasn't perfect.

She shivered despite the heat. Working in LA again...it wouldn't be so bad. She'd be working with one of the most prestigious clients in the world. No longer would her creative writing serve to peddle chicken nuggets, or oat milk, or squirt guns. She'd be working on award-winning campaigns.

Her love of writing would be put to good use, and more than anything, Diane loved to write.

Her career hadn't happened the way she thought it would. She never thought she'd fall into advertising, but the world didn't seem to want any more poets, and her first stab at writing a novel had ended in a long and agonizing slew of rejections.

But advertising had a limitless well of money, because people always needed to buy things. And so there was always a need for writers.

Diane thought of the words she'd scribbled down in her notebook this morning. She couldn't wait to show them to Austin. Writing with him had been wonderful, it was true. Writing had always been a way to process her emotions, and now that she was facing her grief and her losses head-on, writing was saving her. It was everything.

But there was no future in music, obviously. Austin and Kate had encountered some success with Silver Hollows back in the day, but that had all collapsed as their marriage fell apart. Now he sometimes worked north of a hundred hours a week at the Maple Street Diner with Kate, struggling to stop the seemingly inevitable march toward closing their doors.

Music was a wonderful distraction, nothing more. It didn't solve any of the problems at hand. Like the fact that if she returned to LA, she'd leave her family. And every day she was getting a little closer to them.

Was she really going to give that up?

Diane thought of Ramona and Charlotte cheering her name at her first open mic performance with Austin, warmth spreading through her skin.

They hadn't figured it all out, that was for sure.

There was still an enormous amount of distance to bridge between them all. But you didn't solve that overnight, and Diane could be patient. There was just something magical about having your family around.

And as for Austin...

Diane pressed her eyes shut and slowed to a stop. Austin. She was old enough to know that what they had didn't come around often, if ever. He certainly wasn't going to move away with her, not when he was tied down with the restaurant.

There were no easy answers.

The Maple Street Diner was on the corner of Maple & Poplar, a beautifully old-fashioned diner with an outdoor seating area that faced the street, perfect for people-watching. She could see the glistening chrome and red leather of the booths through the large front windows, and the aroma of fresh-brewed coffee and bacon drifted over the warm breeze. Diane's stomach rumbled loudly.

Taking a deep breath, she pushed through the front doors, and was met with a glorious draft of air conditioning.

"Welcome to Maple Street Diner, how many?" asked a chipper young woman at the hostess stand.

"I, ah," she said, caught off guard. What was the plan? Just ask for Kate?

Diane winced inwardly. For reasons that currently escaped her, she hadn't thought about what she was going to say. She wasn't much of an improviser.

The woman smiled patiently. "Yes, one, please," Diane managed, heat rushing to her face. This was a stupid idea. Kate was obviously going to tell Austin that she'd come by. Maybe she could talk to Kate without revealing who she was? Austin probably hadn't mentioned her to Kate anyway.

A waitress came by to take her order. Scrambled eggs, toast, waffles with syrup, orange juice. Diane smiled and leaned back in the booth as she took a long sip of coffee. How on earth was this restaurant failing? Great location, quick service, beautiful decor...

It was a shame. Hopefully Austin and Kate would find a way to keep the place afloat. Diane could get used to a place like this. She watched the people drifting by on the sidewalk outside, and two birds chasing each other through the crystal blue sky. Her phone was shut off in her pocket.

That had to be her favorite part of being here in Marina Cove, away from the constant grind of Los

Angeles, the rat race. She was no longer tethered to her phone like a life preserver. It was freeing in a way Diane never could have imagined.

"Thank you so much," she said as the waitress set down the food before her. She drizzled syrup over her waffles happily and took an enormous bite just as Victoria sat down across from her.

Diane's breath caught in her throat. Suddenly she was in the old Plymouth Duster, Trevor by her side. The horizon was upside down, slowly tilting over as they passed over the guardrail of Mulholland Drive. Glass splintering all around her, the horrible screeching of twisting metal. Victoria burying her head in Austin's chest, the pinched expression of terror on her face, her mouth open in a silent scream.

"Diane," said Victoria.

Diane opened her eyes. Her hands were clutching the table, knuckles blanched white. She was breathing hard. She looked up at Victoria seated across the booth from her. The fire-red hair, the lithe, slender frame, the look of mischief in her eyes, that ethereal air about her.

She shook her head hard. An urge to strike the rubber band she used to wrap around her wrist cannonballed through her. Stop. *Stop.* Not Victoria.

Kate. Not Victoria, *Kate.*

Diane swallowed hard, tears in her eyes. She missed Victoria so profoundly at that moment it physically hurt, like someone had pierced her with a long blade and twisted.

"My God," Diane managed. "You..."

"Look exactly like her?" said Kate, nodding once. "Yeah. I know."

Diane exhaled all the air from her lungs. "I, ah, I'm sorry. I shouldn't be here."

Kate watched her evenly. "What are you doing here, Diane?"

It was hard to catch her breath. Seeing Kate had transported her back to that terrible accident. A flashback. It was like time travel.

"How did you know who I was?" Diane asked. Her voice was trembling.

Kate crossed her arms over her chest. "Austin told me about you. And I know everyone who comes in this place. I put two and two together."

Diane reached for her orange juice and chugged it down, spluttering as she reached the end, coughing hard. "I'm sorry. I just..."

"Austin's not working this morning," she said. Not cold, exactly, but not welcoming. The handwritten note was like an iron weight in Diane's pocket.

"I know," said Diane. "I, uh..."

She took another breath, and then pressed her palms into the table. She hadn't done anything wrong. And if Kate had sent the note, unless Diane said something, it would probably escalate. She could worry about talking to Austin about their meeting later.

"Did you send me anything?" asked Diane.

A line appeared between Kate's brows, her full lips turned downward. Kate lacked the subtle lines of aging that had appeared around Diane's eyes and mouth at some point in the last few years. She was a total knockout, uncommonly beautiful. A nasty flare of jealousy lit within Diane.

"Send you anything?" she asked, her head tilted slightly to one side.

Diane watched her, entranced by her eyes, so like Victoria's. They were even the same deep shade of cerulean, with silver edges. She couldn't think of what to say.

This had been a terrible idea, obviously.

"Never mind," she said. "I just came in to see where Austin spends all his time. He talks about this place so much, and I've never seen it." Diane looked around. "It's a beautiful diner. You've got something really special here."

Kate's expression softened, and she leaned back in the booth. "Yeah. Well. Thank you." She ran a hand through her long hair, and Diane noticed dark circles under her eyes. "I wish other people saw it that way."

A thick silence hung between them. Fifties music drifted lazily through the diner from a speaker near the kitchen. Diane cleared her throat. "I—"

"So things are getting pretty serious between you and Austin, huh?" Kate interjected. She was watching Diane, her eyes blazing like wildfire. Diane's heart beat harder.

"Well, we, uh—"

"You don't look like her," she said, narrowing her eyes. "So I guess he's capable of moving past her after all. How wonderful for you two."

Diane's heart twisted. This woman hadn't deserved what happened. "Listen," said Diane. Kate narrowed her eyes further. "Victoria was one of my best friends in the world. I think about her every day, about the car accident. Austin and I...we both blamed ourselves for what happened. I think Austin still does, in some way. But that doesn't excuse what happened between you two." Diane thought about reaching out her hand, but decided against it. "I know it's not worth much, but I'm really, really sorry."

Kate stared at her for a long moment before turning her eyes down to the table. "It doesn't matter anymore," she said softly.

The words on the note swirled in Diane's mind. She'd made it this far.

"Are you still in love with him?" Diane asked. Her chest tightened.

Kate looked up at her, and tears welled in her eyes. "Yes," she said simply.

"Oh," said Diane. "Okay."

Kate reached for a napkin and dabbed at her eyes. "You don't have to worry, though," she said, reaching for Diane's cup of coffee and taking a long drink. Even Kate's easy familiarity was just like Victoria's. "I'm no fool. It was never going to work out between us. We're not right for each other."

Diane nodded slowly. "So—"

"So," she said, letting out a breath. "If that's why you came here, you can rest easy. I think it's good for him to find someone. Someone who is...enough." Her voice wavered. "I have no reason to try to get back together with him. Austin was never in love with me. He didn't know what he was doing," she said, shaking her head. "And I wish he'd never figured it out. I really do. But it's for the best. I want him to be happy."

Diane nodded, biting back the tears threatening to form. "Thank you," she said quietly. "Honestly, that means a lot."

Kate nodded, and stood up. "I should get back to it. Piece of advice, though," she said, drying her eyes with the napkin. "Austin's a complicated guy with a lot of, ah, baggage. Some other things he's still paying the price for. I don't even know the full story of it all, but if something ever feels off...listen to that voice."

Diane's stomach lurched. "What are you talking about?"

Kate frowned, but then her head tilted up toward the window behind Diane. "I have to go," she said, and turned to leave.

Diane whipped her head around to see what Kate had been looking at. Walking down the sidewalk toward the diner was Austin, a phone held to his ear.

She slapped some bills on the table and looked around for Kate, but she'd disappeared into the kitchen. After smoothing her hair back and taking a deep breath, pushing the new questions out of her mind, she headed back toward the hostess stand and pushed through the front door into the heat.

Austin had his back to her, with his finger pressed in his ear. Something about his body language made Diane stop in her tracks. She knew she should give him his privacy, that this was none of her business, but Kate's words rang in her ears.

"I told you," he said into the phone, his voice cautious, guarded. "I can't talk about this right now, okay?" He shook his head. "We can't do this anymore." He jammed his finger against the phone and shoved it into his pocket, whipping around and nearly running straight into Diane.

"Sorry," Diane managed, "I didn't—"

"Diane," he said, the color running from his face. "What are you doing here?"

Diane's mind raced. She met his eyes and took a deep breath. "Who was that?"

Austin's eyebrows furrowed. "Nothing. No one, I mean. Just some personal, uh, personal stuff." He raised an eyebrow. "What brings you by the restaurant? I needed to grab a few things inside, want to grab a bite? You can meet Kate—"

Diane stepped toward him. "Austin, what are we doing here?"

He tilted his head. "What do you mean?"

She gestured toward his phone. "Are you keeping something from me?"

"No," he said, shaking his head. "I'm not keeping anything—"

"Because I don't want to waste time here, Austin," she said, trying to keep her voice steady. "There's something good here, at least I think there is. But we've got to be honest with each other."

His lips parted like he was going to say something, but then he shook his head again, his shoulders falling slightly. He stepped toward her, and then pulled Diane into a hug, wrapping his arms tightly around her.

"I don't want to waste time either," he said, running a hand through her hair. "I know we haven't talked about...what's next for us. This is hard for me, Diane. I don't even know if you're staying here. I'm trying not to pressure you into figuring out what you want, but..." He sighed. "Maybe we should talk about that. But I want you, Diane. I want to be with you. The personal stuff I'm trying to sort out, it's some stuff between my brother and me, and I'm just not ready to talk about it yet. It's complicated. But it has nothing to do with you, or us. Can you give me a little time to sort through it all?"

Diane let the tension fall from her shoulders and

rested her head on his chest, nodding. She'd been thinking the worst, obviously, that there was another woman, something sinister.

But Austin wasn't like that. She knew it. She had to be patient.

"Okay," she said. "I can do that."

As Austin held her, her mind was spinning. It was clear that Kate hadn't written the note, and now she was no closer to finding out who had sent it.

But really, it didn't matter. It didn't change anything, and right now, Diane had bigger fish to fry. It was time to put all the nonsense here behind, and start to ask the real questions about what she wanted to do next. Everything else was a distraction.

But Diane couldn't stop the feeling needling at her, the little voice in her head, the one Kate had just told her to listen to. The voice telling her that he hadn't been talking to his brother.

That Austin really was lying to her.

13

Natalie cursed inwardly as she trotted over the crosswalk on the way to L'Escalier, the restaurant Theo had chosen on the northeastern shore. He was standing there in a blazer over a gray T-shirt and dark slacks, his dark, wavy hair casually swept over and a warm smile on his face.

She glanced down at her T-shirt and capris and flip-flops. Natalie had never heard of the restaurant, but the name alone should have signaled to her to dress a little nicer. She was going to look ridiculous next to him.

"I'm really sorry," she said as she strode up to him, her stomach in knots for some reason. "I'm totally underdressed."

Theo shook his head. "I think you look fantastic." Heat rushed to her face. On the way over, she'd debated giving him a friendly hello hug, but decided against it now that she was here. She didn't really know him, after all.

"Shall we?" he asked, and gestured in front of him. Her eyes swept over the fingers of his left hand. Still no ring. Her heart fluttered.

Not a date, Natalie, not a date. You don't live here, remember?

The maître d' frowned as he scanned over Natalie's attire, then rolled his eyes and led them to a table in the corner. "Your waiter will come by shortly. Enjoy your meal," he said in a thick French accent. He glanced at Natalie's flip-flops. "*Je suis tellement contente que tu sois habillé pour l'occasion,*" he muttered to himself.

"Je peux vous comprendre," she said. "Je suis désolé d'offenser votre sensibilité délicate."

He raised his eyebrows. "I, ah...my apologies, *madamoiselle.*" He glanced at Theo and quickly swept away, his cheeks red.

"Whoa," said Theo, staring at her. "That was... what did he say?"

Natalie grinned sheepishly. "He said something

about my outfit, and I told him I was sorry to offend his delicate sensibilities."

Theo laughed hard at that, making the people at surrounding tables turn their heads. "Very impressive." He tilted his head to one side, eyeing her. Her stomach tightened. "What other languages can you speak?"

Natalie shrugged. "Uh, Spanish, Portuguese...a little Italian." She ran her hands over her pants nervously, suddenly not knowing where to put them. "I've done a lot of traveling."

He nodded, his gaze lingering for a moment before he looked around. "I hope this place is okay."

"This restaurant wasn't here when I was a kid," she said. "It looks lovely."

An awkward silence hung between them until the waiter arrived, handing them menus and taking their drink orders. After he left, Theo leaned back in his chair and watched her for a moment, making her heart beat harder.

"So," he said finally. "I'm glad you called me back."

Natalie exhaled slowly, nodding. "Well. I wanted to talk to you about your offer to, ah..." She took a quick sip of water. "To maybe come work as a tour guide for a few weeks." He nodded, a small line appearing between his eyebrows. Disappointment? "That's not the only reason I wanted to see you," she added quickly. "Not that I...I just...dinner is on me. I wanted to thank you, for, uh, everything. Saving my life and...whatnot. It's the least I can do." A laugh escaped her suddenly, and her face flushed. "I'm usually much more eloquent than this, I swear."

A smile spread across his face. "Well. I really could use the help. And I'm afraid dinner is on me tonight."

Natalie snuck a glance at the tightness of his arm muscles against his blazer as the waiter came by. "I think we need a minute, thanks," she said. They flipped through the menu in silence.

"So I guess that makes this a job interview, then," Theo said with a sly smile.

Natalie laughed. "Well, I've made a poor first impression, if it is." She set the menu down. "What would you like to know? I'm an open book."

He brought a finger to his chin, pondering. "Hmm. Where do you see yourself in five years?"

"Easy," she said, grinning. "I have no idea whatsoever. And I like it like that."

He smiled, and Natalie blushed again. "What's your greatest weakness?"

Natalie twirled a finger in her hair, pretending to

smack bubble gum in her mouth. "Well, I guess I just, like, care about my work too much sometimes," she said in a ditzy voice.

He chuckled. "Very good, very good." He considered her for a moment. "You wouldn't happen to know how to kayak, by any chance?"

"Kayaks, motorboats, sailboats, rafts, catamarans, yachts, pontoons, you name it, I've operated one," she said. "I've done a lot of outdoor-type jobs like this in my travels. You get yourself a long rope and a parachute, and I'll take people parasailing if you want."

He laughed, shaking his head. "A woman of many talents." A prickling sensation ran across Natalie's forearms. "Now listen," he said, leaning forward. "I'll do what I can in terms of pay, but I don't have a huge budget..."

Natalie waved her hand dismissively. "Anything will be fine. Getting to be outside all day, exploring the island with people? It's gonna be a blast. And besides," she said, taking a drink of water, "it's only temporary."

Theo nodded, but his smile faded slightly. "That's totally fine. I need any help I can get. I've got a new competitor who's really throwing me for a loop. And I have a hard time finding people who know their way around, who are suited to this kind of work. People good in a pinch. I don't want a repeat of the other day." He frowned. "Maybe you could sort of, I don't know, be sort of like a consultant to them. Pass on some of your wisdom?"

"I would love that," said Natalie.

He nodded, the corners of his mouth turning up. "Good. Good. Then it's settled." He reached out and shook her hand. His skin was coarse, weathered, strong. The hands of a man who knew his way around the outdoors. Their eyes met for a moment, and she could swear that color tinged his cheeks. "So where do you go next?" he asked.

"Prague," she said. "I've got friends who will be waiting for me there in a few weeks. I was going to leave sooner, but..." She hesitated, taking another drink of water. "I have an old friend here who I think needs my help. Plans changed a little."

He nodded, and she didn't elaborate further. Silence ensued as they awkwardly flipped through the menu. Natalie shifted in her seat, scanning the items. She had no idea what to order. Over the years, she'd lost her taste for this sort of pretentious fare.

She looked up at Theo to find he was already watching her. Her stomach somersaulted.

"Want to get out of here?" he asked. "I only

brought you here to impress you, to be honest. It's not really my cup of tea. And I'm thinking maybe it's not yours either."

Natalie set down her menu and smiled. "Sure," she said, blushing furiously. "Where do you want to go?"

He grinned. "I know a place."

~

"SYLVIE! Oh, girl, it's so good to see you again." A young, dark-haired woman with two little boys in tow pulled Sylvie into a bear hug as the front doors of The Windmill closed shut behind her, a draft of warm, salty air spilling into the restaurant.

Sylvie squeezed her tight, a thrill running across her skin. "You too, Zara. It really is." She pulled back. "I can't explain how happy I am that you're here."

Zara waved her hands. One of the boys tugged at her shirt, holding a plastic baggie of cheese crackers. "It's nothing, after everything you and Nick have done for me—"

Sylvie shook her head. "No, seriously. We're in dire straits here. You being here...it's a glimmer of hope. One this girl desperately needs right now." She turned to Charlotte and Mariah. "Guys, this is

Zara Clarke. We go way, way back. She was one of our first employees at The Windmill. She heard about us closing and texted me to check in, and so I asked her for some advice." She grinned at Zara. "I didn't expect her to come out here personally. It was an awesome surprise. Truly."

They all shook hands. "Great to meet you all," said Zara. "These rascals are Dominic and Brayden." The boys waved sheepishly. They looked to be about six and four.

Mariah crouched down to meet them at eye level. "Hey, little dudes, I have an idea," she said with a smile. She reached behind the hostess stand and pulled out two plastic packets of crayons and two coloring sheets, then guided the boys to a booth next to them. They began to color happily, kicking their little legs beneath them and munching on cheese crackers.

"Zara here," said Sylvie, "left us for great fame and fortune out in Boston."

Zara laughed. "I wouldn't say that." She turned to Charlotte and Mariah. "I opened a restaurant there a few years back called Sparrow. And then a couple more."

"And she's become one of the most successful restaurateurs in the country," said Sylvie.

Zara gave a small bow, grinning. "She's playing me up here. We do all right."

Sylvie rolled her eyes. "I guess Sparrow's long list of awards means nothing then. Always so modest."

"Well," she said, her face growing serious, "I have you and Nick to thank for that. You guys taught me well."

Sylvie scoffed. "Yeah. Some education we provided. Look around you, honey. Look how great we did!"

Zara's eyes swept over the darkened, empty restaurant, the long front windows all blocked with roller shades. Her fingers ran across the hostess counter, lifting up a coating of dust. She shook her head.

"I'm so sorry to hear what happened," she said softly. "It breaks my heart." She looked up at Sylvie. "What happened, exactly?"

Sylvie blew out a long breath. No way was she getting into all the dirty details. "That, my good friend, is a long and frankly wildly depressing story for another day," she said, shaking her head. "Suffice it to say, Nick and I are clean out of money. There's nothing left. Not for a single day of payroll, not for a single vendor order."

Zara nodded slowly, and took a few tentative

steps into the restaurant. "This is crazy," she said quietly. "I thought this place would be open forever."

Sylvie nodded, fighting tears suddenly pressing against her eyes. "I did, too," she managed. "It, uh, came as a surprise to us." She had no intention of throwing Nick under the bus, even after everything he'd done. She had more respect than that. "Charlotte here was our star pastry chef too, just before we closed. She's an integral part of the business going forward, so she's here every step of the way with me."

Charlotte blushed furiously. "I just want to get back to work. However we can do it, I'm here to help."

Zara nodded sympathetically. "We'll figure it out. I have some ideas."

She glanced over at her kids, who were lost in peals of laughter. Mariah was busy making silly faces, sticking her tongue out and lolling her eyes. "These kids are a good audience," Mariah said, laughing.

Zara grinned. "They're my pride and joy."

Sylvie watched them, some distant part of her aching horribly. A part of her had always wondered what it would have been like to have children of her own. "I'm glad to see you and Peter finally settled down," she said.

Zara laughed, shaking her head. "Yeah, never thought I'd have kids already, but when you know, you know." She turned to Sylvie. "Okay. Let's get down to business, shall we?" They sat down at the counter across the aisle from Mariah and the boys. "Nick still running the back of house? I'll have to talk to him, too. Everything starts there."

Sylvie swallowed a grimace. "Nick is taking a little break from the restaurant. Just for the time being. I'll be running back of house for now." She paused. "Well, actually, Charlotte's sister Ramona has offered to help me too—she's a professional bookkeeper—but I want to know how everything works myself." She let out a breath. "I think that's where I went wrong in the first place."

Zara nodded slowly, and didn't ask any further questions. Sylvie wanted to wrap her up in a massive, crushing hug for that. "I totally get that. I'm the same way. I know how to delegate, but I think it's best that the owners are aware of how everything works."

Sylvie leaned back, pulling her hair back in a ponytail. "So, thirty-thousand-foot view, what are we looking at?"

"Well," said Zara, pulling a notebook from her purse and jotting some things down, "for starters, you need a proper system. We need to know your breakeven, so we know where we stand at the end of every day. We'll figure out inventory control, record-keeping, payroll, profit and loss, all of it." She looked up, her expression softening. "It sounds like a lot, but I promise I'll walk you all through it. Things have to be done the right way. We have to build a solid foundation if we want this place to be around in fifty years."

Charlotte gripped Sylvie's hand. She looked up at her friend, tears welling in her eyes. "That sounds amazing," Sylvie whispered. Charlotte nodded, unable to keep the grin from her face.

Zara smiled. "After everything you guys did for me, I'm happy to help." She jotted something else down on the paper. "I can get you in touch with a few of my vendors. I can have them work with you on credit for now. But we have a larger problem here."

Sylvie nodded. "Yeah. Employees."

Zara furrowed her brows. "That's going to be tricky."

"I've thought a lot about that," said Sylvie. "And I'm going to talk to my staff. Well, my ex-staff, I guess. They're a really loyal bunch, and they want to get back to work. I think I can convince some of them to come back with deferred pay. A small but strong skeleton crew."

Zara raised her eyebrows. "You think they'd agree to that? Because that would—"

"Solve a lot of our problems?" Sylvie sighed. "I think I could convince a couple of them, yeah. At least I hope." She looked over at Charlotte, her heart swelling. "Charlotte is going to help, and Mariah, too, with waitressing, hosting—"

"I can cook, too," Mariah chimed in. "A little, at least. I can operate a spatula, at any rate."

They laughed. "Not only that," said Sylvie, "but Charlotte's sister Diane comes from the world of advertising and has offered to help on that front. Get the word back out. And Natalie..." She met Charlotte's eyes. "We think she might have a background in business, but we haven't talked to her yet. She's only in town for a couple of weeks, so we'll see. Charlotte's mom, Ella, too—"

Sylvie stopped, fighting a wave of emotion. When had she become so lucky, having all these wonderful women around to support her in her darkest hour?

Charlotte gripped her hand. "My mom is crazy

busy these days with her bookstore, but she and everyone has offered to chip in however they can, so we can get our feet back on the ground and start making money again."

Zara reached her hands out to take theirs, clearly touched. "That's amazing, guys. Really. I promise, as soon as the wheels start turning, you'll be off to the races again. This place is already a fixture here in Marina Cove. The hardest part is already done for you." She looked around. "People know and love The Windmill. We just have to get them back in here."

Tears pooled in Sylvie's eyes. "I want that more than anything else in the world. Thank you, Zara, really," she said, pulling her into a hug. "I mean it. I can't thank you enough."

"We'll get you through this," Zara said. "Right now is going to be the hardest time. But it'll be worth it." They pulled apart, Sylvie wiping her eyes with the backs of her hands.

"Well," said Sylvie, letting out all the air in her lungs, "let's get started, shall we?"

14

Natalie and Theo sat on a long stretch of beach, quiet and untouched, happily munching on tacos from a little hole-in-the-wall place that Theo had known about. It was much more Natalie's speed. Night was settling in, the moon painting a glowing path toward the infinite horizon of the dark sea. They'd settled into a nice rhythm, talking mostly about some of the things Natalie would be doing in her new job.

"So, where's Caleb tonight?" she asked, taking a long drink from her soda. "He doing okay after the whole getting lost thing?"

Theo set down his drink and slipped off his shoes and socks. "He's sleeping over at a friend's house. And yeah," he said, staring out over the water.

"He was spooked, but we've talked about it together. He'll be okay, I think. Kids are resilient."

Natalie nodded. A question burned in her mind, the one that she'd wanted to ask but had no business asking. Before she could say anything, though, he turned to face her.

"He's had a little bit of a rough go, the last few years," he said. His brows drew together. "It really didn't come at a good time."

Natalie nodded, feeling the need to look away. Something in his gaze...she was having trouble catching her breath. "Is he all right?"

Theo took a moment to answer, watching the waves splash against the shore. "He struggles with anxiety. I thought going on the tour would be good for him. He and Grayson are good friends...I try to get him to socialize as much as I can. It was hard for me, sending him out there, after..."

He looked up at her, running a hand through his hair. Natalie nodded encouragingly. "I've been homeschooling him for a couple years," he continued. Whatever he'd been going to say, he'd decided against it. "Before all this, before the tour company, I was actually a high school teacher, way back when. And when his problems with anxiety started taking over, his grades were suffering, he was miserable, I decided to take him out, just while we figured out what to do. Teach him myself, temporarily. He sees a specialist for anxiety, and he's been doing better. And so I've been trying to get him out in the world, just to do things, you know? I want to re-enroll him in the fall." He shook his head. "I don't know."

A warm breeze swept over them. Natalie dug her toes deep into the cool sand. "I think that's wonderful that you've been helping him like that. He's a lucky kid having a father like you."

He laughed humorlessly. "I don't know about that. The terrible truth of it all is I have no idea what I'm doing, basically ever. Sending him out was probably stupid. I made him carry a cell phone, but there was no signal out in the woods. When I heard he was lost, it was like my own worst nightmare." He ran his hands over his face. "Zane...I mean, I should have known better. He's not a sharp one, but I can't find good help. I'd take Caleb myself, but I, uh... can't."

Natalie frowned. "Why not?" She squeezed her eyes shut. "I'm sorry. That's none of my business."

Theo took a handful of sand and held it up, letting the breeze carry it away. After a moment, he met her eyes, something crossing over them. "No, it's okay." He took a long, slow breath. Natalie's heart thumped against her chest. "A few years ago, I was out on a new boat we'd purchased for coastal tours with Caleb and Amanda, my wife. There was an accident, and Amanda...she didn't make it." He looked back out over the water. "I was driving the boat."

Natalie swallowed hard. Theo was clenching his hands at his sides. "I'm so sorry," she said quietly.

He ran both hands through his hair, turned to Natalie, and then laughed, shaking his head. "No, I'm sorry," he said. "I'm, ah, disclosing a lot here. Too much. I don't know why I said all that."

Natalie instinctively reached out her hand to take his, but pulled it back at the last moment. "No, I'm glad you did," she said, holding his gaze. "You can talk to me."

Theo let out a breath. "You're easy to talk to," he said softly.

Natalie's heart skipped a beat. "You are too," she said.

He fiddled with his hands in his lap and sighed. "It was something I've replayed a million times in my mind, but there was nothing I could've done to prevent it. A freak accident. But it scared the daylights out of me, to be honest. Life being so...I don't know. Fragile." His voice was hoarse.

Natalie's stomach clenched as she recalled waking up in the hospital. How she never carried her injector. She knew how fragile her life was, but didn't seem to be respecting that fact very much.

She looked up at him, her mouth dry. "So what made you leave teaching?"

He considered it for a moment. "I hated being indoors all the time, I felt like I was trapped. When my dad passed, I didn't want to sell off the company, and it looked like a great opportunity. So with my wife's support, I left my job, and took over the business. And I *loved* it, Natalie," he whispered. "I mean, getting to be outside all day, taking people on these great adventures, and getting paid for it? It suited me perfectly. But after the accident, I couldn't do it anymore. I couldn't go out on the water, I couldn't go out into the woods, I just...*stopped*."

He leaned back against his hands. "So I run the business from the office now. I ended up right back where I started, indoors all the time, doing paperwork and wondering how I got here. And when Caleb started to have nightmares over what happened, when his anxiety started, that became my focus. I'm a hypocrite, though," he said, his eyes dropping to the sand. "I'm setting a bad example for him, holing myself up. But I don't have an answer. I feel like I'm underwater, trying to get back to the surface."

Natalie nodded. That underwater feeling was something she was far too acquainted with.

"I'm sorry you had to go through all that," she said softly. "For what it's worth, I think you're setting a great example for Caleb. You're listening to him, talking to him, trying to do what's best for him. That's what children really need." Her throat constricted. "You're making me miss my dad. He was like that, before he left."

Theo looked at her, his dark eyes illuminated by the moonlight. A little shiver ran over her skin. He looked around, and released a breath. "Want to walk a little?"

Natalie nodded. He stood and reached out a hand. As she took it, a little spark ran from his skin into hers, an actual spark that made her heart beat a little faster. She led the way down the coastline.

It was a beach she knew well; in all the years she'd been gone, it hadn't changed at all. Nonetheless, it felt like she was exploring something new. It was she who had changed, she who was the stranger.

"So," Theo said, glancing over at her, "what

happened with your dad? If you don't mind my asking."

Natalie pushed out a lungful of air. "Right to the core, huh?" she said with a rueful smile.

Theo laughed. "Well, I did just pour my heart out to a perfect stranger tonight," he said, his eyes glittering. "But you don't have to answer that, of course. You barely know me."

"It's funny," she said, "I actually feel like I've known you for a long time." Natalie regretted the words for a brief moment, but then found again that she didn't care. She had no idea what was going on here, but something about Theo made her stop worrying so much about *what it all meant*. There would be plenty of time for overthinking later.

Theo smiled. "I feel the same way." The words carried over the breeze and seemed to caress her skin. She could listen to this man talk for a long time.

They walked in silence for a while. "He left my family when I was younger," she said finally. She reached for a long stick in the sand and began dragging it idly behind her, creating shapes. "We never knew why he left. He didn't tell us. I actually just found out everything recently. Very recently," she added, shivering involuntarily. "It's a long story. But in another way, it isn't. He had a lot of problems, and he wanted to shield us from them. So he left."

Theo nodded, frowning. "I'm sorry that happened to you."

Natalie could feel his eyes on her. Her throat had closed up, and she knew instinctively that Theo was going to let it stand without any more questions. It was exactly what she wanted. That clench in her stomach, the tightness in her shoulder blades told her that the claustrophobic feeling was beginning to set in. She dragged her stick in the sand, at a loss for what to say next.

They stopped near Becker's Pier, its old wooden beams stretching out into the water. Theo watched the waves rock against it for a moment. He turned to her, and Natalie relaxed, her stomach unclenching. "How long are you in town?" he asked, a casual tone in his voice. He'd been able to sense Natalie clamming up and was helping her feel at ease. She could kiss him for it.

"I'm honestly not sure," she said. "And I know that's not great in terms of the job—"

"Hey," he said, shaking his head. "Like I said, I'll be happy with whatever time you can spare. I'm just curious what brings you back to Marina Cove. What's next for you. You've got such an interesting life...I'm pretty jealous. Feel free to not answer, of course," he said, sensing her hesitation.

"No, no, it's okay," she said, casting the stick into the water. The gentle rolling of the waves against the pier soothed the tension pulling at her like tight bands. "I'm going to be starting a joint business in Prague." Her stomach twisted as she thought of Harper.

Poor, poor Harper. She had been so excited to help with the business, before...

Natalie cleared her throat. "A friend of mine, Jess, has a, uh, suitor, I guess you'd call him," she said on a laugh, "and he's providing some startup capital for us. Quite a bit, actually."

"Wow, that's awesome," he said. "What sort of business?"

Natalie grimaced. "Online high-end clothing and jewelry rental. It's stupid. Not my thing, at all."

He raised an eyebrow. "No? That's a really great idea."

Natalie shrugged. "I don't really care what the business is specifically, I guess...I love Jess, but she's a little hapless. I'm going to help with the business side of things just so we don't lose all the money their first week." She hesitated. "I have a business degree. An MBA. Took a while to finish it up with all the traveling, but I figure I ought to use it someday."

"Wow," he said. "A world traveler, a multilinguist, and an MBA, too. You're an impressive woman." Natalie laughed. "I might want to pick your brain on a few things for my business sometime...I can't claim to know exactly what I'm doing, I just try to replicate what worked for my dad."

"I'd love to," Natalie said honestly. "Anytime."

He smiled. "Well, that all sounds pretty exciting to me. Running a business is no joke. Your friend is lucky to have someone with your background. It'll save you all a lot of trouble."

"I guess so," she said, shrugging again. "I travel a lot. I don't like to stay in any one place for too long." That was putting it lightly. "And after the first year or two of getting things going, this would let me go back to traveling, working remotely. Jess wants to settle in Prague, at least for now. So it's a really good opportunity. I need to figure *something* out in my life. I'm not getting any younger."

Theo raised an imaginary glass. "Hear, hear. Life is short, and all that."

She clinked her hand against his. "It's worth a shot. None of us are taking a salary for a good, long while, hence my desire for a little income before I head back."

Natalie released a huge breath she'd been holding, and hopped up on the pier. The water sloshed beneath her. "My dad and I used to come to this pier sometimes," she said, glancing toward the end. Her heart twisted. "We used to skip rocks off the end. It was one of my favorite things to do with him."

She glanced back at Theo, holding her hand out to help him up, and froze. All the color had drained from his face, his chest rising and falling rapidly. His eyes were locked on the water, his fists clenched at his sides. Beads of sweat had formed on his brow.

"Oh, Theo," she said, hopping back down and placing a hand on his shoulder. "I'm so sorry. The water, I didn't think of it..." She trailed off, fighting tears at the terror in his eyes.

He let out a stilted breath, almost a gasp. "I...I can't..."

"It's okay," she said, squeezing his shoulder. "Really. You just told me about your wife, and I'm obviously a terrible listener. Let's just keep walking. I'm..." Natalie debated. "I'm not ready to call it a night yet, if you're not."

Theo's eyes settled on hers, sending a horrible electric shock down her spine. It was the hollow look of a haunted man. He shook his head almost imperceptibly before he sat down hard on the steps leading up to the pier. Natalie sat down next to him. A long moment passed, the only sound the water lapping against the shore.

He exhaled a long breath and ran a hand through his hair. "I'm tired of letting the past dictate my future."

Tears suddenly sprang to Natalie's eyes as Joel's face flashed in her mind. She quickly swiped them away. She looked up at Theo, and nodded.

"I know what you mean," she said slowly. Her mind was screaming at her to stop speaking, to lock it all back up, but she was just *tired* of it all. Something about Theo made it easier. She turned slightly to face him. "I used to be married," she said, her voice catching. He watched her without saying anything, just listening. "A long time ago. Some unexpected things happened between us, and it, ah...it didn't work out. It was my fault." She let a tear trickle down her face. "I carry a lot of guilt."

He kept watching her, his expression knowing, like he was feeling what she was feeling. That awful feeling of claustrophobia was closing in, pressing against her chest, but looking into Theo's eyes kept it at bay for the moment. Her heart thundered so loudly in her ears she was surprised he couldn't hear it.

Natalie felt that old, huge blockage in her throat, the one that made it harder to breathe every time she thought of Joel, of what could have been. She thought of her lockbox, what was inside it. The two things she'd been carrying for what felt like her whole life. She pulled in a sharp breath and swallowed hard.

Enough.

That was enough for now. Any more and she was going to cave in completely, to implode and disintegrate into nothingness.

She took another quick, shaky breath, and held her eyes on Theo's. Time seemed to stand still as silent words passed between them. She swallowed hard.

"I can't stay in Marina Cove," she said, her voice barely above a whisper.

His eyes moved over hers for a moment, his lips parted. He released a small breath, but he didn't say anything.

Natalie's heart twisted. "I can't. Jess needs me. She's gone through a lot lately...she has all my things...I have to start thinking about my future..." She stopped, the words cut off in her throat.

He nodded slowly, the moonlight playing against his dark eyes. She could feel the heat pouring off their bodies, her stomach twisting like a wet dishrag.

"Well," he said, "I'm glad you're here now."

Natalie's throat closed up, and she crushed back tears pressing against her eyes. There was something happening here, something she hadn't allowed to happen since everything with Joel.

Something that made her want to stay.

But it wasn't an option. It just wasn't. She knew the pattern too well. As soon as she got comfortable, the claustrophobia would become unbearable. There was nothing to do about it but push forward as best she could. One day at a time, one step at a time. It would all eventually work itself out.

Wouldn't it?

They sat there under the stars, thoughts unspooling frantically in Natalie's mind. A sensation of freefall stole over her, and she dug her hands deep into the sand to hold on. She was more unsure of what to do next than she ever had been in her life.

15

"Ughhh," Sylvie groaned loudly, scrolling through another long spreadsheet on her laptop. "What am I, a mathematician? I'm never gonna figure all this out."

"We don't need to do everything all at once," said Charlotte. "We'll figure it out as we go along. Zara won't leave us hanging. And besides, with Ramona's bookkeeping background, we'll get there. I promise."

Sylvie rubbed her eyes with her palms and shook her head. She, Charlotte, Diane, and Mariah had been sitting outside on the old wooden picnic bench in the side yard of the Seaside House. The sun was bright and hot overhead. Sylvie looked out over the expanse of cerulean water, sparkling and cool, yearning to strip off her clothes, dive in, and forget all her worries for a while. She released a long and heavy breath.

"Didn't you say Aunt Natalie has some sort of business background?" Mariah asked Charlotte. "I mean, maybe she can help us?"

Charlotte frowned and lifted one shoulder up. "We can definitely ask her," she said, "but she's so hard to pin down. We've barely seen her since she came home."

"And at any rate," said Diane, "she isn't staying long. And knowing her, she could be gone at any moment. Heck, for all we know, she's already skipped town."

Sylvie looked between Charlotte and Diane, her heart twisting. The brief moments she'd seen Natalie, she could *feel* something haunting the woman, something tugging and pulling at her to leave. To flee. And there was some complicated dynamic going on between her and Ella that Sylvie wasn't privy to, and wasn't sure if her sisters were, either.

She pressed her eyes shut. The Kellers had all been fighting an uphill battle for so long. It made her problems seem a little less...impossible.

Ella appeared with a pitcher of lemonade and a large box of chocolate chip cookies. "So what do we think, Sylvie?" she asked, sitting next to her. "Are we ready for the reopening?"

"No, ma'am," she said with a rueful smile. "Not in the slightest. And yet, blind and stumbling, we push onward."

Ella laughed and squeezed her shoulder comfortingly before pouring her a glass of lemonade. Sylvie drank deeply, immediately feeling a little better under the heat of the sun.

The sound of an engine made them all turn. A beat-up white pickup truck rolled to a stop beside the Seaside House. A moment later, a man emerged, wearing paint-stained khaki pants and a dusty white T-shirt that said *Keller Contracting*.

Samuel.

A harsh line appeared between Charlotte's brows as she stepped forward to meet him. "Hey, what are you doing here—"

"I asked him to come," a voice said from behind them. Sylvie turned to see Ramona striding through the sand toward them.

Diane raised an eyebrow. "You?"

Ramona stopped next to her sisters, facing Samuel.

"I should go," Sylvie whispered to Charlotte, and

turned to leave. She didn't want to interfere with a family matter.

"Could you stay?" Ramona asked. Sylvie raised her eyebrows in surprise. "Is that okay?"

Sylvie nodded, touched. "Of course," she said, a small rush of emotion running through her. It meant a lot that Ramona wanted her to stick around for this.

With no family of her own, it meant the world to Sylvie to have a found family, one that each day she felt more and more a true part of.

Ramona turned to Samuel, watching him for a long moment, before she cleared her throat.

"I wanted to thank you," said Ramona quietly. "For what you did." Her eyes drifted over to the beautiful garden paradise he'd restored. "It means a lot to us. To me. My dad, it was his garden..." Her voice wavered slightly. "Thank you."

He nodded, running a calloused hand through his ruffled, windblown hair. "Well, I'm glad I finally got your attention."

Charlotte leaned in toward Ramona. "Are you sure?" she whispered.

Ramona took a deep breath, cautioning one last glance toward the garden, pain in her eyes. She looked back to Samuel.

"I don't trust you," she said.

One corner of Samuel's mouth twitched upward. "Blunt," he said, amusement playing in his green eyes as he raised an eyebrow. Sylvie stifled a laugh. "But fair."

Ramona's eyes crossed over his for a moment before the line between her brows softened. "You can't exactly blame us after what Uncle Patrick has put us through, can you? But we're all here now, and you've been, ah, *persistent*. So what is it you'd like to tell us?"

Samuel bit his lower lip, squinting in the sunlight. "Well, I..." he said, then shook his head. He seemed almost nervous. "Let's take a walk."

They followed Samuel up the sand across the Seaside House lot until they met the small copse of trees that led into the next lot up the coast. Sylvie immediately felt cooler in the shade, and listened to the wind rustling through the leaves overhead. Her mind was whirring as she wondered what Samuel had to say.

Whatever it was...things were going to change. Sylvie could sense it.

They stopped at the base of a huge oak tree, its gnarled and knotted branches reaching into the sky, the leaves whispering in the breeze. You could see the tree from the porch of the Seaside House, but Sylvie had never ventured into the next lot. Somewhere up ahead was an old house, or at least she thought. She was struck with a sudden urge to lie down underneath the canopy of the ancient and beautiful tree, to curl up in the soft grass and let her dreams sweep her into a blissful sleep.

"Remember the tire swing that used to be here?" Charlotte asked.

Ramona smiled sadly. "Dad used to push us on it."

"What ever happened to Mrs. Laurier?" ask Diane.

"She moved, ages ago," said Ella, her eyes lingering on the tree. She seemed to be far away. "Her children inherited it after she passed." She turned to look at Samuel. "Why are we here, Samuel?"

He took a deep breath. "Okay. So I'll do my best to make it brief. My dad..." He shook his head and stared at the ground. "When you guys kicked me and my crew off the property, I didn't understand why. I did a little digging, and suffice it to say, what I found out...it wasn't pretty."

Ramona snorted. "Yeah, that's one way to put it."

He looked up at her. "Well, you probably aren't

going to believe me, but I haven't been privy to what he's been doing. The things he's done. And I'm aware that I don't know the half of it." He stepped toward them. "The short version is that I quit. I no longer run his company. I took a couple of contractors with me and started a new company." He pointed to the logo on his T-shirt. "A clean start."

Charlotte narrowed her eyes. "You don't work for him anymore?"

Samuel sighed. "Look, that's a long story, and not why I'm here. I'm only telling you so that you know there are things going on in the background, and I'm not going to be party to them. I'm here because I've become aware of some things. Things that you need to know." He shifted his weight from foot to foot. "There's no easy way to say it, so I'm just going to say it. This lot," he said, gesturing around him, "now belongs to him."

The words held in the air for a moment. Sylvie's stomach clenched tightly.

"What does that mean?" Ramona asked, her pitch rising. "What—"

"Genevieve Laurier, the owner of this lot and the house that's built on it," he said, "passed her house on to her children, who have never been here, apparently. The house has been abandoned for years. My dad bought the land, because..." He met Ramona's eyes. "He plans on building on it. A chain hotel and resort. A huge one, at that."

The words hung in the air. Sylvie's stomach rolled over. "Oh, God," she said, the words slipping out unintentionally.

"He can't do that," said Ramona. "The zoning—"

"He has connections everywhere," said Samuel, biting his lower lip again. "And unfortunately, that now includes Marina Cove. It's a whole thing. Kick-backs, and whatnot. I don't have all the facts, and they don't matter. But when he sent you guys a letter threatening legal action for payment for the work we did—"

"Yeah, we got that." Ramona looked to her sisters, her voice tight, frightened. "But he doesn't have a leg to stand on, he can't make us pay anything—"

"I know," he interjected. "But it doesn't matter. He knows your family is in a vulnerable position, and if there's one thing my father is great at, it's spotting weaknesses in others. Part of him does want you to spend money on the lawsuit, knowing he can drag it out endlessly, but really, he's moved on from that. Between the 24/7 construction noise of a hotel chain being built right next to your lot, plus the fact that it'll block out the view of the whole coast up from the Seaside House, and the rock-bottom prices he knows he can charge, he knows your inn is going to fail even if you do manage to open it again." He looked between them with a deep frown. "He's going to smoke you guys out, knowing that you don't have the means to fight any of it."

"Why does he want to smoke us out?" asked Diane.

Ramona pushed out a sharp breath. "He wants our land, too."

Samuel nodded. "He wants this whole stretch of coast for additional hotels, all part of a giant resort. It's going to be part of the UHX Hotel & Resort Group chain. Massive. I don't have to tell you what that's going to do to the local hospitality business here, let alone setting future precedent. It hasn't happened yet in Marina Cove...and this will be the first domino." He looked around, shaking his head. "After you guys first reached out to him, he started getting ideas. He knows Marina Cove is basically untouched, that most people don't even know about it. Unfortunately for your family, he knows the potential of this place."

"Oh, my God," said Charlotte. She turned to Ella. "What...what are we supposed to do here?" She turned back to Samuel, her voice rising. "What are we supposed to do?"

Samuel looked down at the ground, kicking the grass idly with his boot. Sylvie had been watching him carefully, knowing the history of what Patrick had done. And she knew that Samuel was telling the truth. She knew it in her bones.

"I'm sorry to be the bearer of bad news," he said quietly. "I don't have an answer for you. I wish I did. But...you needed to know."

"Can't you stop him?" asked Ramona, her voice wavering. "I mean, you know what he's done. Can't you do something?"

Samuel looked at her for a long moment. "I already did something. I left. I gave up my livelihood, my security. I spent my life savings opening a new company that he's almost certainly going to do everything he can to destroy. My dad...I still love him. And now he's most likely never going to speak to me again. That's what I had to give up to try to do the right thing." He shook his head sadly. "I don't have to tell you that he's got too many resources at his disposal. I don't have the means or the evidence to do anything else, even if I wanted to. There's no beating him. I wish I had some answer. Sometimes, there just isn't one."

A horrible silence swirled around them. Finally, Ella spoke. "Why did you do all this? The garden, trying so hard to get our attention. Why are you telling us all this?"

Samuel met her eyes. "Because it's the right thing to do. I knew you wouldn't believe me unless I had a chance to give you some context, to really talk to you. I want to help you guys." His eyes drifted over to the sea, something flitting across his expression. "You aren't the only ones I'm trying to make amends with. To try to make up for the things he's done."

Sylvie glanced at Charlotte. She was biting her lip hard, clearly trying not to cry. Sylvie wanted to say something, do something, but she couldn't think of anything. She was utterly helpless.

After a long moment, Samuel turned back to them. "I don't know when this is happening, but I wanted you to know so you could prepare your-selves. At least now, you know. I'm sorry."

And with that, Samuel turned, and left.

16

Mariah's fingers adjusted the shutter of their own accord as she spun the zoom lens just as the surfer with long blond hair stood on his board, the massive wave cresting just behind him. *Click click click click click.*

She tried to focus on what she was doing, but she couldn't stop thinking about what Samuel had told them. What it would mean for them all. The Seaside House was their home. And for some reason, it seemed like the universe was bent on taking it away from them.

Her mother's face swam in her mind, making her stomach turn over. She didn't need this on top of everything else. The restaurant closing, everything Sebastian had done to her...

Sebastian. Her mind still couldn't square the man who had helped raise her with the man who had sustained a six-year relationship with her mother's best friend. Mariah gritted her teeth, and tried again to push the man out of her mind.

She glanced up from the playback screen just as the wave crashed over the guy, burying him in what looked like a terrifying amount of water. He didn't surface. Her heart beat faster as she looked around.

No lifeguards anywhere. Riptide Cove, as the locals called it, wasn't a public beach. It was just a small group of surfers...and Mariah. She stood and reached for her cell phone, starting to panic.

But then the blond surfer finally shot to the surface, hacking and coughing up seawater, laughing and pumping his fists into the air. The other surfers whooped and hollered. Mariah sat down hard, trying to catch her breath.

She'd hemmed and hawed to herself for a day or two after Keiran made his offer before finally pulling him aside as he and Christian were sawing two-by-fours at the Seaside House.

And then, after an informal meeting at a taco stand later with a man and a woman from *Surfside* magazine, where Mariah showed a few of her photos right off her camera, she had the job.

Her stomach had been in knots the whole interview as she thought about the email she'd written telling Dr. Meyers she'd be back for the start of the upcoming semester. About how she hadn't sent it yet.

The photography gig was just the distraction she needed while she figured out how to move forward, to get back in the saddle. The one that would let her continue med school and move on with her life.

She'd just have to find a way to live with what she'd done.

Mariah swept across the shoreline with her camera lens, looking for Keiran. He was out there somewhere. No harm in taking a little peek.

A second later, she spotted him. He ran a hand through his wet hair, the muscles of his broad shoulders and chest tightening and flexing effortlessly. The long sleeves of his arm tattoos glistened in the late afternoon sunlight. She followed that beautiful form as he pushed himself up on his board and casually caught an enormous rolling wave, a huge grin on his face. He dipped down on his board and softly cut into the breaking wave as it rolled over him, cresting the water a moment later.

Wow.

Mariah sighed. This should be a *lot* more fun.

But hot fire kept rising in her throat as Sebastian's face kept popping into her mind against her will. She ran her hands over her face, trying unsuccessfully to shake away the thoughts.

Her mother didn't know it, but sometimes at night, when she thought everyone else was asleep, Mariah could hear her crying softly.

Mariah's eyes brimmed with tears as she snapped a few more shots, her heart not really in it. Sure, the surfers were all tanned, muscled hotties, but today, it just wasn't doing anything for her.

As the sun dipped toward the horizon, the group parted ways on the shoreline. Mariah quickly swiped away the tears in her eyes as Keiran bounded across the sand toward her, board beneath his arms.

"Hi there!" he said in that delicious drawl. He tossed the board aside and sat down in the sand next to her. The strong fragrance of saltwater poured off his skin. "How're you? How are things looking?"

She fixed a smile on her face and handed him the camera. "Not bad, I think. I'll get a better handle on things as we approach the competition."

He scrolled through the photos. "Are you kidding? These are amazing, Mariah." She ignored the butterflies in her stomach at the sound of her name.

He was grinning as he looked up at her, but a moment later, his face fell. "What's wrong?"

"Nothing," she answered, too quickly. She covered it with a small laugh. "Nothing. Long day is all."

He kept his gaze on her, and something twisted in her chest. It was something in his eyes...she couldn't quite place it. Something that made her shoulder blades loosen a little, made her feel...softer. Like it was okay to be vulnerable.

She opened her mouth to speak, but instead, her eyes flooded with tears. "Oh, no, Mariah," he said, squeezing her shoulder with his wet hands.

Mariah shook her head, swiping away the fresh tears. She looked up at him.

He met her eyes and then stood up, offering her his hand. "I've got an idea."

∼

AN HOUR LATER, they were sitting at a picnic table facing the shore in front of a little burger shack called Mel's. She was holding a gigantic cheeseburger in one hand and a glorious chocolate malt in the other. "This is just *ridiculous*," she said, taking another huge bite.

"I know," he said, grabbing a handful of french fries from a basket they were sharing. "I could live off this stuff. So, Miss Mariah," he said, finishing his cherry Coke, "you're upset about something. If you want to talk, I'm a pretty good listener. I think so, anyway. And if you'd rather just hang out, we can do that too. Your call."

Mariah smiled. She liked how direct Keiran was. She watched him for a moment. There was no talking to her mother about Sebastian, obviously. Her friends were all back home, and besides, she hadn't really kept in touch with them much since she'd started the whirlwind of med school. Sylvie was a blast, but she was dealing with massive problems of her own, so no dice there. And while she adored Christian, she was taking things slow with their budding relationship.

She didn't really have anyone to talk to...and something about the way he was looking at her right now made her think he'd be a good listener.

So Mariah talked. She told him about everything with Sebastian, how he'd lied to her repeatedly in attempts to get her back, how hard of a time her mother was still having even though she was putting on a brave face. Everything with Tex, and the investment that had already been made before Sebastian dragged her mother out to New York under false pretenses. The wretched stab in her heart when she watched the video of police officers escorting him in handcuffs. And now, the prospect of the family inn being ripped away from them. Tears poured from her eyes as she shared everything that had been weighing her down.

She even told him about med school. The impossible hours, the competition between students, the incredible pressure. She left out the reasons she'd left her program.

She wasn't ready to talk about that out loud.

He listened carefully, and asked clarifying questions at all the right moments. He'd been right, he was a very good listener. As she spoke, she could feel the tension lifting from her body, could feel the invisible bands wrapped around her chest and throat finally loosening. She could feel herself blushing despite herself as she felt him next to her, his warm, steady presence.

After she was done, he handed her a stack of napkins to dry her eyes. He blew out a long breath, and for a while they watched the sun setting in the orange and lavender sky, listened to the waves crashing against the shore.

Keiran turned to her. "I'm really sorry, Mariah.

That's...awful. I know it was probably hard to talk about all that." He put a hand on her shoulder, sending a chill down her spine. "I won't say I know what you're going through, because I don't. I can't imagine what all that's like. But I can say I went through something a little bit like that with my dad. He left my mom when I was ten. His secretary...what a cliché." He laughed humorlessly and leaned back on the wooden picnic bench. "One day he just turned up with her and told us he was leaving, and that was that. I never saw him again."

"Oh, I'm sorry," said Mariah softly.

He shrugged. "He was, frankly, a bad father well before then. That was just the final blow. But my mom..." His voice caught ever so slightly, and he looked at his hands. After a moment, he looked up at the water. "I love my mom more than anyone else in the world. She's always been there for me when I needed her. What he did, it really broke her up."

He sat up and looked at Mariah. "She couldn't get past what he'd done. At first. But after a while, things got a little better. And a little better. And then there were whole days where she seemed to be herself again. She was able to carry on. I was so proud of her."

Mariah smiled through her tears. "So she was okay, then?"

He nodded, and wiped a lone tear rolling down his cheek. "It was terrible, seeing what that did to her. Somehow, people who do the cheating, they seem to forget the *incredible* repercussions their selfishness will have on the people around them. How it changes lives. It affects everything. But yes," he said, running a hand through his hair, "as time went on, she was okay. And I think your mom will be too."

Mariah thought of her mother. How she would do anything in the world for her. Maybe she should try talking to her about everything. She hadn't wanted to remind her mother about her own problems, but avoiding it...that was like sweeping it under the rug, like it had never happened at all.

Maybe that was something she could do. She already felt a little better talking to Keiran, and he was practically a stranger.

"You sound like a really great son," she said in a quiet voice.

He looked out over the water. "She was a really great mother."

Mariah turned to him, frowning. "Oh. Keiran, I'm sorry."

He looked up at her. "She died when I was

fifteen. She got sick...really sick." He returned his gaze to his hands, his eyes glistening.

Mariah reached out a hand to comfort him, but retracted it. She didn't want to be too forward. "That's awful."

The last light faded from the sky. "It was a long time ago. But there are times..." He pushed out a breath. "There are times when it really breaks me up. I'd do just about anything to see her, one last time."

Mariah's heart folded over when she saw fresh tears steal down his cheeks. He quickly swiped them away and laughed.

"Geez, I'm really sorry, Mariah," he said, looking up at the sky and shaking his head. "I'm supposed to be making you feel better. I'm doing a horrible, horrible job."

Mariah laughed. "No, actually, you've been really helpful. It helps to talk about it. It really does." Before she knew what she was doing, she took his hand in hers. A thrill of warmth stole across her skin. "Thanks for telling me about her, Keiran. She sounds like a great lady. And thank you for listening to me. It...really means a lot. Especially since you don't really know me very well."

Keiran smiled. "Well, I feel like I know you a

little bit better now." He squeezed her hand and raised his eyes to hers.

Mariah felt her chest tightening. The moonlight shone through a break in the wispy clouds and reflected off those beautiful golden-brown irises. Silence stretched between them as his eyes bored into hers. Her heart pumped harder as their eyes remained locked. She felt like she could fall into his gaze forever.

His chest was rising and falling hard as he opened his mouth to speak. "Mariah," he said a little breathlessly. The vulnerability in those eyes, the depth...it brought fresh tears of emotion to her eyes. She felt like she was looking into his very soul. "Do you—"

"Duuuuuuuuuuude, no way!" a voice shouted from the sand in front of them. Mariah yelped and jumped in her seat, knocking over her chocolate malt on the table with her elbow.

A shirtless guy with white-blond hair raised in high, pointy spikes was jogging toward them. "Bro. *Broooo.* Gnarly waves out there today, yeah?"

Keiran cleared his throat. "Yeah, man, good times. This is Mariah." He gestured to her.

"Right on, right on, photographer, right? Keiran says you take killer shots." He raised his hand for a high five. "You super stoked for the big competish, or what?"

Keiran glanced at Mariah and shook his head, giving her a little smile. The moment between them was gone as soon as it came. Mariah's skin was hot all over. She returned his smile, her heart fluttering.

As the three of them hunched over her camera to look at some of her shots from the day, her shoulder pressing into Keiran's, she silently berated herself. There was no sense in what she was doing.

Yes, something had passed between them; she hadn't misread things. But she couldn't be doing this. She was going back to the real world. Back to her program. There was no future for her in Marina Cove, and there was no sense in falling for some random guy, no matter who it was, or how she felt when he was around. People only left their life plans for some guy they thought they had feelings for in the movies. Real life was a *whole lot* more complicated than that.

Her heart lodged in her throat as she felt pulled in two directions at once. She was slipping, losing her grip on the plan. She had no idea what she was doing anymore.

17

"Listen," said Austin, taking Diane's hand, "I hope you're not nervous to meet the guys. They're super cool, and I promise they're gonna love you."

The sun was dipping lower in the sky over Sunflower Run Park, giving gold and ruby highlights to the wispy clouds. They were making their way across a small bridge over the creek that ran through the park. Diane's palms were sweating as she suddenly couldn't remember any of their lyrics.

"You sure they're okay playing again without Kate?" Diane asked. "I mean, isn't this gonna be weird for them?"

Austin shook his head. "They've been dying to

perform again. All of us have." He looked over at her. "I do sort of wish we'd had a chance to practice all together before tonight. With their day jobs and kids and everything, it just didn't work out." He ran a hand through his hair, and Diane realized for the first time that Austin was nervous.

"Well, there should only be a few people here for this, right? I told my family, but I mean, how would anyone else even know we're performing?"

At that moment they walked through the treeline at the end of the bridge, and turned to face the field they were playing in. Diane's stomach clenched, hard. There were at least a hundred people. They were lying on beach towels, eating snacks, kids running around blowing bubbles and squealing. There were several food trucks at the end of the park where even more people were waiting in line. A magician was pulling a long trail of colored sheets from his mouth to the delight of a group of small children. Everyone was facing an impromptu stage built of a small raised platform, where there were stools, two microphones, amplifiers, and a drum set.

"Oh, no," Diane said, shaking her head. "How did…"

Austin swallowed hard. "I have no idea. I told

like three or four people..." He trailed off, and wiped his palms on his sport coat.

They weaved their way through the crowd toward the platform. A man sat behind the drum set, twirling a drumstick idly in his hands while chatting with another man fiddling with the tuning pegs of a violin.

"You must be Diane," said a deep, booming voice from behind them. They whipped around to find a man with a bass guitar slung over his shoulder.

"Niko!" exclaimed Austin, setting his guitar case down and pulling the man into a bear hug. "It's been way, way too long, brother."

The man grinned and clapped him on the back. "Nice to meet you," said Diane, shaking his hand.

"You too," he said. "Austin's been singing your praises for weeks. He says you've got one heck of a voice. And the guys love the lyrics you two have been writing. I mean, really great stuff."

Diane blushed profusely. "Well, we'll see. I'm not much of a performer..."

He waved his hand. "Just pretend they're not there, and have some fun. You'll do great. Pretty great turnout, though, huh?" he said, gesturing around them. "I asked a few people how they found out. It was just word of mouth. I guess you two have been building something of a following with your open mics lately. All thanks to you, Diane. Everyone knows Austin here is just terrible." He gave Austin's arm a playful punch.

"Ow! At least I know how to play more than one string at a time," said Austin, nodding to his bass guitar. "You ever want some lessons or anything, I don't come cheap, but I'd be happy to help—"

Niko winced, laughing. "Right to the core. I'll have you know I learned a new scale just for you, Austy-bear, but now I'm not gonna play it." He shook his head at Diane. "I don't know how you can put up with him."

Diane laughed as they hopped up on the platform to a few scattered cheers and whistles. Niko bowed, to more cheering. "Always the showman," said Austin, grinning as Niko shoved him.

"Diane," said Niko, "this is Tyson on drums, and Sullivan, we call him Sully, he's our violin maestro." Diane shook their hands, hoping they didn't notice how sweaty her palms were.

"We owe you a big thanks, Diane," said Sully. "For getting this dope out of his writer's block." He nodded toward Austin. "Turns out he's a pretty great writer when someone else is doing all the writing for him."

Diane chuckled as Austin scoffed. "Austin did more than his fair share of the writing," she said. "He just needed to find his inspiration."

"Don't even bother with these fools." Austin shook his head. "They'll never let up. Best to just ignore them altogether."

Diane laughed again, feeling a lot better. Austin had been right, the guys were great. She scanned the crowd, taking a long, deep breath. This was going to be fun.

They chatted for a bit about the order of the songs she and Austin had written. Some of them were incomplete, but Tyson had apparently posted to his social media that they were mostly testing new material for the upcoming Marina Cove Music Festival, so that the audience would expect things to be a little "raw," as he'd put it. Hopefully they would be forgiving.

Austin leaned down, lifted his rosewood guitar from his case, and plugged it into the amplifier. As he looked over the crowd, he took a slow breath, and strummed a single chord. People began cheering and whistling.

"*WE LOVE YOU, DIIIIAAAAAAAAAAAAANE!!!!*

WOOOOOOOOOOOOOOO!!!!!" screamed a familiar voice, bringing laughter from the audience. Heat rising to her face, Diane scanned the crowd to find Ramona cupping her hands and screaming at the top of her lungs, alongside Sylvie and Mariah. Charlotte was whistling through her fingers, and even Ella was shouting her support. Leo was making his way through the crowd toward her family. Diane laughed, feeling strangely emotional. They'd all come out to see her.

Well, everyone except Natalie. Diane brushed away the sting of disappointment. She hadn't realized how much she'd been hoping Natalie would make it. Hopefully she would at least remember the dinner they all planned tonight. They'd wanted to talk to her about Uncle Patrick, about the looming threat to the Seaside House, but she was never around long enough.

Diane shook her head. Now wasn't the time for any of that. She released a breath and let her eyes wander over the crowd, her heart pattering with excitement.

It was a small thing, playing music with Austin, playing at being a real performer. Diane obviously didn't belong in a band; her adult life had mostly been spent leading meetings in corporate conference rooms and huddling over the pen and paper to write things that coerced people to buy things they didn't need.

Yes, it was a small thing, a silly thing, what she was doing here, she knew it. But as she stood there on the platform, the warm sunshine cascading through the oak trees, the clean, bright air in her lungs, the smells of sunscreen and saltwater and fresh-cut grass and barbecue food...her family here with her, right here after so many years spent on different ends of the country, and Austin, the man she was falling in love with, by her side...Diane was overcome with a feeling she'd lost touch with over the long years of adulthood, the feeling that used to come so naturally when she was a child. The feeling of joy.

And so what if she was playing some music for fun? Not everything had to have a *practical purpose*. That way of thinking had dictated Diane's life for too long. When had she become so focused on real life, on the constant dread over the future and regret over the past, that she'd stopped having fun?

Diane met Austin's eyes, and she couldn't help the grin forming on her face. Butterflies danced in her chest as he smiled in return, giving her a small nod. The audience whooped and hollered as Diane lifted the microphone from the stand. Austin turned to the other band members and gave them a nod. Tyson raised his sticks in the air and hit them together.

"One, two, one, two, three, four!"

The next hour was a complete blur. Playing with the additional instrumentation changed their sound dramatically, from a more intimate performance to something that carried real weight, something that made the people on the lawn stand up and pump their fists into the air, the ground trembling with the bass drum, the violin countermelodies swirling through the air, the crash of cymbals coursing through Diane's skin, the sound of her voice rising and falling against Austin's taking on a life of its own, something brand new being created right there on the spot. Diane's mouth was dry and her heart was pounding hard, electric thrills running up and down her spine as they played song after song. Some people were even singing along, singing to lyrics Diane and Austin had written together. Lyrics that had meaning to them, a meaning unique and sacred, but the beauty of music allowed the words to transform into something more universal, something a person applied to their own life, their own fears and heartbreaks and hopes and dreams.

Diane watched her family, clapping their hands, shouting her name, and was overcome with love for them, for their unquestioned support for everything she'd been going through. They'd drifted so far apart over the years...but it was never too late. It was never too late to change, to hold the ones you loved close, to do what you could to use the time you had wisely and to surround yourself with people who cared about you, who loved you in return, as life handed you challenge after challenge.

She looked up at Austin, their voices soaring as they reached the final chorus. Their eyes locked, and tears pricked the corners of her eyes. Her heart was very full. She had fallen hard for him, and there was nothing she could do about it.

This place...this place was magical. Marina Cove was beginning to feel like home again.

The song ended, and the crowd cheered and hollered as fire rushed to Diane's face. Niko set down his bass guitar and came over to Diane, wrapping her in a hug. His eyes were red as he leaned in. "Thank you," he whispered. "You have no idea how much I missed this."

Tyson, Sully, and Austin joined in, arm in arm and leaning toward each other to create a circle as they laughed and grinned like kids. The audience erupted when they got in a line and bowed.

"Thank you! You were a wonderful audience! Goodnight!" Niko quickly yelled into the microphone as they hopped off the platform. Austin shook his head, laughing.

"What a ham," he said, unable to keep the grin from his face.

Niko shrugged. "What can I say? I love attention." He gave Diane a high-five. "What a rush. You were awesome, Diane." Tyson and Sully both nodded. "Austin, you were...fine. I have some notes, though—" Austin kicked him in the shin, making him yelp. "Kidding! Geez. Some people." He pointed toward the food trucks. "I'm starving. Let's get some grub. Mingle with our new fans for life."

Austin's phone chimed in his pocket. He pulled it out, glanced at it, and his face went slack. The color seemed to run from his skin. He let out a hard breath, locked the screen, and tossed it onto the amplifier.

"I'm starved," he said, shuddering. "Diane?"

Her heart thundered in her ears. Suddenly, everything felt very far away. "I'm, uh, gonna say hey to my family real quick, see if they want to stick around..." she said. Her voice seemed too quiet, like someone else was speaking. "I'll meet you guys over there in a few."

Austin kissed her on the cheek. "That was amazing," he said. "We're gonna win at the music festival. I know it." He grinned as he turned to the rest of the band on their way toward the food trucks. "See you in a few," he said, giving her a wave.

Diane watched them walk away, trying to catch her breath. Her mind was spinning as she turned to face his phone, lying on the amplifier.

It was wrong. So, so wrong.

Something she would never actually do.

Diane looked over her shoulder. Mariah and Sylvie were laughing about something, and the rest of them were listening to Leo tell one of his stories, his hands gesturing animatedly. Ella was holding a bunch of daisies he'd brought for her, her cheeks tinged with color as she watched him with sparkling eyes.

Now was her chance.

Before she could stop herself, before she could listen to the voice yelling at her to stop now, that this was the wrong way to go about things, she was already lifting Austin's phone from the amplifier. Her hands were trembling.

She could stop now, and no one would ever have

to know about her moment of weakness. Diane was a grown woman. And this was most definitely wrong, in every way.

But she'd tried to talk to him. And some part of her, call it feminine instinct, told her that whatever he was dealing with had nothing to do with his brother. It was something Diane wasn't supposed to know.

And Diane wasn't about to give up her future, the dream job waiting for her in LA, all of it, for a man who wasn't able to be honest with her. After everything Trevor had put her through, she wasn't about to be lied to again. The stakes were just too high.

The sunlight glared off the phone, momentarily blinding her. It was locked. She cursed to herself. She had no idea what his passcode was.

Her mouth was dry as she went to set the phone back down. A moment of weakness, that was all. She was just going to have to talk to him about it. The right way.

But then his phone chimed. And Kate's words rang in her ears.

If something ever feels off...listen to that voice.

Everything was moving in slow motion as her hands moved of their own accord. A new notification had appeared on his lock screen.

A text message. From someone named Alice Jordan. Diane's vision narrowed to a tunnel.

Beneath her name was the preview of the text. She shielded the phone from the waning sunlight, and read, her heart slamming against her chest so hard it hurt.

It was great to see you again babe <3 <3. I can't wait for you to finally meet our son.

18

"Welcome to Marina Cove Adventures!" said Natalie, beaming. A cool breeze swept off the ocean and caressed her skin, filling her lungs with wonderfully crystal-clean air. "I'll be your guide today as we tackle the raging rapids of the upper Harstow River. Are you ready to have some fun?"

April laughed as she ran up to Natalie and pulled her into a tight hug. "This is so cool, Natalie," she said. "I haven't done something like this in, well..." She frowned. "Forever. Honestly. Thanks for inviting me to tag along."

Natalie grinned as she gave April a high five and guided her to meet the other members of the group.

After an introduction and review of safety rules, they began to gather their gear and board the small shuttle that would take them to the launch point.

Theo emerged from the long bungalow that housed the Marina Cove Adventures offices and gift shop right on the coast. His head was hunched down as he scribbled against a clipboard in his hand, the wind whipping at his wavy hair. Natalie's heart fluttered.

"Whoa, *hello*," said April, and giggled. "Who's that?"

"Theo!" Natalie called. His eyes met hers, and a thrill ran down her spine. She motioned for him to come over.

"Hey, Natalie," he said, a slight color tinging his cheeks. Adorable. "Hi, I'm Theo," he said as he held a hand out for April.

"April," she said, a little breathless. "Pleasure to meet you." Natalie stepped on April's foot playfully, and April shot her a look.

"Likewise," said Theo. "Glad you could join the tour today. Natalie's been doing an amazing job out there."

"Will you be joining us?" April asked sheepishly.

Theo's face tightened, his lips almost white from

strain. "I, ah..." he stammered, running a hand through his hair. "No, ah, you guys have fun. I've got a lot of work to, uh, catch up on." His eyes lingered on Natalie's for a moment, her stomach rolling over as she sensed the terror in his heart. "It was really nice to meet you," he said to April, before turning and heading back into the bungalow.

"What was that all about?" April asked quietly. "Is he all right?"

"Oh, he's fine, yeah," she said, and offered nothing further. She loved April, but what Theo had told her about his late wife and his resulting avoidances wasn't something she was going to share. Natalie valued her privacy above all else, and respected it in others fiercely. "He's just busy, you know. There's a competing tour company that opened up a year or two ago that's been eating his business alive...he's under a lot of stress."

April nodded as they gathered their gear and boarded the bus. As Natalie surveyed the group, about ten people, her heart swelled with joy, with pride. It was hard to believe she was going to get paid to kayak down the river all day.

She and April made small talk as the bus jostled them around on the way up to the launch point at the Upper Harstow. Several chimes emitted from April's phone, and each time, she seemed to get a little quieter, until she simply stared out the window, watching the trees go by along the dirt path.

Natalie gritted her teeth. Obviously, Garrett was hounding her again. He was supposedly watching the three kids at his parents' house again, but was already pressuring April. An awful surge of protective anger welled up in Natalie's chest. Couldn't he leave the woman alone for a *single afternoon*?

As they stood in the clearing before the river twenty minutes later, they put on their helmets and boarded their kayaks, the air thrumming with anticipation. Natalie gave another brief safety review and a reminder of the different sections of rapids and how to navigate them. The group had already been vetted by Theo; these were fairly experienced kayakers, but most had never tackled the Upper Harstow before. Natalie, however, had kayaked the rapids hundreds of times in her life. She knew every rock and eddy, every sweeper and strainer, every undercut and entrapment. She was in her element, and was ready for anything.

"Okay, my friends, are we ready?" she called to the group. Cheers and whistling rippled across them as they paddled in a holding position in the small cove.

"Let's get *wild*!" someone shouted, a fit man in his sixties who'd been kayaking since he was a kid. They all laughed.

Natalie nodded to April, who was grinning from ear to ear. She tightened her helmet and gave Natalie a thumbs up. No matter what April had going on in her personal life, Natalie knew this was important to her, that she desperately missed the adventurous side of herself. And *that* was something Natalie could help with.

"Okay, let's do it!" Natalie shouted, and pushed off the bank and into the rapids.

The section of river they were traveling wound through the thick forest of northern Marina Cove down toward the eastern shore, ending right before a massive waterfall plunged into sheets of rock that led into the Middle Harstow. With a practiced hand, she deftly maneuvered through the first rapids, a sudden shifting of the wide river to a narrow gradient that had them rounding huge boulders and ducking under thick overhangs of trees.

Natalie's heart hammered wonderfully as the water sloshed and splashed across her body, drenching her almost immediately as a swell launched her clean into the air before she sliced back down into the whitewater. She frequently paddled back into a holding position to check on the other kayakers, but everyone had listened to her careful instructions and were whooping and hollering for joy as they swept down the river.

Natalie took a long, slow breath, and looked around. The sun was shining, rays of golden-white light dappling the water, giving it a beautiful, shimmering sparkle, and the air was warm and clean and dry.

Not a bad day at the office.

April suddenly appeared from around a bend, shouting, "*Woooooooohooooooooo!*" as loud as she could, water splashing over her body and her hair flying wildly behind her.

A huge grin broke across Natalie's face. Now this...*this* was a job. She thought about the pain shooting up into her feet after another long night of waitressing, the ache in her back, the tips that were never quite enough. Natalie had been lucky enough to work a few jobs here and there that she'd really loved, driving boats or leading wilderness retreats, coaching groups of rock climbers or scuba divers, collecting useful licenses and certifications along the way. She'd been training as a climb leader at one point during her time living in Nepal, but it hadn't panned out.

As always, she hadn't stuck around long enough, always making her way to another city, another country. She tended to mostly get waitressing jobs, which were easier to find in a pinch.

It sufficed, giving her enough spending money to get by, but as she'd gotten older, she knew she wanted something...*more*. It was the reason she'd jumped at the opportunity to run the new joint business venture with Harper and Jess. A chance to use her skills in a new way, a way that would let her take control of her own destiny.

It was work that fit within her constant moving around, something she had no intention of changing. It suited her disposition perfectly.

Natalie paddled harder as she approached the next line of rapids, carefully avoiding a hidden rock plateau that led to a whirlpool with a strong undertow. She pushed to the left, and skittered down a narrow section that shot her out through two huge boulders at the bottom like a cannon. She screamed into the summer air with joy, laughing. She may not have it all figured out just yet, but right now, this was *spectacular*.

The group made their way down the river in

what felt to Natalie like mere seconds. The very last run was a narrow plunge through smooth rock embankments that funneled out across a mini waterfall and into a stunning, crystal-clear pool, just before a languid stretch that led toward the much larger waterfall before the Middle Harstow. There were buoy lines and several large signs instructing paddlers to get off before the waterfall. Natalie's senses sharpened as she continued to track her group members to ensure everyone ended the trip safely.

"Okay, people!" she shouted before the final run. "Remember, the takeout is directly after the pool. You'll see the signs and the buoys. If for some reason you sweep out too far, there are several safety lines you can catch to get you back to shore before the waterfall. Avoid the lowhead dam about two-thirds into this run, take the left side." She tightened her helmet and met April's eyes. April's face was flushed, a beaming grin on her face so wide it nearly brought tears to Natalie's eyes. She was having the time of her life. "All right, let's do it!"

Natalie led the way, carefully navigating her way down the rapids, anticipation bubbling in her chest as she was rocked hard back and forth, water sloshing over her body. At one point, her stomach lurched as an eddy spun her clean around, nearly tipping her over. The water level was a little higher today after the rainfall last night. She maintained a holding position and ensured the group navigated around it, bursting with pride as they followed her instructions to a T. She held her breath and paddled furiously to get back in front, and before she knew it, the whitewater launched her over the final mini waterfall and into the last pool, her heart stopping as she resurfaced seconds later, whooping into the air.

One by one, her group shot out into the pool, cheering as they held position at the bottom. Natalie scanned around, counting to make sure everyone made it. A few long moments passed, Natalie's breathing getting harder and harder, the blood slowly running from her veins.

April was missing.

Natalie spun around wildly, scanning the safety lines downriver before the waterfall. Had April swept past her, and she hadn't noticed? Was she caught in an eddy above the waterfall? There was no easy way to get back up there, especially since she had to navigate the group to the shore...

"April!" she shouted at the top of her lungs. The other paddlers were waiting beside her, anxious looks on their faces. This had been a terrible idea.

She was going to be responsible for April getting injured, or worse...

But then a kayak launched over the embankment, cannonballing out into the air twice as far as anyone else had. April's paddle was raised above her head, a look of pure joy on her face as a primal scream pierced the air. She plunged into the water and emerged a moment later beside Natalie, an innocent look on her face. Natalie splashed her with her paddle.

"What?" she said, unable to keep the sly smile from her face. "I looped around to get a little more momentum. I think we can both agree, that was pretty epic."

A laugh escaped Natalie's mouth as her heart thundered in her ears. "Let's get going, wild girl."

As they paddled to shore, April's phone chimed, and the grin slipped from her face. It chimed three more times before they got out of their kayaks and began stripping off their helmets. Another surge of anger swept through Natalie.

"April," she said, taking her aside. *Chime.* "Are things okay at home?"

April's face clouded over. "Why do you ask?" *Chime.*

Natalie frowned. "Is that Garrett?" April looked

out over the water, and didn't answer. Natalie took her hands. "April, talk to me. I can help you."

April turned to her, tears pooling in her eyes. Natalie's stomach somersaulted. April opened her mouth to speak.

"Hey, thanks a million, Natalie," interjected a voice suddenly next to her. Jared, one of the kayakers. He held his hand out, and Natalie shook it. "That was incredible. Listen, I wanted to get your advice on something..."

Natalie looked back to April, but she had turned away and was talking to someone else, not meeting Natalie's eyes. The moment had passed. Natalie would just have to try again.

Half an hour later, the shuttle dropped them back off at Marina Cove Adventures. Before Natalie could extricate herself from the group, April had returned her gear and was already heading toward the parking lot.

"April, wait!" Natalie shouted, jogging toward her. But she stopped in her tracks as a massive bright red pickup truck skidded to a stop at the entrance to the lot directly in front of Natalie. Her fists clenched at her sides as Garrett slammed open the driver's side door and began shouting at April, gesticulating wildly and pointing to the kids in the backseat. April looked so small, so helpless against him. Garrett shook his head, his face beet red as he stomped back around and plonked back into the driver's seat.

And just before April got into the truck, she looked back at Natalie one last time, her shoulders slumped and tears rolling down her cheeks, the unmistakable look of defeat in her eyes.

19

"Diane?" asked a voice next to her. Diane was vaguely aware of holding a phone in her hands, which were trembling for some reason. A hand rubbed the small of her back. "Diane, what's wrong?"

Diane turned to the sound of the voice. It was Ramona.

Tears sprang to her eyes. She tried to speak, but nothing came out but a choking sound.

Ramona furrowed her brows and turned to Charlotte, who reached for Diane's hand. "What happened?"

Diane met Charlotte's eyes, tears streaking down her cheeks. Her mouth was like cotton. She held up

Austin's phone for her to see. Charlotte took off her sunglasses and squinted at the screen. A moment later, her face fell.

"Oh, Diane." Charlotte pulled Diane into a hug, her hand against the back of Diane's head, smoothing her hair over. "Oh, no. I don't even know what to say."

Ramona snatched the phone out of Charlotte's hand, her mouth moving over the words as she read, a terrible fury slowly crossing over her expression. Diane squeezed her eyes shut and pressed her face into Charlotte's hair. Ella wrapped her arms around both of them.

"What's going on?"

The women separated to face the voice. Austin stood there, next to Tyson, Sully, and Niko. Niko, who was halfway through a burrito, stopped and frowned as he surveyed the group.

Diane took the phone back from Ramona, marched up to Austin, and shoved it against his chest, hard. "*Alice* sent you a message," she said, gritting her teeth.

Austin's face screwed into a look of utter confusion. He hit a button on his phone, glanced at the screen, and then went white as a sheet.

"It's…it's not what it looks like," he said.

"Please tell me that's not really your response," she seethed. People around them began turning their heads to see what was going on. Diane didn't care. "Are we in some sort of bad movie? *It's not what it looks like?*"

Austin stepped toward her, reaching for her hand. She ripped herself away from him. "Diane," he said, glancing warily at her family behind her, "can we talk about this in private?"

"*NO!*" Diane screamed at him, surprising herself. All the struggles of the last weeks, all the stress, the lost sleep, the constant debating about everything to do, trying to get over Grant and trying to move on with her life, the weight of it all was catching up with her. "No, Austin. I don't care. It doesn't matter. You lied to me—"

"Diane, please, it's complicated—"

"Oh, it's complicated. I'm *so sorry* to hear that it's complicated for you," she said, her voice cracking. "You told me you were dealing with problems with your brother. You lied to me. You lied to me when you *knew* I was vulnerable." Diane brought her hand to her mouth. "You took advantage of me. I've been bleeding my heart out with you, I told you *everything*, and now—"

"Diane, please!" He stepped toward her, his face flushed. "It's a long story, all right? I—"

"Is it true?" Diane asked. She could feel her sisters coming to her side. For the first time in as long as she could remember, she felt supported. She had people in her corner. It made her stronger. "Just tell me. Is it true? You're going to see this Alice woman, the woman sending you hearts, telling you how *great* it was to see you again, and *you've got a son together*?"

Austin opened and closed his mouth, spluttering for a moment. Diane glanced at Niko, who quickly averted his eyes, digging his shoe into the ground. So Niko knew.

It was true.

"Oh, God," said Charlotte quietly, shaking her head.

"It's not that simple." Austin's voice was slightly frantic. "I mean, you don't know what you're talking about, Diane, you take my phone without my permission and *insert yourself* into my private life...I mean, you don't understand—"

"You've got to be freaking kidding me!" shouted Diane. "What don't I understand? Tell me! You're meeting up with an old flame, yeah? She's sending you little hearts, yeah? She called you *babe*, didn't she? And, drumroll...you've got a kid with her? I think I've got the picture—"

"Can we *please* talk about this somewhere else—"

Diane shook her head. "Unbelievable. You're no better than Trevor was. I can't believe I let myself be deceived again." Tears cut their way down her cheeks. "I thought you were a good man, Austin. I really did. But as it turns out, you're just another deceitful, cheating liar."

His eyes flashed, his eyebrows drawing together. "You don't know what you're talking about."

Diane stepped toward him, the words flying out of her mouth. "All right, Austin, then *tell me the truth!* All of it. Right now, or I'm gone."

His mouth worked like he was trying to figure out what to say. He glanced at her sisters, and quickly back at the ground. He ran his hands through his hair as he looked back up at her, speechless.

Diane's shoulders fell. "I'm sure you've got some great reason why this is *all a big misunderstanding*, and I'll never know any better. And it doesn't matter, because you still lied to me over and over again, and now I'd be a fool to trust you. And honestly," she said, her eyes burning into his, "I'm just too old for this sort of thing anymore. I'm not looking for something complicated. My life is complicated enough." She let out a long, slow breath. "This was all obviously a mistake. Goodbye, Austin."

And then Diane turned on her heel, her sisters at her side, and left without another word.

20

Natalie was lost in thought on her way back to the Seaside House, the warm summer air blowing through her hair and the fireflies just beginning to light. She couldn't stop thinking about April. About that horrible, hollow look of defeat in her eyes. As she had been feeling more and more often lately, she found herself having no idea what to do.

Her mind wandered, as it often did, to Theo. She'd stayed late to help him close up, not that she needed an excuse. After he closed up shop, they sat on a wooden bench behind the bungalow, sipping lemonade and getting lost in their respective memories of growing up in Marina Cove, laughing like kids.

Natalie let out a breath, and pushed back the tiny voice that kept needling her, poking her every time she let her guard down. That crucial but stomach-churning voice that she couldn't seem to shut up.

What are you doing, Natalie?

She shook her head. That cabin-fever feeling, the one where she felt like the walls were closing in on her, was growing slowly and steadily every day. Jess had started texting her more regularly, asking when she was coming out. She'd told them she had "a few things to take care of" before they met up in Prague. Jess was supportive but starting to worry— Rami, her rich "suitor," had started asking them uncomfortable questions about their pending business, questions he wanted answers to before he handed them such a large sum of startup money.

Now, he was demanding a business proposal, market analysis, sales strategies...poor Jess, she was like a deer in headlights. *Not a problem at all,* Natalie had texted her. *I can get started on those ASAP.*

A pit had formed in her stomach. She couldn't miss the opportunity of a lifetime while she languished here in Marina Cove. But right now, April needed her, and her family...well, they weren't in great shape, and it felt wrong to leave so soon.

For the first time in as long as she could remember, Natalie didn't like that she had no idea what was next for her. This time, it wasn't a good feeling.

She jogged the last block to the Seaside House, eager to change her clothes and maybe take a solo nighttime stroll along the beach to try to sort things out. The porch came into view in the dim light of the darkening sky, and she froze in her tracks, squeezing her eyes shut.

She'd totally forgotten.

Yanking her phone from her pocket to check the time, she cursed to herself, and then turned and ran.

Five minutes later, huffing and puffing, and Callie's Beachfront Café was just up ahead. A punch of guilt hit her in the stomach as her sisters and mother pushed through the front door.

"Hey, guys, I'm sorry—" she called.

"We waited for, like, three hours for you, Natalie," said Ramona, that line between her brows. "And again, you didn't show up."

Natalie squeezed her eyes shut for a moment. Ramona and Diane had both reminded her several times, saying they needed to talk. But between April and Theo, it had completely slipped her mind.

"I'm sorry," she repeated as they moved away

from the entrance into the sand to let an older couple through. "I had a lot going on—"

"We needed to talk to you," Ramona interjected. "It's about the Seaside House. I just...I mean, come on, Natalie," she said, running her hands over her face.

Natalie looked between them, lifting one shoulder up. "Can't we just talk now? What's the big deal?" she asked. Her eyes landed on Diane's, and something scuttled across her spine. Her eyes were puffy, like she'd been crying. Natalie made a mental note to ask what had happened.

Ella cleared her throat. "We still don't have any way of reaching you," she said softly. "We didn't know where you were."

Natalie bristled, swallowing the swell of anger rising in her throat at the sound of her mother's voice. "I don't really keep my phone on," she muttered.

"So can we have your new number?" Ramona asked.

Natalie hesitated. "Uh..."

"Natalie, what the heck?" Ramona said. "You seriously still won't give us a way to contact you? What do you think we're gonna do, sell your information to foreign governments? Use it to track your every move? I mean, honestly—"

"I think what Ramona is trying to say," said Charlotte, her voice placating, "is we just wanted to see you tonight. We've barely seen you since you've been back."

Natalie shrugged. Her clothes felt tighter, the air hotter. "I've been busy—"

Ramona pinched the bridge of her nose with her fingers. "Natalie, I'm sorry to do this now, but I just don't get it. You barely speak to us, no one knows why you're always on the run, you won't tell us what the heck happened in Ireland—"

"Don't do that," Natalie said, her voice hard. "Don't yell at me—"

"I'm not yelling at you, Nat, I'm *worried* about you—"

"Well, you can stop," Natalie interjected, waving her hand. "I'm fine. And I already told you, nothing happened in Ireland." Her mind flashed to the flames, the smoke. The coughing. The handcuffs clacking into place. "I just needed to get my head on straight. I didn't know I was gonna get the third degree about it all."

Diane shifted on her feet, staring at the sand.

Her voice was strained. "Natalie, that's not what's happening here. I think we just want to talk—"

"Well, I don't really have anything to say—"

"Why do we all keep skirting around everything?" said Ramona, exasperated. "I mean, can't we just say what we really mean here? Natalie, why are you even back home, if you're just going to ignore us—"

"I don't have to do this." Natalie turned to leave. A man and a woman passing them on their way into the café pretended not to be eavesdropping. "I'm not going to stand here while everyone gangs up on me—"

"Natalie," said Ella softly. Natalie bristled again, feeling the fine hairs on her arms standing on end. "You don't have to tell us anything. But you have to understand that this is a little..." Her brows drew together. "Confusing, I suppose." She opened her mouth and then closed it, like she was debating. "You spent an awfully long time who knows where, with no way for us to reach out to you. I mean, that's been hard—"

Natalie scoffed. What the heck was happening here? "Hard? What about me? You don't know the things I've been through—" Her voice caught in her throat as she thought of her lockbox. Ice flooded her stomach. "Look, I appreciate everyone's concern. I really do. I told you, it's complicated, all right? I really don't want to have, like, a whole thing here. I've been doing *just fine*, okay—"

Ramona shook her head. "That's the problem, Natalie." She looked between them all. "That's the problem, with all of us. We've spent too many years not saying what we mean, not being honest. Too afraid to bring up what's *really* happening, what's going on in our personal lives." She let out a breath. "We're all guilty of it. Aren't you guys just a little bit tired of it?"

Diane and Charlotte were nodding. Ella's eyes were fixed on Natalie, her brows furrowed.

"Ramona's right," said Diane. "Natalie, we're not trying to say we're any better off than you, or that we've done all the right things. I mean, whenever we've called each other over the years, it's just... *niceties*." She sighed, again looking down to the ground. "I mean, I didn't even tell any of you when my husband died. That's not okay. And now, Austin..." Her voice wavered as she looked between Ramona and Charlotte. "I don't even know how to begin talking about that. I want to, but it's like I don't know how with you guys yet."

Natalie's heart was pounding hard, that old panic

rising in her chest. She had to get out of here. There was no way she was able to do this right now, not when she was already so far in over her head with everything.

But for some reason she was rooted to the spot, unable to move, like a frightened animal. Like an animal backed into a corner.

"Natalie." Charlotte stepped toward her in the sand. "I know this is probably a lot to take in. You just got here, after we've had a chance to start working to make things better. I have to agree with Ramona and Diane—I know I'd be kicking myself if you left and I didn't get a chance to really talk to you, to at least try." She held Natalie's gaze. "Natalie, we love you. We just want things to be better. I know I don't want to look back and think that I should have done more. That I should have tried harder."

Natalie let out a carefully controlled breath. "I love you guys, too," she said. "You know I do. I just..."

Ella moved toward her. "You can talk to us, honey."

Another surge of anger swelled within her toward her mother, reaching a fever pitch. Her mind was spinning, her heart thundering in her ears. It was like a huge, smothering darkness was closing in on her, and she could either cower and accept it, or lash out. Why was this happening now?

Natalie gritted her teeth. "I don't want to talk—"

Ella took another step toward her. The walls were all closing in now. "Nattie, please—"

"*Don't call me that!*" Natalie shrieked. Hot, horrible tears sprang from her eyes as her heart cracked. Ella recoiled, blinking fast. Several people on their way into Callie's whipped their heads around to see what was happening, but Natalie didn't care. The words were spilling out, out of her control now. "*Don't ever call me that!* That's Dad's name for me, not yours—"

"Natalie," said Ramona, "what the—"

"Is that what this is about?" asked Charlotte. "Is that why you've been gone all these years? Because Dad left?"

Natalie pressed the palms of her hands into her eyes and shook her head, hard, as Joel's face slashed through her mind, ripping her in two. This was unbelievable. She wasn't ready to tell them the real reasons. How Dad leaving had maybe set things in motion, but everything that followed, the worst year of her life...they couldn't understand. They had no frame of reference.

And apart from all that, she certainly wasn't

about to confront Ella. What good could that possibly do? It was too late. There was nothing she could do or say to make up for everything. She wouldn't understand, anyway.

"Please talk to us," said Ramona softly.

A horrible buzzing filled her ears. It was like someone had dropped her into a deep, dark hole, with no way to claw back out. "I can't do this," she said. "You're all obviously a lot further along than I am, I guess, because I can't do this. I just can't." Fresh tears slid down her cheeks. "We're all kidding ourselves here if we think we can just, what, slap a bandage on our problems and make everything all better? It's delusional. That's not how life works." She let out a shaking breath. "I have to go."

"Natalie, don't," said Charlotte, her voice pleading.

Natalie clenched her eyes shut. It was time to leave, really leave this all behind her. Her throat constricted like someone was squeezing it. Everyone was crowding her, cornering her. That itching, strangling feeling was overwhelming, drowning her, smothering her.

It always happened the same way, and she'd known that when she arrived here. It was utterly inevitable. A distant part of her knew she was giving in to that feeling, letting it win out, but she simply didn't know what to do about it. She was broken, irrevocably, and she knew it.

Sometimes there was no answer.

"I'm leaving," she said, her voice defeated. "I'm sorry I'm not who you need me to be."

And then Natalie turned and trudged across the sand, swiping the tears from her eyes as she left.

21

"Are you sure about this?" asked Ramona, a hard line appearing between her brows. "I mean, what are you hoping will happen here?"

Diane kicked a pebble with her shoe, sending it careening down the sidewalk, and shrugged. "No," she said. "I'm not sure. It's undoubtedly a terrible idea."

Charlotte cleared her throat. "It's not too late to turn around."

Diane reached into her pocket and ran her fingers over the note. It was funny, how everything had unfolded. Well, not funny. Horrifying. But a year ago, if someone had told her what was going to happen, the things she was going to do, she would've told them they were insane.

Diane looked up and met Charlotte's eyes. They were all avoiding the topic of what had happened with Natalie. They hadn't seen her since the fight. But her things were still at the Seaside House.

Where had she gone? Had she left for good?

She sighed. Right now, there wasn't anything she could do about that. Right now, there was an unpleasant task at hand.

"I want to do this," she said. "I want to tell Alice that she doesn't need to send any more letters. I want to get the truth, straight from the horse's mouth. No more lies."

Ramona squeezed her shoulder. "I think it seems pretty clear what's going on. I don't want you to get hurt any further."

Diane smiled weakly. "Thanks, guys. I'm glad..." Her voice caught in her throat. "Thank you."

It hadn't been hard at all to find Alice. A simple internet search with their names yielded a reference to an old fan blog for Silver Hollows, back in their heyday, run by a woman named Alice Jordan. A few more searches, and she'd found property records indicating that an Alice Jordan had moved to Marina Cove less than a year ago. She lived right up on the north shore. Charlotte and Ramona had offered to accompany her, and Diane couldn't have been more grateful for the support.

A horrible pang of guilt twisted her stomach as Diane thought of the text she'd sent last night, in the middle of crying herself to sleep. A text to Teagan.

Let's talk tomorrow.

A simple message, but one that was changing the course of her life.

Diane swallowed hard as they turned onto Coldwater Lane, a long road that wound up toward the northern shore. She hadn't told her family yet. But after what had happened with Austin...things had gotten real very fast.

Seeing the text from Alice had woken Diane up from the dream, the dream she'd unwittingly been too afraid to wake herself from. She'd been living a fantasy just playing dress-up, ever since she'd been back.

Real life waited for her in Los Angeles. It was time to stop pretending.

Diane had decided somewhere in the dark hours of the night that she would take the five-year contract with Teagan's agency. She'd be able to save for her retirement, and would send money to her family to help with the Seaside House restoration.

Everyone would win. Diane would make the sacrifice now, on the bet that she could buy herself freedom later.

It wasn't perfect, but life never was. Sometimes you were dealt a winning hand...and sometimes you weren't. No sense in belaboring the inevitable.

And besides, it was only five years. After that... well. Marina Cove would still be waiting for her. Her family would still be waiting for her.

After five years, who knew?

Diane and her sisters finally turned onto Marlowe Street where Alice lived. Hopefully. Part of Diane desperately hoped she'd found the wrong Alice Jordan, and whatever this confrontation was going to be would just...disappear.

"Well, this is it," said Ramona, peering down at her phone. They'd stopped in front of a little red-brick Colonial with white siding, a beautiful oak tree in the front yard. Ice rolled down Diane's spine as she stared at the stone path leading to the front door.

She looked at Charlotte and Ramona, took a deep breath, and before she could change her mind, marched up to the front door and knocked three times.

A few moments later, the door opened, and a

beautiful woman appeared. She had long, dark hair with ruby highlights, matted and slightly unkempt, and trendy blue jeans with high-top sneakers. She wore a Silver Hollows T-shirt.

Alice took one look at Diane, her eyes widening, and she slammed the door in her face.

Well then.

Diane had obviously found the right Alice Jordan.

"Should we take that as a cue and go, maybe?" asked Ramona. Charlotte nodded.

Diane shook her head. "I've come this far," she muttered. Pressure was building behind her eyes. What a mess. No more relationships after this. The universe was clearly trying to tell her something.

Maybe she could become a nun. It was never too late, was it?

She knocked on the door again. "Alice," she said, leaning against the door frame, "I just want to talk for a minute, okay?" She glanced at Charlotte, who gave her a look of encouragement. Diane nodded. "I'm here to tell you that I know about you and Austin. And I wanted to let you know that we broke up."

A long moment passed. The birds sang in the big oak tree behind them, blissfully unburdened and free. Diane gritted her teeth, and turned to leave.

But then the door opened, and Alice stepped onto the front porch. "You know about me and Austin?" she asked quietly.

Diane reached into her pocket and removed the note, unfolding it and holding it up for Alice to see. "You sent this, right?"

Alice frowned, opened her mouth to speak, but then closed it. She nodded once.

Tears welled in Diane's eyes. "Well, you don't need to do stuff like this anymore, okay?" Ramona squeezed her shoulder as Diane wiped her eyes with her forearm. "I thought...I thought Austin and I had something good. But I didn't know. I didn't know about your relationship."

Alice held Diane's gaze for a moment and then looked toward the ground, nodding. "Well," she said softly, "I didn't know about yours. Until a few weeks ago." She dug her sneakers into the ground. "I guess we're in the same boat, then. I thought maybe if I sent you the note...I don't know." She shook her head. "I guess I was trying to scare you off. I don't like confrontations."

Diane nodded, unable to keep the tears from streaming down her cheeks. She hadn't realized until now how much she'd been hoping that she'd read the situation wrong, that there was some other explanation. Now she knew for sure, straight from the source.

Now she didn't have to waste any more time on a man who wasn't worth it.

The women stood there, a thick, knotted silence swirling around them. Diane wiped her eyes, and looked up at Alice.

Alice cleared her throat. "Why don't you guys come in. I just baked chocolate chip cookies. I can't eat them all myself."

Ramona made a sort of strangled snorting sound that very nearly made Diane burst into laughter. "Uh, no," she said, incredulous. "I think we're good, *Alice*—"

"It's okay," said Diane, giving Ramona a calming motion with her hands. "Actually, I think I could use some sugar right about now." She looked into Alice's eyes and nodded. Alice's face drew into a small, sad smile. Diane stepped up onto the porch and followed her inside.

And what she saw made her heart stop beating in its tracks.

22

Sylvie took the long way home, taking a few random turns here and there, her mind working itself into a tangle of knots. Her heart broke for the Kellers, for what Patrick was doing to them. A flare of anger surged through her as she imagined a giant wrecking ball smashing into the beautiful walls of the Seaside House.

What were they going to do?

Her stomach dropped to her shoes. Poor Charlotte. If they destroyed the family home, she wouldn't have anything. Was she going to leave Marina Cove? What would happen to the Kellers?

Tears of despair built behind her eyes. She was already going to lose Mariah at some point, whenever she decided she was ready to return to med school. That one was going to hurt. She supported Mariah, of course, and from the very little Mariah had shared with her, she was going through something significant. But regardless, she and Mariah had become so close in such a short amount of time; they were two peas in a pod.

Who would join her in ogling all the beautiful men of Marina Cove when she was gone?

Sylvie sighed as she turned onto Driftwood Lane toward her home. Her chest tightened as the bright orange tent swam into view. A flurry of thoughts tore through her mind, but she shoved them back into the dark corners where they belonged. There was too much going on right now. Now wasn't the time to think about Nick. What her plan was. Or how she had no plan.

She stepped onto her lawn, her mouth dry. Nick was sitting cross-legged on the grass in front of the tent, reading a book by the light of the waning sun. She walked past him, avoiding eye contact, her heart pounding in her temples.

The lock of her front door clicked open as she turned her key, but she stopped in her tracks, something flitting across the back of her mind. She stood there for a moment, frowning, before she stepped backward, and looked to her right down the length of the front porch.

Sylvie glanced over to Nick. His back was to her, facing the street. She slowly approached the end of the porch, her heart pattering. She stared at the wooden swing, suspended by two shining galvanized steel chains that mounted into the eaves above. Her stomach twisted as her eyes fell back on Nick.

Years ago, who knew when, the chain had rusted through, and one particularly windy day, it had snapped, bringing the swing down with it. They'd never bothered to fix it; no one sat there anyway, because the way the house was situated, the setting sunlight beamed directly through an opening in the trees onto the swing, too bright for comfort. She'd had an idea for a roller shade and had asked him to install it, but he'd never gotten around to it. The swing had become something of an ongoing argument between them; whenever Sylvie looked around and felt they weren't keeping up with things, she'd begin to harp on Nick to fix this, or install that, or clean whatever. He'd kept the house in reasonable order, but never seemed to get around to certain things. And so she'd harp on him some more.

Sylvie ran her fingers over the brand-new chains, over the freshly sanded and polished wood, guilt pooling in her chest. Looking back, he'd been so busy with the restaurant, always putting in long hours taking calls and helping the cooks on the line and doing paperwork, so much paperwork that was part of running a business like that.

She'd given him such a hard time about the few things he wasn't doing. And now that he'd been gone, it had become readily apparent all the many, many invisible things he'd been doing around the house that she'd never noticed. Or taken the time to notice. Things were falling apart in there. She'd been so wrapped up in her own stress, her own long hours and hard work and exhaustion, that she'd taken it out on him without realizing it.

Sylvie looked at Nick, whose back was still turned to her, and eased herself into the swing, immediately feeling the relief of the weight released from her feet. She leaned over and pulled down the brand-new canvas roller shade he'd installed, perfectly filtering the unforgiving sunlight cutting through the trees. Her heart leaped a little as she noticed the little end table he set up next to the swing, a candle in the center.

She pulled it up to her face, and breathed in deeply. Rainwater and moss, her favorite.

Her throat tightened a little. It was a simple

gesture, but it said a lot. Nick did care. He always had. Sylvie closed her eyes and rocked, listening to the whisper of the breeze through the trees.

Nick had let her down horribly. There was no doubt about it. He had a long pattern of not listening to her, of not taking her seriously, of being dismissive. His terrible relationship with time, the years of not letting her know where he was, his stubborn belief that he was always right.

But maybe, just maybe, the experience of tanking their business had humiliated him enough to humble him a little. People changed all the time, didn't they?

Or was she kidding herself? Were things really going to be any different than they had been?

Sylvie couldn't just let him languish on their front lawn forever. At a certain point, she needed to make a decision.

She thought of the Kellers. They'd been slowly working through things, beginning to really support each other. They had each other.

As for Sylvie...well, she had no family. Sure, the Kellers were becoming her family, but there was a hole a mile wide inside her where her own mother and father should be, used to be. They were long, long gone, so long that she wondered sometimes if they hadn't been a beautiful dream. Being alone...it was something she convinced herself she could do, but truth be told, nothing terrified her more. She'd overcome so much, had built a good life for herself. But lately, she was in freefall, and wanted it to stop.

She could make it stop. It was up to her.

One simple decision, and it could be over. She wouldn't have to be alone anymore.

Sylvie rose from her seat, padded over to the front door, and pulled it open. Nick turned around at the sound. She stepped just inside the door frame, stopped, and turned around, meeting his eyes. He slowly set his book down on the grass, holding her gaze.

"Well," she said, "are you coming in, or what?"

A small smile broke across Nick's face. He stood up, and began to walk across their lawn toward her. Sylvie's stomach tightened as she felt a shift in the air.

Things were changing. Like it or not, she was taking the first steps into the unknown.

23

As Diane surveyed the inside of Alice's home, several things hit her all at once.

First...the smell. It nearly knocked her off her feet. It was as if a thousand litter boxes had been sitting in a piping hot greenhouse for a year. She immediately pulled the top of her T-shirt over her mouth and gasped for air. Two cats sat on the couch, a third walked out of the kitchen, and a fourth brushed against her shins, making her yelp out loud.

The second thing was the incredible clutter. Boxes were strewn all about, clothes and dishes and broken furniture and more boxes. Old dishes were piled sky-high on every surface. Diane could see into the kitchen, where a mountain of dishes poured from the sink onto every available surface.

But the thing that struck her most of all sent stripes of confusion and horror through her, a jumbled mess of thoughts and emotions that made her head spin. She spun around, speechless.

The walls. They were lined with Silver Hollows posters. There were Silver Hollows T-shirts, hats, framed records. There were CDs, lanyards, hundreds and hundreds of pieces of Silver Hollows merchandise.

And alongside it all, Alice had framed dozens and dozens of close-up shots of Austin.

Her mouth fell open. Austin performing with the band. Austin in the park, strumming his guitar. Austin walking down the street, laughing with Niko. Austin leaving the Maple Street Diner.

Diane slowly turned around, her heart slamming against her chest, to find a huge, blown-up framed selfie of a very young Austin, his arm wrapped around Alice, smiling into the camera.

"Oh, dear God," said Charlotte from somewhere behind her.

Diane watched with a detached fascination as Alice swept past them into the kitchen. "I'm sorry it's such a mess in here," she called. "Make yourselves comfortable."

"We've got to get out of here," whispered Ramona.

A moment later, Alice reappeared, gesturing toward a table in what was probably the dining room. It was honestly hard to tell with all the clutter. She set down three bowls, a gallon of milk, and a box of cereal. "Here we are," she said in a melodic voice. "Sorry, the cookies aren't done yet. This is all I've got. Hope everyone's hungry."

Diane took a long, slow breath as it all began to dawn on her. Her mouth felt like it was filled with hot dust.

"Alice," she said slowly. "Can we, ah, talk for a minute?"

Alice nodded. "Sure. What can I do for you?"

They sat down at the table. Ramona was jamming her thumb toward the door, but Diane waved her away. *It's okay,* she mouthed to her sisters.

"Alice," said Diane. "You and Austin...how did you meet?"

A wistful smile appeared on her face. "Oh, we go way back. Way, way back." She poured herself a bowl of cereal and began munching on it. A cat appeared out of thin air and settled itself on her lap, grimacing at Diane. "I followed Silver Hollows all over the country. Austin...he's a dream, isn't he?" She turned to face one of his posters on the wall, her cheeks bright red with color. "I finally got the courage to talk to him after one of his shows. We dated for a while, and then he broke up with me. I never figured out why." She turned to Diane, her face suddenly serious. "But we're right for each other. I know it. Austin...he just hasn't seen it yet. But he will."

Diane nodded slowly. "Did you...see Austin recently?"

Alice nodded. "Oh, yeah. I moved here for him, so, you know. I had to slash his tires to get his attention this time." She set down her spoon and tilted her head slightly. "Listen, Diane, I'm sorry I sent that note. I was shocked when I saw you guys together for the first time. I feel terrible. But Austin and I are meant to be together."

Charlotte was looking between Alice and Diane, her eyebrows raised to her hairline. "Uh, you slashed Austin's tires?"

Alice grimaced. "Yeah...I didn't want to have to do that, but he agreed to talk to me when I did. I know I'm not supposed to do that sort of thing anymore...but look. When love is on the line, well, wouldn't you do whatever it took?"

Ramona shook her head. "I wouldn't do that," she muttered to herself.

Diane scooted her chair closer, wincing as the smell of litterboxes filled her lungs. Seriously, it was like she was trapped in the world's oldest dumpster on the hottest day of summer. "Alice..." she started.

"Yes?" Alice stroked her cat's fur. The cat gave Diane a look of incredible superiority, a look of utter disdain that only cats were capable of.

"Alice, can you tell me about your and Austin's son?"

Alice stopped stroking. Her eyes widened slightly as the color ran from her already pale skin.

"How...how did you..." she stammered. Her hands gripped the table surface, her knuckles turning white as she shook her head. "He *told* you?"

Diane debated for a moment, and then reached across the table, taking Alice's hand in hers. "You can talk to me."

A choking sound came from Alice's throat, and then tears pooled in her eyes. In one motion, she shot up from the table, the chair kicking back behind her and the cat hissing and leaping onto the table, spilling milk and cereal everywhere.

Alice ran her hands through her dark, knotted hair, and paced back and forth, tears streaming down her cheeks. Charlotte and Ramona both stood up, looking anxious.

"Alice, it's okay—" said Charlotte.

"Oh, man," Alice began to mutter to herself. She continued to pace, her face in her hands. "Oh, man, oh man oh man oh man." She stopped, her eyes falling over the posters on the wall. She put a hand to her mouth and slowly turned, looking all around her as if seeing the room for the first time. As she faced the framed picture of her and Austin, her body began shaking with sobs.

"What should we do?" whispered Ramona.

Before Diane could form a response, Alice moaned, and turned to face them, wiping the tears from her eyes. Her chest was heaving up and down. "I told him that a few weeks ago," she said, the pitch of her voice rising. "He caught me following him around again. But I wasn't going to do anything... years ago, I had sort of, uh, given Kate a hard time, I guess..." Her shoulders slumped. "That's putting it lightly. I stole her dog for a week. And I might have set her front lawn on fire. And, uh, a few other things…it's sort of a blur. But I waited to move to Marina Cove until after the restraining order expired. I was trying to respect him."

In the corner of her eye, Diane caught Ramona eyeing the front door. Diane nodded toward Alice reassuringly. "And then what happened?"

"Well, he threatened to file another one. I didn't know what else to do. And so I…" She choked out a sob. "I'm a fool. I told him that we had a son together. That back when we dated for those few months, I'd gotten pregnant and never told him. And so he agreed to meet with me a few days ago to talk about it. I didn't know what to do, so I stalled." She buried her face in her hands. "I just texted him again, too. Oh, God. I don't have any idea what my plan even was." Alice's eyes wandered over her home, her look of pain so intense that Diane's throat constricted. "I mean, what am I doing here? *What am I doing here?*"

Diane looked to her sisters, helpless.

Alice met Diane's eyes and shook her head softly. "I'm not crazy, you know."

Diane stepped toward her. "I don't think you're crazy."

She scoffed. "It might not seem like it, but I do know what this all looks like. At least, I do sometimes. I can't explain it. I get these obsessions with people, and it just sort of..." Her body seemed to deflate. "It sort of takes over. Austin isn't the first person I've had this problem with. I don't know what happens. I wish I could stop...I really do." She pinched the bridge of her nose with her fingers. "Frankly, I'm surprised Austin told you about me, after what happened with Kate. But I swear, I wasn't going to do anything. I'm trying to change."

"Why would you be surprised he told me the truth about you?" Diane asked, then immediately regretted it.

Alice looked into her eyes. "Well, he told Kate, and the way she would look at me..." She shuddered. "I was being respectful, following from a distance. But she knew. She knew who I was, and I couldn't handle it. She looked at me like I was crazy. With that stupid fear in her eyes. I guess I sort of, uh, had a hard time with that." Her shoulders slumped. "Which does sound crazy, I know. But that's when I started to try to scare her off. I didn't know what else to do, you know? He wasn't leaving her. I was getting desperate."

Diane's mind was reeling as she tried to recon-figure the events of the last weeks in her mind. Austin taking the phone calls, the look of concern on his face, the deflection when Diane asked about it. How he'd left that night of their first open mic to take a phone call, that look of fear in his eyes. How Kate had said that Austin had a lot of baggage, that there were things in his past he was still paying the price for. She took a long, slow breath, and let it out.

Austin had been trying to protect her.

Diane glanced at Ramona and Charlotte, who gave her an encouraging look. She watched Alice for a moment, and then approached her slowly, pulling her into a hug.

"It's okay," said Diane, her voice soothing. Her heart broke for this woman. She clearly didn't like being this way. "I'm sorry you're going through this."

Alice clutched her, and broke down, tears spilling down her cheeks. "No, I'm sorry," she said. "I've never had anyone in my life. I've never had anyone who loved me." She looked up at Diane, her eyes wide and sad and hollow. "All I've ever wanted was for someone to love me."

Charlotte sniffled behind her. Diane bit back tears as she rubbed Alice's back comfortingly. The poor woman felt like she'd never been held before in her life. Diane wondered what had happened to her that had led to her obsessions.

No one ever wanted it to be true, but Diane knew

all too well how a painful past could come back to haunt you in strange ways if you buried it for too long. She recalled the years of her own obsessions, how she'd avoided influencing anyone's decisions around her for fear of endless guilt after what had happened with Victoria, how she'd gone as far as putting tracking devices in her kids' cars, the endless time spent hunched over the computer refreshing the traffic accident reports when they were driving. Never letting Grant leave the house if she didn't know exactly where he was every minute he would be gone. The years snapping that rubber band around her wrist any time she felt the past bubbling up, the horrible, painful emotions she didn't want to feel.

Yes, a buried past could come back to haunt you in ways you never expected.

"I think..." Alice began, and pulled back from Diane, wiping her eyes. "I think I might need some help." Alice then laughed humorlessly, shaking her head. "I mean, that much is clear. I don't want to be like this. I never did."

Diane nodded. "We can help you with that," she said.

"I could give you a couple of recommendations," said Ramona. She approached them, and put a reassuring hand on Alice's shoulder. "I've been working through sobriety, and the best thing I ever did was to get some help."

Alice nodded as fresh tears pooled in her eyes. "Thank you," she whispered. "No one has ever tried to help me before."

They exchanged phone numbers. "You're going to be okay," said Diane.

Alice lifted one shoulder up slightly. "I hope so. And listen," she said, looking up at Diane. There was a lot more awareness in her expression than met the eye. "Will you just talk to Austin for me? Tell him the truth...about what I told him about our son. I shouldn't reach out to him again." She blew out a breath. "This has gone on way too long. I can't live like this anymore."

Diane held her gaze. "Yes," she said. "I'll talk to him. And thank you for telling me everything. I know that was hard."

They hugged again, and Alice saw them out. A few minutes later, the three sisters walked back down Coldwater Lane in heavy silence. Diane's mind was racing.

Austin had been trying to protect her, especially after what Alice had been doing to Kate. He'd told Kate about Alice, and just the fact of her *knowing* about Alice had drawn her ire, had made her a target. Austin clearly had no intention of repeating the past with Diane.

Diane wondered if he had believed Alice about them having a child together. He'd probably wanted to figure that out before he came to Diane with everything.

She pressed her eyes shut. Austin had been in a bad predicament. Yes, he'd lied to her, but now she understood why. She didn't necessarily agree with his approach, but he was shielding her, not wanting to complicate things or scare her off if he could handle the problem on his own, like he'd done in the past. Diane was sure Alice's unpredictability was a huge source of anxiety for him.

Yes, his behavior was suspicious, and that text hadn't been great. Austin probably could have found another way to handle things. He could have trusted her not to draw Alice's attention while he figured out how he was going to deal with her.

And Diane's own issues with trust had stopped her from letting go, from seeing what she had already known to be true. That Austin was a good man. That what was developing between them was true, and real, and wonderful.

They both had work to do.

But that was the way it worked. You didn't get things right on the first try, or the second. You kept trying.

That was what made all the difference.

"I'm calling him," said Diane. Ramona and Charlotte nodded emphatically.

Diane dialed his number. Straight to voicemail. His phone was off. She dialed a second time, a third. Nothing.

"He's not answering," she said, unable to keep the anxiety from her voice. What if she'd ruined everything? She'd said a lot of things...

Diane fired up her social media app, punched in a search, and sent a message.

Niko, it's Diane. Where is Austin? He's not answering, and I need to talk to him.

A brief moment later, he responded.

Hey, Diane...I don't know where he is. But he left town. I think he needed to clear his head. He's not answering his phone. I'm sorry.

Diane slid her phone back into her pocket, furrowing her brows. Where would he have gone? Was he going to talk to her again? She didn't blame him for taking off, after the fight they'd had in the park. After the things she'd called him.

She stopped in her tracks as she thought of her

exchange with Niko. The first edges of a plan formed in her mind.

"Are you okay?" asked Charlotte, looking concerned. "What can we do?"

"I think I know what to do," said Diane, her heart pattering. "I have an idea."

24

"All right, ladies and gentlemen, here for his sixth year, looking ready to conquer it all once more in our next heat of this round, it's Dylan Tyler!"

The announcer's voice drifted over the loud PA across the north shore of Marina Cove. Mariah turned a dial on the telephoto lens and snapped a few shots as Dylan lifted his hand in a wave, cheers and whistles pouring from the spectators packed behind lines of yellow tape. He paddled out to meet two blond guys and a young woman in a bright green wetsuit as they treaded water on their boards for the right waves, biding their time as the minutes of the current heat counted down.

Dylan narrowed his eyes as he surveyed a wave building in strength, kicked off and paddled hard, then pushed himself up on his board. The crowd cheered as he swept up above the wave and cut back into it, disappearing into the barrel for a brief moment before blasting out and cutting a twisting maneuver against the glassy water.

An audible gasp emitted from the spectators as the wave built in power and suddenly knocked Dylan head-over-heels across his board into the depths of the sea. Mariah's heart thudded hard as an oncoming wave obscured her view. She breathed a sigh of relief as his head emerged several long and agonizing moments later. The waves were no joke today.

"I don't know about you, Jax," said the second announcer from their platform next to the judges' tent, "but I'm gonna say that one was at least an eight, maybe a nine. That's gonna be hard to beat."

"It sure is, Ryder," Jax responded. "We'll see if the judges agree. And how about these waves today? They are *intense*, my good friends. I don't think I've ever seen anything like it up here. These surfers are gonna have to be careful out there."

"As we wait for our judges to post their scores,"

said Ryder, "let's talk about our next surfer, Steven 'The Axe' Delgado, a man who needs no introduction, folks..."

Mariah rapidly flipped through the photos on the playback screen, frowning. An even higher shutter speed, maybe. She flicked the dials and lifted the camera, taking a few more shots and checking them, nodding. Perfect.

She rubbed her eyes, still bleary. She'd arrived on the beach at five a.m., after another night without sleep. The day was beautiful; rays of golden-white sunlight splayed across the sparkling crystal water, and a warm wind washed over her skin, whipping at her hair. She inhaled deeply and dug her bare feet into the damp sand, smiling. Not a bad way to spend a day, not by a long shot.

The first heat ended, and Mariah's heart fluttered as she spotted Keiran jogging out across the sand toward the water, the crowd cheering. "And that's Keiran James," Jax bellowed into the PA, "back to prove himself this year after his heartbreaking elimination in the quarterfinal round last year."

"Look at him, you can tell he's got fire in his belly this year," said Ryder. "I'm thinking he might just give Dylan Tyler a run for his money..."

Keiran turned to the crowd and pumped a fist, sending more cheers into the air. Mariah turned her camera on the crowd and snapped a few photos.

"*Keiran! We love you, Keiran! Wooooooooooo!*" Mariah turned her camera to find girls screaming for him, a trio of young blonde women in tiny bikinis that left nothing whatsoever to the imagination. Mariah rolled her eyes, and laughed. Desperate.

But still, she couldn't help the tiny twinge of jealousy as they jumped up and down in the sand, cupping their hands and shouting his name. She pushed it back, smiling to herself.

Get it together, Mariah. You've got no claim on him.

Keiran deftly maneuvered his board across several waves, his tight muscles pressing hard against his black wetsuit, a look of intense concentration on his face. Mariah snapped a stunning shot just as Keiran catapulted above a wave, the sunlit whitewater forming a halo around his body. Heat rushed to her cheeks.

"Wow, what an aerial," said Jax. "A risky move on a wave of that height."

"That's right, Jax," said Ryder. "Who can forget last year, when Dax Foster fractured his spine after that nasty wipeout?"

"Oooof," said Jax. "That one still gives me nightmares. And yet, here he is again, ready to compete this year…"

Keiran's two best waves were scored, and he advanced to the next round. Mariah knew next to nothing about surfing, but it was clear that Keiran was unusually talented, at least based on the announcers' commentary. As the next heat began, she watched as Keiran paddled out beyond the break, positioning himself in the lineup.

The sun marched across the sky as the rounds advanced, the announcers droning on until they faded pleasantly into the background. Mariah felt the world slow down around her. The seagulls squawking overhead drifted away into the wind, the waves cresting seemed to stop in their place. Keiran paddled out for the next heat, running a hand through his hair, shining droplets of water cascading down around him. He pushed himself up onto his board and rode the next wave, moving like a glacier, his hand reaching out to touch the glassy surface of the wave, his fingers rolling gently across it. As he turned his board up toward the lip, the hard muscles of his body tightened, and he shot himself clean into the air, spinning a full rotation before slicing smoothly back into the sparkling water.

It was just her, and Keiran. She imagined her hands gliding over the wetsuit clinging tightly to his skin. Her fingers lingering over the deep ridges of his abs, pushing her hands through his hair as their eyes met, the sunlight dancing in his irises. The soft feel of his lips touching hers, his hand on the small of her back, pulling her closer, ever closer, the heat pouring from his body as she brought her lips to his neck, caressing his tanned skin...

"Helloooooo, anyone in there?" said a voice. Mariah yelped and dropped her camera into the sand, her heart thundering in her ears.

"What? Nothing!" she heard herself cry out. Christian was standing next to her. He looked out into the sea, directly toward Keiran, and then back at Mariah. He wiggled his eyebrows.

"Well, well, well," he said thoughtfully. "What do we have here?" Fire rushed to her cheeks as she shoved him, a smile breaking on her face. "Hey!" he yelped. "Listen, they don't make 'em like Keiran anymore. He's a fine young lad—" He barked a laugh as Mariah shoved him again.

"A fine young lad, huh?" said Mariah, shaking her head and laughing. "Is that right?"

Christian chuckled and plopped down in the

sand next to her. "Take a load off," he said, gesturing next to him.

Mariah sat down, and leaned back on her arms. "Where's Mom?"

He pointed to a spot near a large yellow canopy in the middle of the crowd. Charlotte jumped up and waved to her. "She didn't want to interrupt you. I'm not nearly as polite, though."

Mariah looked up at him. "I'm glad you're here."

He smiled and wrapped an arm around her. "Wouldn't miss it. This is pretty cool. I'm proud of you, kid."

Mariah's heart cracked as she leaned into him. Was she really supposed to leave, just as she was developing a relationship with him, her father, her real father?

He was here, right here. A real man.

Not the sorry excuse for a man who was Sebastian, the man currently working out his legal defense with a team of lawyers so he could stay out of prison for securities fraud. Mariah swallowed hard.

"Hey," he said, tilting her chin up. "What's going on?"

Mariah's eyes welled up, and she looked down at the sand. "I don't know," she said. "Everything's a mess. I think...I think I, uh..." She stopped, not wanting to say it out loud.

Christian gazed at her for a long moment before a look of understanding washed over his expression. He gently pulled Mariah into his arms. A tear rolled down her cheek.

He really had a way of making her feel so safe.

"I know what it's like to have to make the hard choices, Mariah," he said quietly. Mariah nodded as she thought of Christian's older brother, Elliott. How he'd died in combat, and how Christian had enlisted in his stead. How her mother had been left behind. "Everyone supports whatever you want to do, sweetheart. Your mother, she'll understand."

Mariah looked up at him. "And you?"

Christian wiped a tear from her cheek with the pad of his thumb. A few moments passed. "You don't know how much this has meant to me," he said quietly. "I can't tell you how happy I've been, having you come into my life. The most wonderful surprise a man could ever dream of." He gestured around. "But nothing is permanent. It's a brutal lesson to learn, but we can only control so much. The choices you make...if you think too hard about the long-term consequences, all the ripple effects, you do one thing but you could've done another, second-guessing it all endlessly...you'll drive yourself mad." He shook his head. "Take it from someone who knows a thing or two about it."

Mariah nodded, her heart in her throat. "So what should I do?"

Christian's eyes met hers. "All we can ever really do is what we feel, *in our gut*, is the right thing to do. Forget about everyone else. Forget about their expectations, and forget about your own, too. You've got to learn to trust your instincts. So ask yourself. What do you *really* want, right now?"

Mariah turned to look around at the beautiful seaside scenery. She felt the balmy sunshine against her skin, the breeze in her hair, the crashing of the waves against the shore. The warmth of her father's arms around her, the man who was here with her, really here, right now. She thought of her mother, who had the biggest heart of anyone she'd ever known, her mother who loved her unconditionally and who would do anything for her.

She looked out across the water to find Keiran. Something was there. She was sure of it. An electric shock stole through her as he turned toward her, his eyes landing directly on hers, glittering in the sunlight. He raised his hand in a wave before getting back on his board to paddle to the next wave. Butterflies fluttered in her chest.

Mariah looked up to Christian and nodded, resolute. "Thank you," she whispered. He pulled her closer, stroking her hair. Right now, everything felt *right*.

An awful, ear-piercing scream from the beachfront tore Mariah from her thoughts. She and Christian jumped up from the sand. "What the—" Christian said.

Mariah's blood ran cold as she scanned the water frantically. To the spot where Keiran was just a moment ago.

"*Keiran!*" she screamed. She turned to Christian. His face had drained of color as he watched just over her shoulder. She whipped her head around to see a jet ski blasting through the water, crashing over the lip of a huge wave before landing beyond the break and out of Mariah's field of view.

The camera fell from her hands into the sand as she began to move toward the water, her mind a blur. She registered more screams from the crowd. A strong hand gripped her arm and stopped her.

"No," said Christian, his face grave. "You can't go out there, the waves are crazy today—"

"*We have to help him!*" Mariah shrieked. But he

pointed toward the water just as the jet ski plowed back over the break. Tears burst from her eyes at the sight of Keiran's lifeless form on the gray and yellow rescue board, towed listlessly from the jet ski as it crashed through the waves.

She yanked herself from Christian's grip and tore across the beach toward the water's edge, kicking up plumes of sand behind her. Two lifeguards met the jet ski and pulled Keiran away from the water and into the sand. Her body went numb as one of them leaned over Keiran's face and gave him a rescue breath.

Mariah arrived just as the other lifeguard was chattering into a radio. "He must've hit his board when he wiped out, he's unconscious," he was saying. Mariah watched his mouth move in fascination, everything coming on too quickly. "He's aspirated water, not breathing, get down here as soon as you can—"

She watched the lifeguard leaning over Keiran, pressing the heel of his hand against the center of his chest. "*One. Two. Three. Four. Five...*" he was saying. Beads of sweat had broken out all over the lifeguard's forehead, his voice tight with anxiety.

Mariah felt very far away, her eyes losing focus as it all seemed to fade away.

"*Fifteen. Sixteen. Seventeen. Eighteen...*"

"*Stop!*" Mariah heard herself scream. They looked up at her.

"Please move away from the scene, ma'am," the man speaking into the radio said, his voice icy.

"You're doing it wrong!" she shrieked. The lifeguard administering compressions looked up at her.

"Someone get her out of here!" he screamed. "Nineteen! Twenty! Twenty-one!" The man on the radio moved toward her, fury in his eyes.

"You've got to listen to me!" she said, shoving past the man and kneeling next to Keiran.

"Ma'am, *get out of here—*"

"Your hands are too high," she said, a swell of outrage coursing through her. "Your compressions are too shallow, his chest isn't recoiling completely, your pace is too fast, and his freaking chest didn't rise during your rescue breaths!"

The lifeguard's eyes widened as he looked down at Keiran helplessly. "How—"

Mariah pushed him out of the way. "You!" she said to the man on the radio. "Where are the paramedics? Where's the AED?"

"On its way, any second now," he said, his eyebrows rising.

Mariah let out all the air from her lungs, knelt

over Keiran, and tilted his head back. She watched his chest rise as she gave him the first breath, and then the second. She leaned back, placed the heel of her hand on the lower half of the breastbone, inter-locked the fingers of her other hand, and began compressions.

"One! Two! Three! Four!" Her mind emptied of all thought: the crowd forming around her, the voices in the radio, the crashing of the waves, every-thing except her med school training.

Come on, come on, Keiran.

"Thirteen! Fourteen! Fifteen!"

Tears spilled from her eyes as she depressed the center of his chest. "Please!" she shouted. Her mind flashed for a moment back to that night, the night when everything changed. She pushed the thoughts down as far as they would go. "Twenty-nine! Thirty! Come on, Keiran, please!" she cried.

She tilted his head back again and leaned in. One breath, two. Her heart slammed so hard against her chest it hurt as the minutes dragged on endlessly. Where in God's name was the freaking ambulance? She began compressions again, feeling the hope drain from her body like liquid, like blood from a wound.

"Sixteen! Seventeen! Eighteen!" she cried, her

body shaking with sobs. She had to do it. She had to redeem herself.

He had to make it.

"Twenty-seven!" she screamed. "Twenty-eight—"

And then Keiran's eyes popped open just as he choked out a mouthful of water. He leaned over, his body retching as he coughed out more and more seawater, his face bright red and his eyes watering.

"Oh, thank God, thank God," Mariah breathed out as Keiran sat up, drawing huge lungfuls of air. The lifeguard who had started CPR sat down hard in the sand, the color gone from his face, sweating profusely and breathing hard. Keiran coughed again, hard, spluttering as he clutched the sand with his hands, looking around wildly.

"What...what happened..." he choked out, before his eyes met Mariah's.

Her stomach somersaulted as he looked at her, his eyes brimming with tears. His lips parted, his head tilting ever so slightly as their eyes locked. He was looking at her like he was seeing her in a new light, really seeing her for the first time. The whole world disappeared around them as she lost herself in his eyes.

"Mariah," he whispered. "I—"

And then someone nearly fell on top of him,

kicking sand into Mariah's eyes. "Hey—" she started, but the words dried up in her throat.

A pair of arms were wrapped around him, a long mane of blonde hair whipping in the wind. One of the beautiful young blonde women she'd seen earlier, screaming his name.

"*Keiran!* Oh, Keiran, baby, I thought you were gone," she wept, her body shaking against his. She ran her hands through his hair and kissed him hard on the mouth.

Mariah sat back in the sand, hard, the wind suddenly knocked from her.

The blonde woman suddenly whipped around to face her and leaned over, pulling Mariah into a hug.

"Thank you, *thank you*," she whispered. Mariah watched herself from a distance extricate her limbs from the woman.

"It's okay...uh..." Mariah managed, meeting the woman's eyes.

"Leilani," she said, letting out a harsh breath. She turned back to Keiran, took his hands in hers, and squeezed. "I'm his fiancée."

A buzzing sound filled Mariah's ears as two paramedics pushed through the crowd that had formed around them in the sand, helping Keiran to his feet. She stepped back into the crowd, stunned.

She didn't know why she'd assumed he wasn't already in a relationship.

She'd been a fool.

Her mind spun as she replayed everything between them. Keiran had never been anything but a gentleman the whole time, had never crossed any lines. What she'd taken for something developing between them...it was simply the actions of a kind and caring man who'd been listening to her.

Nothing more.

Mariah had never in her life felt so stupid. She hadn't thought to wonder if he was seeing someone because she hadn't been considering Keiran as someone she could even *be* interested in, since she was inevitably leaving. But what felt like mere moments ago, as she watched him out in the water, as their eyes met...something had shifted within her.

She shook her head, and weaved her way through the crowd. It didn't matter anymore. It had never mattered.

All these distractions...they had to stop.

It was time to go back. Back to Boston, back to where she'd been running from, her tail tucked between her legs. Time to face the music, one last time.

Mariah looked back only once. Keiran was sitting up on a stretcher as one of the paramedics listened to his chest with a stethoscope. He was staring right at Mariah, a line between his eyebrows.

It had been a great summer vacation here in Marina Cove, that was true. But all vacations eventually came to an end.

Mariah looked at Keiran for one final moment before she turned and left.

25

For what felt like hours, Natalie walked with no sense of purpose or direction, her thoughts spooling out endlessly. Her throat screamed with pain; it was like someone had shoved an iron spike right through it, blocking it.

How had she gotten herself into such a mess?

She slowed to a stop and squeezed her eyes shut. She'd gotten into this mess by coming home. Being back here...it had been a huge mistake. The moment the shoreline of Marina Cove swam into view, she'd known, but she'd persisted. And now, everything was worse. Natalie couldn't remember why she'd even wanted to come home in the first place.

Hiding out at April's place these last days while she figured out her next steps hadn't helped things.

April had clammed up entirely, unwilling to even talk about Garrett anymore, despite Natalie's gentle attempts to find a way to help. There was nothing else to do.

At any rate, she was only stalling now. It was time to leave.

She checked the time on her phone. Enough time left to catch the late ferry.

The night air swept across her sweaty skin as she continued her aimless wandering. She wanted to absorb it all before she left. She swallowed hard, willing her tears to just come already, but they stubbornly refused.

It would have been so much better just not knowing. Not knowing about April, about Garrett. Not knowing how hard of a time her family was really having.

Not knowing about Theo.

How against her will, against everything in her telling her there was no point to it, no future for them, her feelings for him had been deepening.

She let out a huge breath, and looked up to find that her feet had carried her to Marina Cove Adventures. Her heart sank as her eyes scanned over the long bungalow. All the lights were off, the door shut. A part of her had desperately hoped he'd still be here before she left for good. A chance to say goodbye.

It was probably better this way, anyway. Natalie had never been one for goodbyes. Better to make a clean break.

She padded through the sand sparkling in the glow of the moonlight down toward the waterline. The night was warm, but a cool, refreshing breeze swept off the water, breaking goosebumps across the skin of her arms. Her eyes wandered across the sea, dark and beautiful and infinite.

Natalie swallowed against the spike in her throat. It was going to be very hard to leave this place.

She let out a slow breath, and then something moved in her periphery. Her heart thudded against her chest as she whipped her head toward the wooden picnic table behind the bungalow. Sitting cross-legged and staring out into the sea, a look of intensity in his dark eyes, was Theo.

She was frozen in place for a moment before Theo turned toward her, his eyes falling on hers. A thrill ran up her spine.

"Natalie?" he asked, his brows drawing together.

Natalie pulled in a shaky breath, that terrible pressure building behind her eyes. She slowly made her way toward him, not breaking his gaze. His eyes scanned over hers, and his expression softened. He motioned for her to join him on the table. She sat down, the words in her throat swept away like dust in the wind.

Theo silently took Natalie's hand in his, and softly squeezed it. And something broke within her.

Hot tears sprang to her eyes. His strong presence next to her...it was like a lifeline. Something to keep her from slipping beneath the surface.

Natalie lowered her head, her eyes pressed shut. She'd had relationships over the years, but this time, something different was happening to her at the prospect of leaving. Something black and wretched and despairing.

Whatever was unfolding between them would have ended anyway, as soon as the claustrophobia, the cabin fever took over and sent Natalie running to the next place.

Lather, rinse, repeat.

And she was powerless against it.

It was only going to get worse if she forced herself to stay longer. Better it be now than when things got more complicated. Natalie bit her bottom lip, and her gaze met his, tears pooling in her eyes.

"I have to go, Theo," she said softly. Her heart twisted like a wet dishrag. "But I don't want to."

Theo's eyes didn't leave hers, but a tightness appeared between his brows. His lips parted slightly.

"Then don't," he whispered.

The pressure in her throat sent stripes of pain into her face. She shook her head quickly, her mind a whirlwind of grief and longing and regret and despair. "I…" she started. "I can't…"

His chest rose and fell sharply, his eyes boring into hers like he could see into her soul. "Natalie," he said quietly. "What made you leave Ireland in the first place? Why did you come back?"

Natalie watched him for a long moment, trying to etch his features into her mind. It was hard to recall ever feeling worse than she did at this very moment.

As they looked at each other, her heart folded over. She was sick and tired of holding it all in. Natalie needed someone right now. Even if she was leaving, she needed someone. The pressure crushing her needed to be released.

And Theo…there was something about the way he was looking at her that made her know she was safe.

Natalie looked out over the water, and shook her head. "It's a long story," she whispered.

26

THREE MONTHS EARLIER

Natalie grimaced as she pulled a brush through her hair, glancing at the clock on her dresser. She was going to be late for her shift, again. Esther wasn't going to be pleased. To say the least.

She yanked her O'Donnell's T-shirt over her head, part of the hideous bright green uniform they'd recently switched to at the pub where she'd been waitressing, shaking her head at the reflection in the mirror before pushing through her bedroom door into the common area. She frowned at the sound of giggling.

"You're too much," Jess said into her phone, giggling again. She was sprawled on the couch, her feet dangling off the edge, rocking back and forth. "Naughty, naughty man!"

Harper huffed from the recliner in the corner, snapped her newspaper shut, and got up. She rolled her eyes as she passed Natalie on her way into the kitchen. Natalie snickered.

She stood over Jess, raising an eyebrow. Jess looked up at her and shrugged. "Listen, Rami," Jess said, injecting a slinking, lascivious melody into her voice. "I've got to run. Call me later." She hung up the phone, sat up, and stuck her tongue out at Natalie. "What?"

Natalie shook her head, laughing. "If Tucker ever finds out about Rami..."

Jess pursed her lips into a pout. "What do you take me for? Nothing's ever happened between me and Rami."

Harper scoffed from her seat at the kitchen bar with a cup of coffee. "Tucker's not gonna see it that way if he ever hears the way you're leading Rami on," she said.

Natalie leaned back against the bar next to Harper. "I mean, when Rami finds out you already have a boyfriend, what's your plan? He's going to pull our funding." She pushed down the frustration bubbling up within her.

The stakes just weren't as high for Jess and Harper as they were for Natalie. They seemed to stumble into opportunities wherever they went. They had more of a...flexible moral compass than Natalie.

Their new business venture might not mean as much to her friends, but to Natalie, it represented a fresh start. A way to use her talents in some meaningful way. A chance, maybe, to even settle down. For a while, at least.

"Rami will never find out about Tucker," said Jess. "And honestly, he just likes the attention. He's a big flirt. He knows it ain't gonna happen with me. Besides," she said, heading into the kitchen and pouring herself a glass of orange juice, "he wouldn't just pull our funding. He knows we've got a good idea. That we're gonna make him even more rich. We'll make sure he can't screw us over when we draw up all the paperwork."

Natalie frowned, then grabbed Jess's orange juice and slugged down the rest of it. "I hope you're right," she said as Jess flicked her arm. "I like Tucker. Don't screw that up."

The wry expression fell from Jess's face. "I won't," she muttered. Tucker had been following Jess around from country to country, their on-and-off-again relationship the source of endless strife between them, but Natalie could see the way Tucker looked at Jess. He really loved her. He'd been the one to buy the house in the Irish countryside they were all currently living in.

Jess somehow always seemed to draw wealthy men who fawned over her, delighting in spending their money on her, spoiling her. Natalie and Harper teased her endlessly about it, but privately, Natalie thought Jess was playing a dangerous game.

She loved Jess; she was a thoughtful friend and had a big heart, but sooner or later, someone was going to get hurt.

As Natalie grabbed her purse and said goodbye to her roommates, Jess's phone rang. Natalie clicked the door shut just as Jess's giggling resumed, a pit of unease roiling in her stomach.

∼

"ALL RIGHT, MISS HARPER, OL' buddy ol' pal," said Natalie, her heart hammering in her chest. "You ready for this?"

Harper was grinning ear to ear as she pulled on the straps of her parachute pack and then saluted Natalie. "Ready, boss! Let's do this!"

The early morning wind whipped at them hard as Natalie looked around the grassy cliffside north of Donegal, feeling like she was standing on the edge of the world. The Atlantic stretched on infinitely beneath them, its glittering surface reflecting the pale sunlight peeking through the dense clouds. Natalie had done hundreds of jumps over the years, but never from these cliffs. Her mouth was dry as dust as she inhaled the cold air, her lungs sparkling and her skin electric with anticipation.

"Okay," Natalie said, grinning. "One. Two. Three!"

And Natalie and Harper took several long strides, pumping their arms and legs hard, and heaved themselves over the edge of the cliff.

The beautiful sensation of freefall tugged and pulled at Natalie's core, those sensational moments of pure weightlessness sending an explosive, icy thrill up and down her spine, a feeling of pure joy and adrenaline cascading through her. She had only a few seconds of freefall before she had to release her chute; the cliff gave them only about four hundred vertical feet before ending on a short, rocky slope that led to a second seven-hundred-foot drop.

She whipped her head around, trying to take in all the stunning beauty of the northwestern Irish coast, the sea stacks and the long lines of cliffs, the earthy smell of incipient rainfall, the cold wind fragrant with saltwater, the huge boulders peppering slopes of heather and bright green grass.

Jumps like these were so different than skydiving; they were over much more quickly, but there was something about leaping directly off the sheer face of the earth that made her feel *alive*.

The seconds after she leaped seemed to stretch to eternity, the ground suspended beneath her, the beach below them only visible during low tide just a tiny collection of rocks a million miles away. And then Natalie released her chute, the wind roughly shoving her back up into the air and everything rapidly pulling into harsh relief around her, her senses sharpened and her mind racing as her training took over and she began to navigate to the tiny landing spot below.

Natalie turned her head to find Harper, the grin on her face so wide it almost hurt, her heart pattering like a jackrabbit.

But Harper was nowhere to be seen.

A cold sweat broke over Natalie's skin. "*Harper! Haaaaarper!*" she screamed into the wind, her eyes skittering wildly over the cliffside. Had she chickened out? No one was standing on the top of the cliff. Natalie scanned the ocean, thinking the worst.

And then her body went numb as her eyes fell to the base of the first vertical drop, to the crumpled red and white chute draped over the rocky slope leading endlessly down to the ruthless and unforgiving sea.

∽

NATALIE SWALLOWED against the hard lump in her throat as she stood in the nearly empty bedroom. Shafts of weak sunlight fell listlessly through the pale gray cloud cover and dappled the dusty hardwood floor, making the room appear even more desolate than it was.

She pulled open the bottom drawer of Harper's chestnut dresser, carefully lifted out the haphazard collection of sweatshirts and jeans, and sat down, beginning to fold them carefully. Several cardboard boxes lined her empty wall, the square dust outlines of old movie posters and framed pictures of her adventures all over the world smattering its surface.

Natalie let out a careful breath as she set the first sweatshirt into the box, an old gray hoodie that

Harper had worn what seemed like ages ago, but in reality was only a matter of days.

Tears welled in Natalie's eyes. The last time Harper wore this, she had no idea what was coming, no inkling of it. Carrying on, day in and day out, happily thinking of the little things that filled a day, where to eat for dinner, what television show to watch, what time to get to bed to start it all over again. Having no real sense of how fragile it all was.

Natalie squeezed her eyes shut. She was pushing her luck, she knew it. She could dial things back, though. Yes, it was time to reassess, to learn from what happened. To be a little more cautious. Despite what had happened to Harper, she knew she couldn't stop it all, not really. The thrill-seeking...it was the only thing that made her feel something.

It was the only thing that could make her forget.

She set the last of the clothing into the cardboard box, taped it up, and pushed it against the wall. Her knees cracked and groaned as she stood up, her throat tight and her thoughts tumbling. She tapped on the connecting door that led to Jess's bedroom, and pushed in.

Jess was lying on her bed, laughing into the phone. Natalie rolled her eyes. Rami.

"You really think so?" she was saying, holding up

a finger to Natalie. "I mean, maybe if I was really, really drunk..." She giggled into the phone as Natalie shook her head. "Hang on one sec, Rami," she said, holding her hand over the phone. "Hey, Nattie, what's up?"

Natalie held back her anger. There was only one person who could call her that. "Can you help me load up some of Harper's boxes, please?"

Jess's face fell, her eyes clouding over. "Yeah, of course," she said. "Sorry. I didn't know you were working on that again. Give me two minutes."

Natalie nodded and left out Jess's other door that led to the common room, Jess's voice more serious now as she softly clicked the door shut.

She turned, and ran headlong into Tucker.

Natalie yelped in surprise. "Tucker!" she said, her eyes skittering to Jess's bedroom door. "Why... what are you doing here?" He'd clearly been standing in front of her door, listening.

How much had he heard? A shiver ran down her spine.

Tucker's face was a stone as he towered over Natalie, staring at her for what felt like an eternity. "I have to go. Tell Jess I stopped by." Something Natalie couldn't quite place flitted across his expression.

With one last glance toward the bedroom door, Tucker turned and left.

∽

"COME ON, COME ON," Natalie said as she impatiently tapped the steering wheel, stuck behind a long line of cars. She glanced at the clock. Late again. Esther was going to have a conniption. The late shift was already short-staffed.

She groaned, and flicked on the radio to distract herself, her mind racing.

Weeks had gone by without anything seeming to change between Tucker and Jess. They went out, he slept over, they carried on like usual. Jess had assured Natalie that Tucker didn't hear anything, that she was worrying over nothing. Natalie began to wonder if she'd imagined the look on his face as he stood before her door.

A cold, hard tightness stole over her. It was all beginning to be too much. She'd taken what happened to Harper a lot harder than Jess had; Natalie and Harper had been closer, and despite the fact that she'd done nothing wrong, Natalie couldn't shake the gnawing, eroding feeling that she was somehow responsible.

If anything, Harper had been a *more* experienced jumper than Natalie...she hadn't talked her into anything. They both knew the risks.

Yet, the feeling remained. The whole experience had spooked her more than she was letting on to anyone else.

And now that she'd talked to Aunt Maura, had found out everything that had happened with her father...well, it hadn't made things *easier*, that much was certain. Natalie had been like a zombie ever since, stumbling in and out of the days, barely aware of her surroundings.

She'd known deep down for a long time that Dad had died, but she'd never been able to fully extinguish that tiny spark of hope that he was still out there somewhere, perhaps thinking of her, regretting that he'd missed it all, everything. Natalie's whole adult life.

Her heart broke all over again as she listened to all that he'd been going through. Learning what had happened...it helped fill in the holes in her knowledge.

But it didn't bring him back.

The tires of her car screeched as she tore into the parking lot of O'Donnell's. She took off her seatbelt, but then stopped, clenching the steering wheel for a moment.

Prague. Prague. She closed her eyes. It was the fresh start she so desperately needed. She had to think about her life, which had begun to feel like it was spinning out of control, dovetailing toward something that was surely going to end poorly.

More than anything, Natalie needed an anchor.

She grimaced. She'd taken to calling the old Seaside House landline, but every time Ramona answered, something had locked up inside her, the words crumbling in her throat. She hung up before she said anything, but always felt a little bit lighter upon hearing a familiar voice. Something to hold on to.

Natalie got out of the car, groaning at the dark heaviness that seemed to wrap itself around her body lately, and pushed through the front door of the pub. She froze in her tracks as Esther marched toward her, that permanent scowl etched even deeper across her face.

Uh-oh.

"Natalie," Esther seethed in her thick Irish lilt. "We need to talk."

~

Ten minutes later, Natalie trudged back toward her car, dazed. She'd been late one too many times.

There was no one else to blame but herself.

She slumped into the driver's side, shut her eyes, and blew out a long breath. It was the sort of irresponsibility that belonged to a careless teenager, not a grown woman. Natalie hadn't even argued. Esther had done the right thing.

It was no way to be. Something inside her had just been dragging her down, affecting her decision-making, making her care just a little bit *less* about everything. She was getting careless, reckless.

Her blood ran cold as she thought of Harper. The image of that crumpled parachute blazed through her mind like wildfire.

Maybe they shouldn't have gone out that day. Maybe it really had been too windy. Neither of them had said anything. They hadn't taken the very real threat to their lives seriously enough. And for what, a few seconds of an adrenaline rush? Why did people do this? There were other ways to get thrills, safer ways. Had it been worth it?

It seemed, without ever really realizing it, that Natalie didn't quite value her life enough.

She leaned back, that familiar burning pressure

building behind her eyes. Enough was enough. It was time to take things a little more seriously. It was time to look at the next steps. To start thinking about her future, instead of acting like she didn't have one to consider.

Natalie nodded once to herself, resolved. Getting fired was a good wakeup call. She needed to have a conversation with Jess. It was time to push all this nastiness away, get back on track. Get out of Ireland. It was lovely here, but she'd been here far, far too long.

She'd do her best to get another job for a couple months, save some money, and talk to Jess about moving sooner rather than later. Get things rolling with the business. Already Natalie began to feel better, the horrible tightness in her neck and shoulders loosening a bit.

Natalie pulled out her phone to check the time, wondering what she was going to do tonight now that she was free. But as she saw the list of notifications on her lock screen, she felt like someone had dumped ice water into her stomach.

She had dozens of texts and missed calls from Jess.

Her heart lodged into her throat, she frantically

punched Jess's name to call her. On the first ring, Jess answered, shrieking.

"*Natalie! The house!* The house, the house..." she wailed. "I can't believe it, I don't...Natalie, what do we do, *everything we have*—"

"*Jess!*" Natalie hissed into the phone. "Take a breath! What happened to the house?"

A sob escaped Jess's mouth, followed by ragged, heavy breathing. She was hyperventilating. "Tucker...I can't...he heard me on the phone with Rami...I can't believe he did this...He set our *freaking house on fire*, Natalie!" she screamed. A terrible moan curled through the phone, and then Jess broke into fresh sobs, her breath shuddering in tiny gasps.

Natalie felt all the blood drain from her face as the world seemed to slam to a halt around her.

Her lockbox.

It was under her bed.

Natalie watched herself from a distance fling the phone into the passenger seat, turn the key in the accelerator, slam her foot against the gas pedal. She watched herself tear through the streets of Ireland, the world passing curiously slowly around her. The phone rang again and again, fading away into the background. Her heart no longer seemed to be beating. All she could think of was the lockbox under her bed, holding the only two things in the whole world she truly cared about. Her mind was bent on them, everything else filtering out into a white, blank void.

Natalie watched herself tear into their gravel driveway, yanking her body from the seat and leaving the door open behind her. The night was cool, a fine mist of rainfall just beginning to drift down from the dark sky. She faced the house she'd called home, things popping into relief one at a time.

A wave of heat, hitting her body like a thick blanket, wrapping around her. The sharp bite of smoke already filling her nostrils, the tendrils creeping into her lungs.

The fire shooting up into the sky like a blowtorch, igniting the air in an orange, almost pleasant glow.

Without stopping to think, Natalie tore off her O'Donnell's T-shirt, dunked it in the decorative fountain in the small garden next to the driveway, and held it up to her face, marching directly toward the front door. The fire hadn't spread yet from the back of the house to the front. Some distant part of her mind wondered if Jess had thought to ring for a fire crew. They only had one reasonably close neighbor down the road. There might not be anyone coming for a while.

Natalie closed her eyes, took a breath, and then shoved her way through the front door and into the house.

Thoughts came too slowly as she stood in the living room, her eyes sweeping over everything. The lights were still on, the black-and-white clock still ticking away on the wall. It all looked strangely intact.

It *was* a little warm, perhaps.

Natalie's heart was a drum in her ears as she moved through the living room toward the back of the house. Toward her bedroom. She pressed her eyes shut.

Please. Please still be there. Please.

Natalie stood before her bedroom door and reached for the handle, yanking her hand backward immediately and screaming. She lowered the shirt from her face to the polished brass and turned, feeling the heat through the fabric as she pushed the door open with her foot.

Heat slammed out from the doorframe against her body. Tears poured from her eyes as she dropped to the floor, smoke billowing from the room. She quieted the distant screaming part of her saying it was too late. Natalie didn't care. She didn't care what it took.

She had to try.

Natalie squinted through the smoke. The back wall of the room was engulfed in flames. Her dresser had caught fire and tipped over, partially blocking her path.

A burst of hope shot through her like a torpedo. Her bed wasn't on fire yet.

Natalie pressed her shirt to her mouth, took a huge breath, and stood up, leaping over a pile of flaming clothes that separated the distance between her and the box under the bed. She momentarily cursed herself for not investing in a fireproof box. What had she been thinking—

It didn't matter now. She ducked back under the smoke line, dropped to her stomach, and crawled, her body shaking with sobs as she pushed harder than she'd ever pushed in her life.

Finally, she took another huge breath through her shirt and reached under her bed, sweeping both arms around frantically. She screamed wildly.

It was gone.

Something cracked and fell behind her. There

was no time left. There wasn't going to be any oxygen left in the room, even if she did manage not to succumb to the smoke.

She shook her head violently, squeezed her eyes shut, and shoved herself halfway under her bed, a primal scream erupting from deep within her before her fingers found the smooth metal edges of the lockbox, the heat searing the palms of her hands.

Tears of relief fell from her eyes and dappled the wooden floor as she located the small black handle and pulled.

Natalie shimmied away from the bed, her eyes skittering across the room. Something crashed and fell directly outside the bedroom door, kicking up bright red and yellow flames, making her scream in terror, in desperation.

She was trapped. This was how it all ended. After everything.

Her lungs heaved up and down as a sickening lightheadedness stole over her. Her mind flashed rapidly as she pressed the wet T-shirt to her nose and mouth. Her father, his laugh. The small crinkles in Joel's eyes when he'd smile. Harper, her wild eyes, the crumpled parachute. A thousand memories, a thousand regrets.

She clenched her fists. Her sisters. How she

missed them, what she'd give to talk to them, to hear their voices. Her mother's face swam in her mind, her chest suddenly constricting, her heart cracking.

Natalie's body shuddered with grief as she thought of her father. At the end of it all, more than anything else, she wanted to see him. To be held, one last time.

She gritted her teeth.

No. This wasn't how it ended. She had unfinished business.

Natalie had always been a fighter...and she wasn't about to go down that easily.

She stood up, hunched over, and scanned the room frantically before her eyes fell on the far corner of the back wall. The muscles of her body went rigid in preparation. And then she took one last breath in her T-shirt, held the lockbox close to her chest, and ran as fast as she could toward the window. She aimed her shoulder out, her heartbeat stopping, and slammed through the glass and out into the cool, wet grass of the backyard.

Natalie rolled several times, her hands seared and raw, before crawling away from the house backward, gasping for breath. A cry of joy tore from her throat and into the night as she gripped the lockbox against herself, hugging it like a child.

A moment later, she caught something in the corner of her eye, against the side of the house, against an old wooden trellis. Unable to stop herself, she rose to her feet and ran over to it, lifting it in her hands.

A bright red gasoline canister.

Natalie shook her head slowly. She would need this. The police needed to see it.

Tucker was going to pay for what he'd done to Jess.

She turned to walk away from the house, and froze in her tracks. Standing there, a look of horror on her face, was her neighbor, Ailbhe.

Natalie opened her mouth to speak, but clamped it shut as Ailbhe's eyes wandered down to the gas canister in Natalie's hand and widened. She turned and bolted away, back toward her house.

Oh, no.

"Ailbhe!" Natalie shouted. "*Ailbhe!*" She began to run toward her, but tripped over a rake someone had left in the yard, sending her sprawling. She scrambled to her feet, and glanced at the plastic gasoline canister now tipped over on the ground. Now it had her fingerprints on it. And Ailbhe had seen her at the scene of the crime, with the gasoline in her hands.

A feeling of being trapped washed over her. That claustrophobic feeling, hands around her throat, squeezing until she could no longer breathe. The old instinct to run.

Without hesitation, Natalie got into her car, turned the key, and drove away.

27

"And then what happened?"

Theo was leaning toward her on the wooden bench, his brows pinched together. Natalie met his eyes.

"And then," she said, her voice wavering, "I called the Seaside House over and over as I drove away. I didn't know what to do, where I was even going. I wasn't thinking clearly." She rolled her head around on her shoulders. "The police caught up with me not too long after that. I was arrested, and tried my best to explain what happened. I showed them my texts from Jess, explained why I went into the house in the first place. While I was being held, they interrogated Jess too. Apparently when they got to Tucker, he confessed immediately. Ultimately, they let me go."

Theo exhaled a huge breath, like he'd been holding it the entire time she'd been talking. He frowned and shook his head before looking back up at her.

"What was in the lockbox?"

Natalie fought back tears as she thought of the two items inside the lockbox. The ones that were part of the very fabric of her heart.

The little red box, and the notebook.

She opened her mouth to speak, but then closed it. Tears welled in her eyes as she thought about what she'd done all those long, long years ago. A horrible swell of guilt built in her stomach.

She wasn't ready to talk about that yet. And she probably never would be.

"I'm sorry," Theo said, moving closer to her and putting a comforting hand on her shoulder. "That's none of my business, obviously. I didn't mean to ask. I just..." He ran his hands over his face. "That's terrifying, Natalie. I'm so sorry you went through all that. I'm really, really sorry."

Their eyes lingered on one another's for a long moment, the only sound the lapping of the water on the shore, before they pulled each other into a hug. "Thank you, Theo," Natalie whispered into him.

A long moment stretched between them before they pulled apart. Theo leaned back on his hands, watching the water. "Well, it's a good thing you were able to break through that back window. I don't think I would've been able to think that clearly if it were me." He turned to her. "You're lucky to be alive."

Natalie nodded, but then froze. Her breath caught in her throat. "Oh, my God."

Theo sat up straight. "What is it?"

Natalie's mind was racing. She hadn't been able to think clearly when she was in the room.

Something else had made her stand up and fight.

Natalie shook her head. "I thought I was going to die, Theo. And the last thing I thought of was my family. How much regret I had. That I wasn't ready... I wasn't done." Her voice cracked. "When I thought it was all over, I wanted to see them. To see my mother. Because..." Her eyes pinched shut. "Because I didn't want it to be over before I'd had a chance to talk to them...to her..."

She shot to her feet. All the long years, and she'd been avoiding talking to her family. All the time she'd been running, and she had never tried, even once, to talk to them about some of the things she was thinking.

About why she was so furious with Ella.

"I've got to go," she said breathlessly. "I'm so sorry. I have to go talk to them."

Theo's eyes scanned over hers, and then he nodded. "Good luck, Natalie."

Natalie nodded back, and then left, back toward the Seaside House. She was done holding it all in. She had no idea what would come of it, but at least she was going to try.

It was time to confront her mother once and for all.

~

"LADIES AND GENTLEMEN," said a booming voice over the microphone. "Welcome to this year's Marina Cove Music Festival! *Let's make some noise!*"

Beads of sweat broke on Diane's forehead as several thousand members of the crowd began cheering and whistling, the ground practically rumbling with their combined applause. The sun was just beginning to set over the expansive Silver Tide Beach, the sky an incredible teal and scarlet and tangerine. Waves splashed against the shoreline directly behind the enormous stage that had been constructed right on the water, bookended by two giant columns of lights and speakers taller than Diane. The smells of barbecued food and sunscreen drifted through the air, people dancing to music playing from portable speakers and bouncing giant beachballs to each other across the surprisingly large crowd.

That summertime spark was in the air, that feeling that surged through everyone, that intangible excitement for a good night to come. Diane swallowed hard.

"He'll come," said Niko, standing beside her. Diane looked up at him. He gave her a thumbs up and nodded. "I know he'll come." Tyson and Sully gave her a reassuring look.

The last few days had been an absolute blur. Austin still was nowhere to be found, and had shut his phone off. Diane had stopped at the Maple Street Diner, but Kate had said only that Austin had worked it out with her to take some time off to "figure some things out." She didn't know where he'd gone. Or at least, she hadn't told Diane.

But Diane had Niko leave him a message, asking Austin to meet up with him at the music festival to watch the performances together, now that they wouldn't be performing. Diane had asked Niko not to say anything about her or what they had planned; she didn't want to risk him not coming if he thought she would be there.

"I hope so," Diane said, scanning the crowd for that familiar tousled hair, that familiar angle of his jaw. Those beautiful eyes that held mystery and amusement all at once. Her heart twisted. She missed him badly. "I think maybe this was a stupid idea. I mean, I called him a deceitful, cheating liar and then left him, when he was just trying to do what he thought was right. I wouldn't blame him for not wanting to talk."

Niko shook his head. "No way. I think it's really sweet. Super romantic." Tyson and Sully exchanged glances, snickering at Niko. He made an obscene gesture with his hands toward them. "What? I love love. What do you want from me?"

Diane laughed, happy to have the guys there with her. They had a way of making her feel more at ease. The emcee was explaining the audience vote for the grand prize, based on the crowd's reaction as the song was being performed. "And so make sure you really give it up for the band you think deserves to win!" he continued.

He paused for a moment, bringing the microphone closer to his mouth. "On that note. After a last-minute sponsorship from our friends at Don's Refrigeration, we're pleased to announce that the cash prize for the audience vote has been raised to *fifty thousand dollars!*"

A surprised murmur swept through the crowd, followed by a huge applause.

"I know!" said the emcee. "A huge thanks to Don Murphy, and please remember to call the team at Don's Refrigeration for all your, uh, refrigeration needs!" He grinned, and held up a notecard. "So without further ado, please welcome to the stage, The Wild Rabbits!" The crowd burst into a wave of cheers and applause as the band took to the stage and began playing an upbeat rockabilly tune.

"Oh, my God," said Sully. "Fifty grand."

Niko whistled. "Not too shabby," he said, turning to them. "How are you guys gonna spend your cut after I take my eighty-percent manager's fee?"

Tyson punched him in the arm, making Niko yelp. Diane laughed, but her stomach tightened. Her share of the money would have done a lot of good toward reopening the Seaside House.

Without Austin, though...it wasn't going to happen. Before everything, they might've had a chance. He was the lifeblood of their music.

All she could do now was follow her gut, do what she thought was right tonight.

"Diane!" shouted a voice from behind her. She whipped around to find a grinning Charlotte threading through the crowd to meet her, Mariah following closely behind.

"Good luck up there," Mariah whispered, hugging her for a split second too long.

Diane frowned at the faraway look in Mariah's eyes, the stiff tension in her body. She should ask her about that later.

Ramona appeared from behind them, holding Lily's and Danny's hands. Her sisters hugged her tight.

"I'm so glad you guys are here," she said into Charlotte's hair.

"It'll be great," said Ramona. "I really hope he comes."

They pulled Ella into their hug as she appeared behind them. Sylvie waved to her as she followed Christian through the ever-growing crowd toward them.

Diane raised her eyebrows. Nick was at her side. Apparently, he and Sylvie had made up.

Her mouth went dry as she looked around at all the people who had come here to cheer her on. Who were there for her. Just a few months ago, she'd been toiling away in Los Angeles, lost and adrift, tired and lonely.

It was incredible how quickly everything could change. All she'd had to do was take the first steps. Those first steps had been the hardest.

The next hour and a half flew by in a blur as they listened to act after amazing act, the sky slowly darkening as the sun slid down toward the horizon. Diane could barely focus as her eyes skittered over the throngs of people, her hope slowly waning as Austin failed to appear. She did her best to keep her head clear, to pay attention to the music.

There was true talent tonight, a wide array of performances from blues to country to pop. Diane could only shake her head in amazement as a twenty-member lineup performed an incredible acapella rendition of "Wonderful Tonight" by Eric Clapton, tears welling in her eyes.

It hadn't mattered after all. Up against this sort of competition, they'd never really stood a chance, even with Austin.

And that was okay. Tonight was about something more than that. Even if he didn't show, at least she had tried. That was all she could control.

Before she knew it, Niko was gesturing for her,

leading them through the crowd toward the stage. "Good luck, Diane!" her family shouted. Diane's palms were sweating, her throat parched.

And she blinked her eyes, and she was suddenly following Niko onto the stage, the crowd erupting in applause. Tyson sat down at the drums as Sully quickly tuned his violin. Diane felt weak as she walked through a river of molasses to get to the microphone. She turned to Niko, who plugged his bass into the huge amplifiers surrounding them.

You know what to do, he mouthed to her, giving her a small thumbs up. A surge of emotion swept through her. She was so used to doing everything alone for so long...having people around who supported her, who weren't just trying to see how they could use Diane to get themselves ahead in some way...it was nothing short of pure magic.

Diane grinned in spite of herself, gave him a thumbs up, and turned to the microphone.

28

Natalie groaned into the pillow and turned the music up in her headphones, shaking her head. Mom and Dad were downstairs arguing again, the muffled sounds carrying through the old inn. It had been happening more and more lately, it seemed, but her siblings didn't seem to notice. Or if they did, they hadn't said anything.

She ripped the covers off, the humid summer air pooling upstairs and making her sweat. She turned the music up further and leaned back in her bed, staring at the ceiling.

Her mind wandered to her date earlier, and a slow smile spread across her face. It was hard to believe how fast her senior year had gone. It seemed like only yesterday when she'd looked up during the first day of

French class to find a cute boy watching her. She'd grinned as he hastily looked down at his paper, blushing furiously.

And now...

Natalie's stomach clenched as she thought of college looming before her, only a few weeks away now. They were going to try it, to stay together during college. The dreaded long-distance relationship. She wondered what would become of them.

In her mind, she and Joel were meant to be together.

Natalie frowned as she heard the front door close downstairs through the music in her ears. She pulled off her headphones, and listened for a while. Nothing.

Moving as quietly as possible, she tiptoed through her bedroom and down the stairs, avoiding the creaky ones. She froze as she turned to the common room, her legs locking beneath her.

Dad was sitting alone at the old upright piano, his face buried in his hands.

Natalie's chest tightened. She silently backpedaled, badly wanting to get back upstairs. There was something about the way he was holding himself...it was like she was intruding.

But she stopped, and shook her head. Maybe he wanted to talk.

"Daddy?" she asked softly.

His head snapped up, his eyes landing on hers. Immediately, Natalie's throat closed up, like someone was pressing on her windpipe. He had a horrible thousand-mile stare in his eyes. Exhausted, weary. Like a man who had nothing left to give. Natalie's blood ran cold.

"Natalie," he said, his voice hoarse. "What are you still doing up, honey?"

She stepped toward him tentatively. "Daddy," she said, "what's wrong?"

He let out a slow breath. "Oh, it's nothing, sweetheart," he said, shaking his head softly. He reached for the rocks glass resting on the top board of the piano, his favorite glass with the little dimples at the bottom where he ran his thumb over when he was thinking, and took a long drink. "Just working through some things, that's all."

Something pinched her stomach tight. "Something with Mom?"

He shook his head. "Oh, no, no. It's, ah..." He glanced up at her, like he was debating. "I'm just dealing with some issues with my family. Nothing you need to worry about."

Natalie swallowed against the lump in her throat, and nodded. She knew not to ask about his family. She knew almost nothing about them, but it was clear to all of them that they were a great source of pain for him.

And Natalie would do anything to keep him from being sad. She loved him more than life itself.

He watched her for a long moment, his eyes scanning over hers. Tears pricked the corners of her eyes. It was like...like he was trying to etch her face into his memory. Her stomach somersaulted.

He tore his eyes away from her and tilted back the rest of his drink. Natalie ignored the pounding of her heart and sat down next to him on the piano bench, resting her head on his shoulder. A few moments passed before his body seemed to tighten, and then shake with silent sobs. Tears fell down her cheeks as she buried herself deeper in his arms, breathing in his scent, wrapping her arms around him and squeezing tightly.

Natalie had no idea what was wrong, but something dark and heavy opened up in her stomach. Something that took the ground from beneath her feet. She closed her eyes, and listened to the rise and fall of his chest. They held each other on the piano bench, two hearts beating together across the long and lonely night.

NATALIE SHOOK her head hard to snap herself from her reverie, and shot up from the wicker chair. She gritted her teeth as she paced across the porch of the Seaside House. That terrible pressure had built behind her eyes again, a dam about to burst. But she couldn't cry. It was like someone had her throat in a vise, squeezing the breath from her.

She yanked out her phone to check the time. The concert would be over soon. A fresh wave of fury blazed in her chest like wildfire as her mother's face swam into her mind. She pushed it out with all her might, swallowing hard against it.

One way or another, tonight was the night. The night she would get it all out. It was time to put on her big girl pants, roll up her sleeves, and have a frank conversation with her family. To say what she really felt, whatever it would mean for all of them.

~

"Uh, hi," said Diane, a high-pitched whine of feedback looping through the amplifier that made her wince. She stood back slightly. "I'm, ah, Diane, and this is, uh, Silver Hollows," she said, gesturing behind herself. "Most of Silver Hollows, anyway."

Cheers and whistles burst from the crowd. Never in her life had she been in front of this many people. Her eyes wandered over everyone, hoping against hope to find Austin. Her chest tightened. He was nowhere to be found.

Diane cleared her throat, and pushed on. "This is a new song...I wrote it for someone who, uh, someone who means a great deal to me. Austin, I don't know if you're here, I really hope you are, but this song is for you." More whistles and cheers. The corners of her mouth turned up as she spotted her sisters cupping their hands and cheering for her.

"Austin," she said into the mic, taking a deep breath. "I love you."

The crowd went wild, a chorus of *awwwww*s and hollers filling the humid nighttime air. Heat scorched her cheeks as she squeezed her eyes shut for a moment, taking it all in. Then Diane turned to Tyson, nodding. He lifted his drumsticks in the air, hitting them together, shouting, *"One, two, one, two, three, four!"* Diane held the microphone between her palms, and began to sing.

"Never knew
Never knew how tired and lonely I've become
Just waitin' for a change
Another day, another night has come and gone..."

Sully slowly drew his bow across the violin, breathing life into her words, the horrible tension in her back loosening. The crowd seemed to blur in her vision as she lost herself in the lyrics she'd written. They told a story of a woman lost, a woman who had struggled her way through the ups and downs of life. A woman who shared a complicated past with a man who was now back in her life, and how they had grown together, faced their most painful parts of themselves together. How they'd leaned on each other and how together they were more than the sum of their parts.

"I should have known
That you'd be there
Always there by my side..."

The bass and drums kicked in as she closed her eyes, letting the music wash over her. Diane had poured her heart out into the words she'd written for him, trying to communicate through her writing what she often had difficulty facing in real life. Writing had always unlocked her ability to face her own pain in a way that she'd lost touch with in her advertising career.

It was something she'd fallen back in love with, letting her begin the slow but critical process of moving on.

"We can hold on
Hold on just a little bit longer
Together through the storm
Through the nights cold and long..."

Tyson and Niko dropped their playing for the

final outro, leaving only the swirling notes of Sully's violin against the rise and fall of her voice. Diane's heart thundered in her ears as she breathed the powerful emotions she was feeling for Austin into her words, holding nothing back.

"Cause it's you
'Cause it's you, my sweet love
It's always been you..."

Diane closed her eyes and stepped back from the microphone as Sully swept his bow across the final note, the sound ringing out into the night sky just beginning to light with tiny pinpricks of starlight.

The crowd roared with a tidal wave of exuberant cheering, the peals of whistling cutting through the air, sending shivers down Diane's spine. And then a moment later, the crowd began chanting as Diane's eyes wandered over the beach, searching.

"Austin! Austin! Austin! Austin!" they shouted, calling for him. Diane's breath caught in her throat as the chants rippled across the beach, people turning their heads and calling for him to come on stage to meet her. A long minute passed as Diane stood there at the microphone helplessly, her heart sinking further and further. Finally, the chants began to die away. A collective murmur of disappointed *"awwwws"* threaded through the crowd.

Diane let out a slow breath.

He hadn't come.

She turned to Niko. He shook his head, mouthing *I'm sorry* to her. She nodded once. Tyson, Sully, and Niko approached her, giving her a hug to another burst of applause and cheering.

"That was incredible," said Niko away from the mics. "I'm proud of you, Diane. You and Austin will figure it out eventually. I know I give him a hard time, but he's a good guy." He looked into her eyes. "Thank you for this," he said, gesturing toward the crowd. "Me and the guys...we missed this terribly. It was great to have one last night of it all."

Diane hugged them and led the way across the stage to leave, fighting tears. At least she'd gotten it out of her system. All she could do was hope they could work through it someday, that she forgave him for lying to her, that she understood why he'd handled things the way he did. And she hoped he would forgive her for not giving him a chance to explain, for letting her own issues with trust get in the way of something wonderful.

Austin was a man worth fighting for. Diane would have to find another way.

As Diane took the first step down the stairs leading to the back of the stage, a surge of cheers and applause rippled through the crowd for the next act. Sully and Tyson gave her high-fives as they gathered around.

"We're sorry again about not saying anything about Alice," said Niko. "We didn't even know the full story...Austin was pretty spooked about the whole thing, and kept things close to the vest. We didn't want to interfere."

Diane nodded, waving her hand through the air. "All water under the bridge. It wasn't your responsibility. It's a sad situation." The next act began to play, the first chords of an acoustic number ringing out across the beach to a chorus of whistles and shouts. "I'm glad I went over there. Alice needs help. I only hope that—"

"Last night I dreamt you were still here with me..."

Diane froze, her heart skipping a full beat. She looked up at Niko, whose face was almost comically twisted in confusion.

"Right here, holdin' me tight..."

A shiver ran through her body. She jumped over a bundle of cables in the sand and pushed her way around the side of the stage so she could see with her own eyes.

Standing there in the middle of the stage, his old

rosewood acoustic in his arms and singing into the microphone, was Austin.

"I could feel your heartbeat against my chest

Could feel the warmth of your skin, your hand locked in mine..."

A rush of cheers broke out as his fingers crossed over the fretboard, his brow furrowed in concentration. Diane's mouth went dry as she listened to him sing the words they'd written together, only he'd changed them up, a new interpretation. She watched herself wander through the crowd toward the center of the stage.

And then Austin looked right into her eyes, and continued singing.

"Fighting to stay asleep, 'cause I know when I wake

You'll still be gone, long gone, my love

But just for now, no one can take you away..."

Diane laughed as tears of joy welled in her eyes. She felt a gulf widening around her as members of the audience stepped back to see who Austin was singing to. Their cheers seemed very far away right now.

Austin strummed a chord, letting his voice ring out against it, before picking notes in hesitation. His eyes bored into hers, sending goosebumps up her arms. He asked the question with his expression, and Diane nodded. A huge chorus of cheers spread across the beach as Austin approached the edge of the stage, reached out both arms, and helped hoist Diane up to meet him.

Her cheeks were on fire as he looked into her eyes. He glanced at a second microphone stand that had been placed next to him, and Diane knew. Before she could overthink it, before she could stop herself, she stood next to Austin at the second microphone as he began strumming the chords for the next verse, and then they both began to sing the words they'd written what seemed like a lifetime ago, but now held new meaning.

"And I'll hold you,
Yeah, I'll hold you, my darlin',
Through the good times, the hard times
No matter the changing winds, the shifting tides..."

As they faced one another, Diane's voice rising and falling in harmony with his soulful, gravelly voice, everything seemed to melt away around them. Right now, it was just the two of them, the only two people in the whole world, and nothing else mattered. The words they sang swirled between them, everything they'd wanted to say to one another but had been unable to now bridging the gulf that had threatened to separate them permanently. And Diane knew that the words she'd spoken into the microphone were true.

She loved him.

A clarity fell over her, a clarity that had been eluding her for too long. Everything she'd been torturing herself over, caught between two worlds, between Marina Cove and Los Angeles, between her perceived future and her family, her career and love.

Los Angeles...it was a complicated place for Diane, an amazingly fun, wonderful, and awful place, an absolute playground of a city with unlimited potential for those who were willing to sacrifice everything else, a place full of memories great and painful. The city she'd called her home for so many years...it was already beginning to fade in her mind, a dream upon waking.

Maybe it was time for a change. People did that all the time, didn't they? Diane had already filled an entire lifetime's worth of experiences into the time she'd been on earth. But that didn't mean she wasn't ready for a new life.

There was nothing stopping her...provided she was willing to let go.

And maybe it was time to let go.

Diane's eyes were blurry with tears as they sang the final outro together, Austin's fingers plinking against the steel strings, sending a hauntingly beautiful melody swirling around them.

"Yeah, I'll hold you close,

Be right here with you, darlin',

Never let you go,

No, I'll never let you go..."

Austin picked out the last chord, not letting his eyes fall off Diane's. She couldn't tear her gaze away from Austin. He leaned into the microphone, his eyes welling with tears.

"I love you, too, Diane," he said, his voice echoing across the beach.

Diane's face broke into a grin and she laughed through her own tears. A roar of applause and cheering tore through the air. Austin pulled the guitar over his head and set it down, swept toward Diane, and pulled her into his arms, pressing his mouth hard against hers as the crowd went wild.

And in that moment, Diane couldn't recall ever being happier.

After a long, beautiful moment that seemed to stretch into eternity and back, they pulled apart, Diane's heart skittering. She lowered her voice so it wouldn't be picked up by the microphone. "When did you—"

"I left to get my head straight," he said, lifting

one shoulder up. "I left to think, to do what we talked about. I wrote. And I knew I needed to show you how I felt." His eyes softened. "I signed up to perform days ago. I didn't know if you would come tonight. I can't explain it...I just had this feeling. And so I took a chance." He stepped toward her. "I had no idea you were going to do this. You have no idea how much that means to me."

He took her hand, raising it in the air for one final eruption of cheers and applause, before they walked toward the end of the stage together, hand in hand. As they stepped down into the sand, he stopped her, his eyebrows furrowed.

"Diane, I want to tell you the truth about what's been happening—"

"Austin," she interjected, wincing. "I already know. I, ah, went to talk to Alice."

His eyes widened. "What?"

"I know that's horrible," she said quickly, her heart beating harder. "I know that's a huge breach of privacy. And I'm sorry. Call it temporary insanity. But I had to know. A while back, I got this in the mail." She pulled out the letter from her pocket and handed it to him.

He mouthed the words scrawled against the paper. *Austin is lying to you.*

"Oh, geez," he said, shaking his head.

"Between this, and your behavior lately, plus that text I saw...well, I went to talk to her. And I understand everything now. I know you were trying to protect me." He nodded and began to speak, but she took his hands. "We can talk through it all later. But I need you to know something first." She let out a breath. "Alice wanted me to tell you that she lied. You don't have a son together. She was trying to keep you in her life, even if just for a while."

He pulled in a huge breath, and let it out in a *whoosh*. "I figured as much. But I wasn't sure. She can be pretty...convincing." He ran a hand through his hair, shaking his head. "It's not the first time she's done something like this, but I agreed to talk to her because I had to know, even if there was only a small chance." He squeezed her hands. "Diane, I am so sorry I lied to you. I know there were better ways to handle all this. I know it. I honestly didn't know what else to do. I didn't want her to start up with you and scare you off. She's unpredictable. It's a mess."

Diane nodded. "My sisters and I are going to work with her to try to get her some help. It was her idea. I think she wants to change. Time will tell, I guess."

The crowd kept on cheering. Diane stepped

toward him. She could feel the intense heat of his body so close to hers. "We have so much to talk about," she said, her voice wavering from the adrenaline coursing through her. "But right now, what I really want to tell you, Austin, is that I'm staying."

His lips parted as his eyes suddenly glistened. "You mean..."

Diane nodded. "I'm going to stay. It's the right thing to do. I know I'm meant to be here. With my family." She looked deep into his glittering eyes. "With you."

He grinned and kissed her again, sweeping her clean off her feet. And all the burdens she'd been carrying on her back, the horrible weight of it all, seemed to whisper away into the wind.

"*Whoa, whoa, okay, folks,*" the booming voice of the emcee echoed across the sand. "You've been wonderful tonight, just a terrific crowd. Let's give it up one more time for all our talented performers!"

Boisterous cheers and shouts swelled through the throngs of people in the sand, people raising their hands in the air and clapping hard. In the heat of the moment, Diane had forgotten all about the competition.

The emcee raised his hands in the air, and the cheers died down in anticipation. "All right, then.

Without further ado. The audience favorite for tonight, based on your reaction and participation." A thick silence hung in the air. "I've spoken with the judges, but it should come as no surprise. The winner of the audience favorite vote, and a fifty thousand dollar cash prize courtesy of Don's Refrigeration—thanks again, Don—is our final performance of the night. Let's give it up for Diane Keller and Austin Hall!"

Diane's skin went numb as Austin pulled her into a hug and gripped her tightly against him. "I can't believe it," he whispered. "We did it, Diane."

The crowd went wild as Austin led her up the stairs to the stage, butterflies dancing in her chest. Fireworks launched into the starlit sky, bursts of red and gold and white, a kaleidoscope of beautiful streaming light. She glanced out to the crowd below and spotted her family, whistling and shouting for her.

Tears glistened in Diane's eyes as the emcee handed them a stunning bouquet of flowers and a giant novelty check. Confetti swirled around them as the fireworks continued bursting in the sky and the crowd cheered endlessly around them. Austin reached his hand around the small of her back and pulled her against him, their mouths locking, tears falling down her cheeks and electricity crackling across her skin.

So much in her life had changed. And there was still so much unanswered, so much left to figure out. But never had she felt such hope, such promise for the future.

And life would undoubtedly hand them more challenges, more heartbreak and grief and difficulty. But that was what made life so rich, so beautiful and complicated and hard and wonderful. Diane was here in Marina Cove, home with her family, the home she'd never truly left. She was here with the man she loved, and who loved her. After everything she'd been through, all the twists and turns and surprises, it had all led up to this.

And Diane knew in her heart that she was exactly where she was always meant to be.

29

By the time the figures of her family swam into view, Natalie's thoughts had become such a knotted, tangled mess that she could barely breathe. Everything that had been happening to her, being on the run for so long, her fears over her future, losing Harper, the problems with April, her confusion over Theo...it was all coalescing.

Something had to give.

Natalie knew it probably wasn't smart, what she was doing. That she should take a night to think things over, to come to her mother, her sisters when she had a chance to calm down.

But she knew in her bones that if she didn't talk

to them tonight, she was never going to. She'd finally mustered up the courage, and couldn't stop now.

For the first time ever, she was going to let it all out. Break the momentum, finally, of a lifetime of never being forthright. Of always running when things got too hard.

She'd been running for too long now, and she wanted to stop.

Her chest hurt as her family stepped up onto the porch. Ramona froze in her tracks as she reached for the front door, Diane nearly running into her, holding a bouquet of flowers and wearing a thousand-watt grin.

"Natalie?" Ramona shook her head. "What are you...we thought..."

Natalie swallowed hard. They were all here: Charlotte, Ramona, Diane.

Mom.

It was now, or never.

"I don't know how to do this," she started, her throat already tight. "But I want to try anyway."

They looked at her with puzzled expressions as she drew a deep breath. Natalie sat down in an old wicker chair and gestured for them to sit, running a hand over her face.

"Are you okay?" asked Charlotte as they sat around her.

Natalie looked at her for a moment, and then shook her head.

"No, not really," she said, her voice warbling. She turned to Ramona. "You said we should start saying what we really mean. That we all skirt around everything. That we need to be more honest with each other. And I think you're right."

The porch was silent for a long moment. Natalie was overcome with a feeling of unreality.

"I think we're basically all islands of our own," she continued, "and that we're living this sort of weird, collective lie where we're all just *strong women* who can handle it all." Her voice cracked slightly. "That's ridiculous. Can't we be strong *and* need help? I mean, does it have to be so black and white? We can talk about how we support each other, but how much of what we say is the *real* stuff, the painful stuff?"

Natalie met Charlotte's eyes, and nearly broke down when she nodded softly. There was a look in her expression, something so raw and vulnerable. Natalie knew that her sisters understood, that they wanted the same thing. They might have progressed along without her in the last few months, but everyone was still tiptoeing around everything. Around the hard things, the difficult, ugly things.

If there was any hope of changing the way things were, to have something real, they were going to have to dig a little deeper. No matter how much it hurt. Natalie loved them too much not to try while she still could.

"We've been trying," said Ramona softly. "It's not so simple."

"But shouldn't we, I don't know, try a little harder?" Natalie asked. "We've all been through some of the most awful things people can go through, and we've told each other about them, sure, but we don't..." She raised her hands, exasperated. "We don't really *talk* about it, like you said the other night, Ramona. It's sort of like, here's this horrible thing that happened. *Oh, are you all right?* Yeah, I'm getting through it. *Okay, well, we're here for you.*"

Natalie shook her head and stood up, pacing. "It's just words! I mean, for example, why don't we ever fight? That's crazy, right? Families are *supposed* to fight sometimes. You wouldn't look at a husband and wife who never fight and think, oh, they've got it all figured out, right? We all worked so hard to never create ripples over the years, to just smooth everything over, *everything's hunky-dory*, and what do we have to show for it? A splintered family who, as it turns out, don't really know each other at all."

The words echoed across the porch. "I want things to be different too, Natalie," said Charlotte. "I think we all do." She motioned for Natalie to sit down on the wicker chair next to her. "What is it you want to say?"

Natalie shook her head. She didn't want to sit down and lose momentum. Hot tears were threatening right behind her eyes, but she was still unable to release them. Decades of grief and loss and despair swirled in her mind in a wretched, confusing scramble.

"I'm sorry I'm doing this now. I know this is coming out of nowhere, but I realized recently that I've held too much in for way too long...and I don't want to regret not trying to make things better when I had the chance. None of us knows how long we have." She thought back to the fire, to the moment she thought it was all over. "So I'm going to try. I have things I want to get off my chest, and I'm afraid if I don't do it now, I never will."

"That's good," said Diane. "We've all spent too long trying not to rock the boat. Not trusting each other. I think we all want the same thing here."

Natalie nodded. "All right. Look. In the years

after Dad left, I was having some problems. Actual, serious problems. I tried to talk to you guys several times. But you were all so wrapped up in your own stuff that no one bothered. I know we were all hurting in our own way, but no one asked...no one tried. Like, at all." She shook her head, looking between them. "I mean, didn't anyone wonder why I ran away?"

A thick silence filled the porch. "I always thought it was because Dad left," Diane said softly.

Natalie let out a frustrated sigh. "Well, it wasn't. And so you guys all just assumed the same thing, and I was left to figure everything out on my own. I mean, things fell *apart*, guys—"

"We tried to call you, I mean, hundreds of times, right? And you never answered your phone," Ramona interjected. "You basically ignored us—"

"That's not how it started, and you know it. None of us talked to each other. We basically all went our separate ways. I wasn't ignoring you, I was trying to figure out how to stay above water. You have no idea—"

"*You* all went your separate ways," Ramona spat. "While I was left here holding the bags. Did you reach out to me, see how Mom and I were doing here?" Her voice was wavering. "We were falling apart over here, too—"

"Natalie," said Ella, "can you try to see things from our perspective? Maybe we didn't know what you were going through, but you should always know we're there for you—"

"*No!*" Natalie shouted. Ella recoiled in her seat. "*Please*. Please don't give me that, Mom, the family party line. We're always here for each other? One great big happy family?" Natalie's face was suddenly on fire, rage coursing through her veins toward her mother. She could feel she was losing control, but couldn't stop. "You guys weren't there for me, not when I really needed you—"

"I've always been there for my children," Ella interjected hotly.

"*No, you haven't, Mom!*" she shrieked, the words echoing on the porch. It was all coming out now. Tears were struggling hard to release from her eyes, but it was like a dam holding fast. "You weren't there! After Dad left, *you* weren't there when I needed you, when I needed *someone!* You don't even know what I was going through, you had no idea—"

"Natalie, please, take a breath," Ella said, tears welling in her eyes. "I know I was having a hard time after your father left us, I know that—"

"No," said Natalie, gritting her teeth. Something hard and hot wrapped itself around her chest. "You weren't there, *at all*. I tried. I tried, but you were stuck in the freaking bedroom, you didn't care about us—"

"Hey, come on, Natalie," Ramona interrupted. "You're not being fair—"

"Natalie, I'm...I don't..." Ella started. "I don't know what to say. I did care. I..." She pressed her eyes shut. "I didn't know you were going through anything. You're right. What happened?"

They all looked at Natalie. No way was she getting into that. "No. No, no, *no*. It's a little bit too late for all that. It doesn't matter anyway," she said, biting back her tears. Joel's face flashed in her mind. A terrible hopelessness was settling over her. "You were supposed to be my mother. I needed you, and *you weren't there*."

A tear fell down Ella's cheek. "Look, I didn't know what I was doing when your father left. I just didn't. I didn't plan on him leaving us out of the blue, there was no roadmap for that. I was doing my best." Her voice trembled. "I know I let you kids down. I know I could've done better. I don't know what to say, your father leaving...it was devastating—"

"Oh, yeah, Mom?" Natalie burst out. "*Then why didn't you do more to stop him from leaving us?*"

The words rang into the air, filling all the spaces between them, a black pit of despair and heartbreak. Natalie's chest rose and fell rapidly.

"Oh, no," whispered Diane.

"Natalie," said Charlotte, her voice thick, "Dad leaving us wasn't Mom's fault. He left us without any warning."

"No, he didn't," said Natalie, her body shuddering. She turned to Ella. Until now, she hadn't known how to articulate it. But it was all pouring out of her now, the confusion and rage she'd held in for so long. "I heard you arguing with him *constantly*, Mom, before he left. Giving him a hard time about his drinking. About the finances, the upkeep of the Seaside House, everything—"

"I...I don't..." Ella stammered. She shook her head, wiping her eyes with a handkerchief. "Natalie, I don't remember that. I mean, this was almost thirty years ago—"

"Well, I haven't forgotten!" she shouted. "And now we might know more about why he left, but it was always obvious, always. It was because he didn't trust us! We didn't do enough. I knew something was wrong. I could've said something, *done* something, and I didn't. None of us did. We didn't do enough, but *you* held the keys, Mom, *you* should have seen what was happening to him! He wouldn't have left if he thought he had any other options—"

"Natalie, please—" said Charlotte. Natalie waved her off, drawing in a lungful of air and crushing back her tears.

Natalie knew she needed to stop. A part of her knew that she was being unfair and horrible, but a darker part of her was taking over, a scared, angry, utterly heartbroken girl that she'd kept locked up for her entire adult life.

"But I didn't know," Ella said. "I didn't know what was really happening to him. You don't understand, he was..." She searched the air for the right words. "He was so private; I couldn't read his mind. I did the best I knew how, I supported him fully. Natalie, *he* left *us*! No one made him do that!"

Natalie balled her fists up. "How in God's name did you not see what was happening to him, Mom? How is that even possible—"

"Your father didn't leave us because we fought," Ella said, her voice strained. "He left you kids, but he left me too, you know. I'm sorry you think I didn't do enough to support him, or that I should have seen it coming, but I loved him, honey, I *loved him*, so much.

I would have done *anything for that man*—" Her voice broke, and she covered her eyes with her hands.

"Natalie, you've got to stop," said Diane, tears in her eyes. "This isn't about Mom. You're upset and hurt and angry, I get that, but you're not being fair here. You know that no one could have stopped Dad. He made his choice. That's not our fault—"

"It is, it is our fault," she said, her voice shaking. "We have no freaking idea how hard it was for him, the horrible things he was going through. I loved him and I couldn't help him." She clenched her teeth hard against the flood of tears fighting desperately to pour from her, remembering the night on the piano bench. "And you know what? It would have been really, *really* nice if he'd been around when I was having the *worst freaking year of my life*—"

Natalie clenched her eyes shut, her fists balled up so hard her arms were throbbing. Her father's voice cut through her mind, shearing it in two, the memory of their day at the waterfall slamming into her like a ton of bricks. The sunlight reflected off his eyes, the feel of his hand holding hers, the wonderful warmth that spread through her at the sound of his laugh.

It was too much, it was all too much.

Natalie looked up at her mother. Ella's eyes were scanning over hers. And then her expression changed, like she'd just understood something.

The claustrophobic hands gripped Natalie's neck and squeezed as her mother closed the space between them.

"Honey," she said, her voice just above a whisper. "You have to let it out. You have to let it out, or trust me...it'll eat you alive."

The pressure behind her eyes was so intense her head was throbbing like a gong being struck. She couldn't breathe anymore. "Let what out?" she choked.

Ella held her gaze. "Natalie, sweetheart. Let it out. It's okay." A tear trickled down her cheek. "It's okay to be angry with him for leaving."

The words tore through her like a hurricane. Her heart cracked completely as she thought of his arms around her, the ache for it so powerful and bone-deep that it knocked the wind from her. Fire-hot tears spilled from her eyes as she fell into her mother, wrapped her arms around her tight, inhaling her scent, burying her face in her hair like a lost child.

"*I needed him!*" she shrieked. "*I needed him! He*

missed everything, and he's gone! He's gone!" Her body shook with sobs as she clutched her mother like she was a life preserver. She buried herself deeper into her mother's strong, warm embrace. She was lost at sea, and her mother was the only thing keeping her hanging on.

"I know, baby," Ella whispered, stroking Natalie's hair. "I know."

Natalie was vaguely aware of her sisters appearing at her side, their comforting arms around her, holding her along with her mother. "Why did he leave," she cried into her mother's shoulder. "Why did he leave us, Mom? *Why?*"

Ella's body began to shake as she let out a quiet sob. A long and awful silence stretched between them as they held each other in the darkness.

"I wish I could answer that, my love," she said finally, her voice thick with emotion. "Your father was a wonderful man, he was such a good dad to you and he was a wonderful husband. But he was also flawed. He was dealing with horrible issues. He had his demons, all the things that led to some moment we'll never know, some breaking point that made him react to his situation the way he did. And he left us. He left me, and he left you kids, too." She released a harsh, exhausted breath. "He shouldn't have left."

Natalie's mind was spinning as she swallowed hard against the devastating realization tearing through her. That she'd spent years carrying so much anger toward him for abandoning them, so long believing her father could do no wrong, idealizing his memory as though he bore no responsibility for what he'd done.

Ella held Natalie for a long time, stroking her hair, soothing her as she wept. She finally pulled back, wanting badly to hide her tear-streaked face, but she didn't.

"I'm sorry," Natalie whispered. "I'm so sorry. I think I...I needed someone to blame. I was wrong. You deserve a lot better than that."

Ella dabbed at her eyes. "Well, I could have tried harder when your father left. I was barely hanging on myself. I have a lot of regrets. I know we all do. We fell apart when he left." She looked up at Natalie. "I can't change the past. Your father was flawed, and I was too. I still am...we all are. All that really matters is that we keep trying. We can all do better."

Natalie nodded. "I've been horrible tonight. I hope you can forgive me."

Ella tilted her chin up. "There's nothing to

forgive, honey. It's a mess. None of us knows what we're doing." Natalie glanced at her sisters, who were wiping tears from their own eyes and nodding in agreement. "Sometimes, there isn't an easy answer. If there was, everyone would have life figured out. Real life is messy. We'll stumble through it together. And sometimes, it's not going to be pretty."

A laugh escaped Natalie's lips as the corners of Ella's mouth slowly turned up. Natalie wiped her eyes with her arm. "Well, this is definitely not pretty."

Ramona laughed, wiping her eyes with her sleeve. "I think it worked, Natalie. We had a fight. And look." She gestured to their mother, to Charlotte and Diane. "We're all still standing."

Natalie pulled Ramona into a hug. "I'm sorry for everything I said." She looked up at her sisters. "All of you."

"We're sorry, too," Ramona whispered. Natalie looked up at her mother, seeing her in a new light. Her mother who was here, now, there for her even when she'd been wrong and said awful things and been ungrateful. She was still there for her.

And in the end, that was what mattered.

Ella took Natalie's hands. "I love you, sweetheart.

And listen," she said, her eyes lingering on Natalie's. "Whenever you're ready to talk about what you went through...what happened after your father left... we'll be here."

She let out a breath, and after a long moment, nodded. "I love you too."

Natalie, her mother, and her sisters held each other tight, and talked deep into the night. The cabin fever feeling, the claustrophobia, it was still there, but perhaps not quite as strong. It wasn't going to be solved overnight.

But tonight...it was an important first step.

She squeezed her eyes shut, and thought of Joel. That deeper, more powerful urge was tugging at her. To talk about the terrible year. To try to explain some of what had happened. To explain to them the real reason why she left.

Some things had to wait. Some things didn't have to ever come out at all. Maybe it didn't matter.

Maybe that wasn't part of Natalie's story. Time would tell.

But as Natalie sat there with her family, the family she loved and who loved her in return, she felt lighter and freer than she had in a long, long time.

30

N atalie cursed to herself as she yanked a third time against the front door of the Seaside House, before a horrible squealing grind of wood against wood tore through the house like thunder.

Great. She'd probably woken them all up.

As quietly as she could, she pressed the door shut behind her, swept down the steps into the sand, and breathed in the cool night air, shivering slightly. The moon shone high in the sky, clear and brilliant, painting the sea with sparkling diamonds. She turned and headed down the coast, trying to clear her mind.

After her family had all gone to sleep, she'd tossed and turned on the downstairs couch for what felt like hours. She'd known she wasn't going to be able to sleep.

She still had no idea what she was going to do next.

Natalie let her feet guide her aimlessly down the coastline, the cool sand crunching beneath her bare toes. If anything, her newfound closeness to her family had made things *more* difficult, not less. She stopped for a moment, squeezing her eyes shut.

She had hoped against hope that what had happened with her family tonight would help ease the feeling she had to run. But it simply hadn't. Whatever it was that was going on inside her...it wasn't over.

Hours seemed to pass as she wandered the coastline, her thoughts spinning and ricocheting against each other. She raised her head to find that she'd wandered all the way down to Becker's Pier. A memory popped into her mind, a sunny afternoon skipping rocks from the end of the pier with her father. How he'd given her a sneaky grin before turning and leaping off the pier into the cold water, fully clothed, laughing that booming laugh of his.

A brief surge of anger tore through her before settling into heartbreak. Anger only masked the hurt, the hollow, aching grief she felt at his absence.

What she wouldn't give to hear that laugh again.

Natalie stopped cold in her tracks at the sight of a figure standing on the shore at the base of the pier. She raised her hand up to shield the moonlight from her eyes. And then her heart folded over.

It was Theo.

He had that faraway look in his eyes, that haunted look as he gazed down the pier and out over the sea. The same pier he'd been unable to step on with Natalie, unable to go out over the water after what had happened to his wife, her ghost still haunting him.

Natalie's stomach twisted as she thought about what that must have been like for Theo. Her accidental death ripping the rug from underneath him. To have the shock of it poison the things he loved to do most, to force him into a life of avoidance.

She and Theo, they were the same. They ran from the things that had hurt them.

Natalie's breath caught as Theo looked up, right at her. His bloodshot eyes glistened in the moonlight.

"I'm sorry," she called. "I didn't know—"

"I've been thinking about what you did," he said, his voice almost lost in the wind.

Natalie frowned, taking a step toward him. "What I did?"

He nodded, turning back toward the sea. "How you keep fighting...after you've been through so much. I don't know all of it, obviously, but..." He sighed, his shoulders falling. "Your dad leaving, your friend Harper. I mean, you broke into and broke yourself out of a burning house, all to protect something you cared about." He turned his head to look back at her, sending a shiver across Natalie's skin. "You went to go talk to your family tonight, when I could see that it was the last thing in the world you wanted to do, but you did it anyway." He shook his head, his eyes falling to the sand. "Sometime after Amanda died, somewhere along the way...I stopped fighting."

Natalie started to move closer but stopped herself. "Theo," she said. "You didn't stop fighting. You fight every day for your son. You're there for him. You didn't leave him when things got tough. Trust me," she said, letting out a sharp breath. "That's what really matters."

A long moment passed. Theo pressed his eyes closed and gritted his teeth. "I can do better." He looked up at the pier, intensity blazing in his eyes. "I will do better."

And then he stepped up onto the pier.

Natalie rushed toward him. "Theo, you don't have to—"

"It's okay," he said, his voice shaky. "Really." He pressed his feet into the wood. "I need to face these things sooner or later." He turned to her, his face white as a sheet. Natalie's throat constricted as he held out his hand, forcing a weak smile on his face.

She looked at his outstretched hand, debating, and then took it. He took another breath, and they made their way down to the end of the pier, slowly, wordlessly. Natalie's heart was pounding hard, her mouth dry.

They sat down on the end, letting their legs dangle over the edge. Theo's eyes were pressed shut, and his breathing was slow and controlled, his knuckles blanched white from gripping the wood beneath them. After a few minutes, he opened his eyes, letting them wander over the dark sea surrounding them.

"This is beautiful," he said softly. "I missed this."

They watched the waves roll against the pier, the light shimmering on the water. "I admire you," said Natalie. "I wouldn't claim to understand what you've gone through, but I know how hard this must have been for you."

Theo turned to face her. "Well, I have you to thank for that." His eyes lingered on hers. "Thank you."

Natalie turned her eyes toward the sea, unable to hold that gaze. "I didn't do anything," she said quietly.

She could feel his eyes on her. "Yes, you did," he whispered.

Natalie shivered, that caged-in feeling gnawing at her. An awful scorch of anger ripped through her, directed at herself this time, her heart in her throat. An awful urge to cry took hold of her.

It wasn't supposed to be like this. She didn't want to be like this, panic seizing her every time she got close to someone.

Her mind drifted to Joel against her will. What could have been, had things been just a little bit different. The decisions she made that had changed everything afterward, irrevocably.

To her lockbox, now safe and sound with Jess.

The little red box, and the notebook.

Her heart sank as she thought of the number in her phone, the only other number alongside the Seaside House landline. The one silently burning a hole in her pocket, needling at her whenever she stopped long enough for the white noise to take hold in her mind. A nasty flood of guilt ripped through her. She was fully responsible for the mess she'd found herself in.

It wasn't going to happen. But that didn't stop the desperate longing to finally dial that number after so long.

Natalie brought her eyes up to meet Theo's, gazing into those honest, knowing eyes. And something gave within her.

It was so exhausting, the constant static, the constant debate of when to drop it all and leave. She didn't know what was going to happen next, and frankly, she was sick and tired of letting the back and forth rule her life.

Here and now, tonight...it was all she needed to focus on.

"Natalie," said Theo, his voice barely audible over the cool wind. He opened his mouth to speak again, but then closed it, something pained and unspoken crossing over his expression.

Natalie swallowed hard as tears pricked the corners of her eyes. She sighed and leaned into Theo, letting her head rest on his shoulder. Her heart fluttered as he paused, and then wrapped his arms around her, holding her close. She breathed in his scent, her body seeming to melt in his embrace, his quiet strength. A tear trickled down her cheek as the clawed fingers of claustrophobia gripping at her throat dissipated and slowly drifted away.

There were going to be complications later. Some things she was going to need to face. But what she knew, here and now, was that she was where she belonged.

Natalie closed her eyes and let the tears fall, the tears of relief, of hope. She'd taken the first steps, and she knew from experience that those were the hardest. She didn't know yet what to do about her family, about April, about the past that still haunted her, the future in Prague.

About Theo.

Natalie wasn't going to leave Marina Cove just yet. Maybe she wouldn't leave at all. She didn't have that answer yet.

But right now, it didn't matter. As she and Theo held each other under the brilliant starlight, for the first time in as long as she could remember, she didn't want to run. At this moment, everything was right.

And for now, that was enough.

EPILOGUE

"How is it?" asked Sylvie.

Nick stopped cutting for a moment and met her eyes. "Delicious. Really." A moment passed. "Thank you."

An awkward silence ensued as they ate. They were seated at the dining room table, candles lit, soft music playing in the background. The sound of the waves crashing against Decker Beach drifted in through the open windows, a soft evening breeze cooling the house and caressing her skin.

Sylvie glanced up at him, and then back down at her food. It should have been more relaxing, but it was like she was eating dinner with a stranger. It was Nick...but not Nick.

She sighed inwardly. It was to be expected, after

all they'd been through. They weren't going to just pick up where they left off.

Patience, *Sylvie*. Patience.

She opened her mouth to speak, but he spoke first.

"Sylvie," he said, a line appearing between his eyes. He looked up at her.

"Yes?"

Something shifted within her as she looked at him, the familiar features of his face, the stubble on his cheeks, his slightly disheveled hair, the old twinkle in his eye. Something was there now in his eyes, something she was sure had never been there before. Something unsure, like he didn't know what he was doing. A broken confidence.

Her heart twisted. She reached out her hands and took his, running her fingers over his skin. "Talk to me," she said.

He ran the pads of his thumbs over her fingers. "If we're going to do this," he said slowly, "if we're really going to do this, I want to do things right."

Sylvie nodded. "I agree. I want that too. I know we've got a long way to go. But we've gone through a lot, haven't we?"

He laughed, and nodded. "Yeah, we have." They looked at each other for a long moment, her heart beating harder. She missed him, badly. Maybe they could figure things out after all.

The smile slipped from his face. "Before we move forward, though, I want us to be honest about everything. I want us to be honest with each other."

Sylvie frowned. "I have been honest. I told you. There's a trust problem, obviously. You can't blame me for that." She squeezed his hands. "I guess, if I'm being honest with you, there were a number of times I really considered leaving, Nick. Like, ending things for real. I guess I've never told you that."

He nodded, a small flash of hurt passing across his expression. "I don't blame you for that," he said slowly. "Of course. And thank you for saying that. But I was talking about me." He leaned toward her, his eyes holding hers. "I want to be totally honest with you. A fresh start, so I can get everything off my chest. I want to start things off again on the right foot."

The fine hairs on the back of her neck stood on end. "Okay," she said, unable to keep the fear from her voice. "What is it you want to tell me?"

His chest rose and fell, hard. "When I left, I said I went out to Nevada to stay with Judah."

Sylvie's heart lodged in her throat. She pulled her hands away. "And?"

Nick's eyes crossed over hers, his shoulders slumping slightly. "Well, that was true. I did go stay with Judah." He squeezed his eyes shut, and let out a slow breath. "But that's not the only place I went."

~

"AGAIN!" Niko shouted, just as Tyson crashed a drumstick against the cymbal marking the end of the song.

Diane laughed as Austin, Sully, and Tyson all groaned in unison. "Dude, *please*," said Sully. "You're going to ruin music for me."

"Honestly," said Tyson, taking a long drink of water from a bottle. "You're obsessed."

Niko scowled. "Hey. It's not my fault you guys gave up our chance to win all that money. You dropped the ball. I could be sipping margaritas by the pool right now, fanning myself with hundred-dollar bills. And," he said, turning to Diane and Austin, his frown deepening, "it's not my fault that these two stole the grand prize from under our feet—"

"I said I was sorry, Niko," interjected Austin, amusement dancing in his eyes.

"Me too," said Diane. She affected a pouty face.

"Please forgive us. It was for love. You can't hold that against us."

"And soooo," continued Niko, pretending he hadn't heard them, "we *go again*. I'm not going to lose next year. I'm the only one in this band with any real talent, so you're all going to have to try a lot harder to keep up—"

Tyson set down his drumsticks and got up. "Well, with all that talent, you shouldn't need us at all. Best of luck," he said, shaking Niko's hand and heading toward Austin's front door.

"Wait, wait, wait," Niko said, pushing through the living room and blocking his exit. "I mean, let's not be hasty—"

Austin met Diane's eyes and gestured with his head toward the back patio. They made their way through the living room as the rest of them bantered over their next "direction," what they wanted their sound to be. Austin poured them two cold drinks and led the way out to the patio where they sat down on an old wooden swing together.

"They'll be at it all night," he said. "Want me to kick them out?"

"Nah," said Diane. "Let 'em have at it. I wonder how long it'll take them to notice we're gone."

Austin laughed as Diane rested her head on his

shoulder, watching the breeze rustle through the trees. She could just make out the sound of waves crashing against the shore, the air warm and salty. Austin wrapped an arm around her and pulled her close, making Diane's heart flutter.

It was all so much to process. After it all, after everything, she was going to be moving to Marina Cove. She was terrified, of course, but knew in her heart that it was the right call. She would be with her family, and now, she would be with the man she knew she was supposed to be with.

There was still so much up in the air, but things could be a lot worse. Austin had wanted Diane to take all the money from their win, but Diane had refused, insisting on an even split. He and Kate had taken on a lot of debt as the Maple Street Diner continued to struggle in recent years, and they needed it. He'd eventually relented, and Diane noticed an extra skip in his step lately.

And now that she was moving, she was going to sell her house. It was going to be brutal, saying goodbye to the home she'd shared with Grant, but the time had come. With market appreciation, she'd have enough to pay off the balance of the second mortgage against it, with enough left over to give her a little breathing room to get by on, a little bit to stick into her nonexistent retirement funds, and most importantly, a little to put toward the Seaside House restoration. It wasn't going to solve anything overnight, but alongside her share of the grand prize money, it was a good start.

Things were looking up, that was for sure. The tension in her life had been pulled so tight that she'd thought it would snap at any moment, but for now, it had eased a bit.

Diane's chest tightened hard as she recalled what Samuel had told them under the old oak tree. How Patrick was out to ruin them. It might not even matter if they restored the family inn at this point. The Kellers were in a horribly vulnerable position, and he was taking full advantage.

Something powerful and convincing had been needling her, a strong feeling that they really weren't ever going to open it again. Too much was stacked against them.

She sighed. It was a feeling she might never get used to, having so much left uncertain. Taking steps into the darkness, not knowing if she'd stumble and fall...it went against her nature.

But sooner or later, you had to face the fact that there was only so much you could control. All you could do was what you could, to do your best. The rest was left to fate.

She pressed her eyes shut, thinking of the voice-mail she'd left for Jamie this morning. After some serious internet sleuthing, she'd finally found her son's number. His new number.

And so she'd called him.

It had been a long time since Diane had systematically and unknowingly ruined her relationship with him. She couldn't change the past. But she was trying to do what she could moving forward, and that was what mattered.

Maybe he would call her back. Maybe not. She would just have to wait, and see.

Austin sat up suddenly, and turned to face her. "What is it?" asked Diane.

He stared at her for a long moment, then placed both hands on the sides of her face and brought his mouth gently to hers. She kissed him deeply, her body light with newfound relief, with possibility.

"Nothing," he said as they pulled apart. "I'm just happy."

Diane grinned. "I love you," she said softly.

"I love you too," he whispered, before pulling her into another kiss.

The back door barged open, and Niko, Sully, and

Tyson poured onto the patio, arguing over something. "Whoa, whoa, whoa, get a room, you two," said Sully as he plopped down across from the swing.

"Are you sure about him, Diane?" Niko raised an eyebrow. "He's really your final choice? Because I could set you up with someone *a lot* better than this fool—"

Austin groaned. "Do I need to give you guys a time out? Can't we get a little privacy?"

"We're hungry," said Tyson. "Food. Food time."

"I guess you guys all made up, huh?" said Austin. "How sweet."

"Fooooood," said Tyson.

Austin laughed and turned to Diane. "I'm starved," he said. "Shall we?"

Diane shook her head. "You guys go ahead. I've got some stuff I want to work on."

"Oooh," said Sully. "A new song?"

"No," she said. "It's a, uh, personal project." She didn't elaborate.

Niko stood above her, shaking his head. "Going solo already. Not gonna lie, that one hurts."

She laughed. "Nothing like that. And also, none of your business." She stuck her tongue out at him.

He barked a laugh. "Fair enough," he said.

"Come on, Austin. You're flush with cash now, so you're buying."

Austin kissed her goodbye as the rest of the guys made their way through the back door, pushing and arguing about something again. A smile broke on her face. She was going to be seeing a lot of them, and that was good in her book. They were striking up a real friendship.

After the music festival, a few record producers had reached out to Austin, wanting to talk. After discussing it with the rest of the band, they'd declined any meetings. It would entail going on tour, traveling all the time, and none of them were interested at this point in their lives. They had families, roots here in Marina Cove. But that didn't mean they were going to stop; they'd keep making new music and play locally, where they'd built up quite a following.

They were going to play, just for fun.

Diane shook her head and laughed inwardly, leaning back against the wooden swing. Fun. A fairly new concept for Diane. Doing something without some practical end purpose. Playing music simply because she enjoyed it.

The back door opened, and Austin swept through it, lifting Diane from the swing and pulling her into another kiss. Her heart burst with happiness, with joy, with hope.

"See you in a bit," he said as he pulled away to leave. His face was flushed as he gave her a small wave and turned through the back door.

Tears pricked the corners of her eyes. After all she'd been through, after all the heartbreak and confusion and after so many mistakes, everything had finally clicked into place.

Diane watched the sunlight dance against the grass for a while before she leaned over to the end table and grabbed her notebook. The notebook where she'd been writing her lyrics, pouring her heart out, working so hard to process what she'd gone through.

She flipped to a blank page and pulled out the pen clipped to the spine, her mind swirling with thoughts.

Diane thought back to her first foray into creative writing. Poetry, mostly, but also short stories, a play, and at one point, the novel that she'd written to completion. After countless rejections, she'd given up hope, and eventually landed in her career writing advertising copy.

Writing had always meant everything to her. It was her way to work through all that happened in her life. After so many years without it, Austin had helped her rediscover it through writing lyrics. And the more she wrote, the more she knew in her bones that it was what she was meant to do.

Diane took a long, slow breath, and lowered the pen to the blank page.

Chapter One, she wrote.

She leaned back, staring at the words. When she'd written the first novel, she'd been so young. She had no way of realizing it, but she'd barely experienced anything of what life really had to offer. The joys, the sorrows. The sweet and beautiful anguish of falling in love, and losing love. The highs and the lows, how you didn't know what you were truly capable of until you lost everything.

Diane was older, and wiser. This time, when she wrote, the authenticity of her words would come through. Authenticity...it was everything. It was what made them *feel* something.

And now, Diane had a deep, deep well on which to draw.

Probably no one would ever read her novel. But she would try. And maybe try again. A smile lifted Diane's cheeks as the setting sun warmed her skin.

It was all coming together.

She looked down at the blank page, took a deep breath, and began to write.

∿

NATALIE INHALED the fragrant air sweeping off the bright blue sea, savoring the gritty feel of the sand against her toes with each step she took down the coast. A warm glow was coursing through her. She'd just taken a long beachside stroll with Theo after she'd finished up leading a tour through Miller Woods. They'd talked about their lives, the past. Their dreams, their joys, their regrets.

She smiled as she thought of his laugh, the way he ran a hand through his hair when he was thinking, the way he watched her when he thought she wasn't looking. Each moment she spent with Theo drew her inexorably closer to him. The man was impossible to resist.

And so she stopped resisting so much. Let future Natalie worry about the rest.

Life was looking pretty good.

Natalie pulled out her phone, and after a long hesitation, opened her texting app and started typing.

Hey Mom, there in five :)

A flash of something black and knotted curled through her as she hit *Send*, her chest constricting like someone was trying to crush it, but it disappeared as quickly as it came.

After everything, she had decided, finally, to give her family her number. Something fundamental had shifted between them, something powerful. She was starting to question the old rules that had up until now guided her life...and Natalie was ready to open up her heart, really open it up and let the ones she loved in.

As she pushed her phone back into her pocket, her fingers brushed against something smooth and foreign. Her heart skipped a beat as she recalled her family standing around her at the hospital, the looks in their eyes. It felt like it was only yesterday, but so much had changed since then.

After a candid internal debate, Natalie had decided to fill the prescription that Dr. Grenier had given her. The one for the epinephrine injector.

It didn't matter if it made her feel weak, or defective or shackled or whatever other reasons she'd had for not carrying one over the years. It was time she started viewing her life with a little bit more care and gratitude. It was an incredible gift, just being alive.

Natalie raised her face to meet the warm rays of sunlight cascading down, and smiled.

Change was in the air.

The Seaside House appeared up ahead as she wound through a small meadow running through a copse of birch trees. Her mother and sisters were spread out on beach towels, laughing and eating snacks and soaking up the sun slowly inching down toward the horizon.

Natalie's heart swelled with love. They'd made plans for a girls' night, to watch the sunset together and then order in and watch bad movies until they fell asleep.

It was going to be great, and Natalie wasn't going to miss it for the world.

"Hey, Natalie!" Ramona's face brightened as Natalie padded toward them. "You've been every-where. Settle an argument for us." Charlotte snick-ered behind her as Ella smiled and shook her head. Natalie sat down in the sand next to her mother and leaned back on her hands. Ramona shushed her sisters, and forced a straight face. "Truth or myth: toilets flush backward in Australia."

Ella burst into loud laughter as Natalie grinned. Her mind went to a particularly wild summer she spent in Melbourne, ages ago. One memorable night with a couple of girls she was rooming with involving roller skates, a smoke machine, and a confetti cannon. She laughed.

"I think you're thinking of the Coriolis effect," she said. "And no, my friends, it doesn't affect the toilets."

Charlotte squealed as Diane buried her face in her hands, pretending to be ashamed. "I swear, I read that somewhere," she said, shaking her head.

"It was in that one movie," chimed Ramona. "With that guy...what was it called..."

"*Gone with the Wind*," joked Charlotte, to a chorus of laughs.

"You guys are lame," said Natalie on a laugh, reaching for a slice of watermelon that they'd prepared. She glanced around. "Where's Mariah and Sylvie? I thought they were coming too."

"Mariah just texted me, she's on her way," said Charlotte. "I think she wanted to talk to me about something first, so I'll have to step away for a sec when she gets here. As for Sylvie..." Her smile faded almost imperceptibly as she paused, not quite long enough for anyone else to notice. "She, ah, hasn't gotten back to me yet. I stopped over at her house and she wasn't home. I'm sure she's just busy planning for The Windmill reopening."

Something tickled the back of Natalie's neck at the look in Charlotte's eyes. But as she opened her mouth to speak, she yelped out loud and shot to her feet as a terrible, grinding roar ripped through the air around them. Diane screamed.

"What in God's name is that?" yelled Ella as they all leapt to their feet. Natalie could barely hear her over the horrible, wrenching squeal. It sounded like someone was feeding gravel into the world's largest garbage disposal.

Something moved in the lot just up the coast from the Seaside House. They plugged their ears as the sound seemed to shake the ground beneath their feet. Natalie's eyes darted around, trying frantically to find the source of the sound, her heart slamming against her chest.

Her stomach rolled over as her gaze landed on the giant old oak tree in the neighboring lot. It looked different, somehow. Like it was slightly askew. Almost as if…

"Oh, no," moaned Ramona. She looked at Natalie, her face white as a sheet, tears in her eyes. "No, no, no no no no!" Ramona tore through the sand toward the oak tree. Natalie dug her fingers into her ears and met Ella's eyes. Her throat constricted at the despair in her expression, the fear. A cracking sound tore through the air.

Natalie's mind ran to something she'd totally forgotten about, a memory of her father pushing her on an old rubber tire swing suspended from an oak tree. The sun was cascading languidly through the canopy of leaves above them, dappling the ground in a beautiful dancing pattern. His laugh as Natalie screamed with wild glee as he pushed her higher and higher. Tears welled in her eyes as she squeezed them shut, trying to etch into her memory the look on his face, his eyes glittering in the sun. Another cracking sound tore through the air as Natalie opened her eyes.

"They're starting," yelled Charlotte over the roaring sound. A tear fell down her cheek, a look of pure misery in her eyes. "They're razing the lot. It's all starting now."

"What?" yelled Natalie. "Who's razing the lot?"

Charlotte bit her lip. "We've been meaning to tell you—"

They both jumped as a second grinding roar cut into the air. Natalie and her sisters watched help-lessly as a final horrible *crack* reverberated all around them. Ramona had disappeared into the copse of trees surrounding it, but Natalie already knew that nothing was going to stop this.

The old oak tree swayed and groaned one last time before it tipped over and fell, crashing to the ground and shaking the earth beneath their feet.

And Natalie knew that something awful had just begun.

∽

MARIAH LEANED FORWARD on the bench on Shannon Pier, her happy place, and ran her hands over her face. The nostalgic clicking of the rotating Ferris wheel and children laughing and running around behind her did nothing to quell the horrible nausea tearing and twisting its way through her stomach. Her heart was beating so fast she was feeling lightheaded.

She shoved out a breath, leaned back, and pulled out her phone. Her eyes scanned over the email she'd drafted to Dr. Meyers but had been unable to send. A buzzing sound filled her ears as her fingers hovered over the Send button. But she still couldn't push it down.

A thousand thoughts tore through her mind. Christian, that glint in his eye, the strength of his arms around her. Sylvie, the wonderful tinkling melody of her laugh.

Tears welled in her eyes. Her mother's face. The look of authentic concern when Mariah would come to her with something, that indelible feeling of safety that only a mother could provide.

Her eyes squeezed shut as she thought of Keiran. How stupid she'd been to let herself think that something was happening between them.

She thought of the night in the hospital, the night that had changed it all. The rhythmic pounding of the heart monitor. That horrible, wretched tinge of disinfectant, the fluorescent lighting slicing into her eyes. She gasped for breath as the thoughts swirled into a frenzy, swallowing her whole.

Mariah suddenly shot up from the bench, her eyes streaming with tears, and screamed out into the water at the top of her lungs. Several people around her whipped around to see what was wrong, but she didn't care. She swiped the tears away, gritted her teeth, and jammed her finger down on the Send button, her heartbeat slamming against her temples.

There. See, that wasn't so hard, huh? She needed to get it together, to grow up and face the music.

It was the right thing to do. She knew it.

Mariah put her phone away and leaned against the railing, watching the sun march toward the horizon, swallowing against the panic rising from deep within her core. A wretched feeling that she'd just made a horrible mistake stole over her before she crushed it down. It was just the fear talking.

She would get over it. She had to.

As she leaned forward and buried her face in her hands, she ran over the words in her mind she'd prepared. The words she would use when she told her family that she was leaving. Fresh tears forced their way into her eyes, and she let them fall.

Mariah felt the hairs of her neck stand on end. She whipped her head up, and her eyes landed directly on Keiran's. He was making his way down the pier toward her, something in his gaze she couldn't quite place.

She groaned inwardly. Keiran had stopped over to see her after the incident. He'd been shaken badly by the event, and had thanked her profusely. She hadn't told him her decision to leave yet. Something had stopped her, but she wasn't sure what.

It didn't matter anymore. None of it did.

"I thought I'd find you here," he said. "Can I sit?"

Mariah nodded. A long time passed as they watched the water in silence. She took a deep breath and ran her hands through her hair.

"I'm leaving, Keiran," she said softly, the words carrying in the breeze.

After a moment, he nodded slowly.

"About that," he said. Mariah's heart skipped a beat. He turned toward her, their eyes finding each other's in the fading light. "Can we talk?"

~

NATALIE CLENCHED the old wooden railing of the front porch until her hands hurt. The moonlight seemed to envelop her as she fixed her tear-stained eyes on the waves sloshing against the shore.

Her body trembled as she replayed the phone call she'd just received, the words tearing through her mind over and over until she could no longer breathe. She clamped her hands over her mouth as a fresh sob broke from her throat.

The door squealed open behind her, and Natalie clenched her eyes shut. She had tiptoed out as quietly as she could, her heart pounding too hard as she'd pushed through the front door onto the porch to take the call. The sound of the chainsaws hadn't ceased until late into the night, effectively ruining their time together. They'd all fallen into an uneasy sleep from which her ringing phone had ripped her.

"Natalie?" a voice called softly.

Natalie tried to draw a breath, but nothing came. Her hands shook against the wooden railing.

Ella came up beside her, placing a hand on her shoulder. "Natalie, baby, what's wrong?"

Natalie's stomach somersaulted as she shook her head. "I can't believe it," she whispered. "Oh, Mom." She swallowed hard against the wretched tightness in her throat. "Oh, God..."

Ella gripped her hand. "Natalie, you're scaring me," she said, panic rising in her voice. "Talk to me."

Natalie looked up slowly to meet her mother's eyes, her heart breaking.

"I have to leave," she choked, the tears falling down her cheeks. "I have to leave *right now*."

~

THE STORY CONTINUES in book six of the Marina Cove series, *The Changing Winds*.

Sign up for my newsletter, and you'll also receive

a free exclusive copy of *Summer Starlight*. This book isn't available anywhere else! You can join at sophiekenna.com/seaside.

Thank you so much for reading!

~Sophie